Also by Kris Ripper

The Love Study Series

The Love Study

Rocky Fitzgerald

One Dead Vampire
Two Black Cats

Queers of La Vista

Gays of Our Lives
The Butch and the Beautiful
The Queer and the Restless
One Life to Lose
As La Vista Turns

Scientific Method Universe

Catalysts
Unexpected Gifts
Take Three Breaths
Breaking Down
Roller Coasters
The Boyfriends Tie the Knot
The Honeymoon
Extremes
Untrue
The New Born Year
Threshold of the Year
Ring in the True
Let Every New Year Find You
Every New Beginning
Surrender the Past
Practice Makes Perfect
Less Ordinary

Kith and Kin

New Halliday

Fairy Tales
The Spinner, the Shepherd, and the Leading Man
The Real Life Build
Take the Leap

The Home Series

Going Home
Home Free
Close to Home
Home for the Holidays

Little Red and Big Bad

Bad Comes First
Red Comes Second

Erotic Gym

Training Mac
Teasing Mac
Taking Mac

Stand-alones

Gun for Hire
Fail Seven Times
Runaway Road Trip
The Ghost in the Penthouse
Hold Fast

THE HATE PROJECT

KRIS RIPPER

Recycling programs for this product may not exist in your area.

ISBN-13: 978-1-335-50917-8

The Hate Project

This edition published by arrangement with Harlequin Books S.A.

For questions and comments about the quality of this book, please contact us at CustomerService@Harlequin.com.

Carina Press
22 Adelaide St. West, 40th Floor
Toronto, Ontario M5H 4E3, Canada
www.CarinaPress.com

Printed in U.S.A.

The Hate Project includes depictions of anxiety and panic attacks. It's not a quirky plot point; it's just the way Oscar goes through the world, like so many of us. He's still got anxiety at the end of the book—anxiety and depression can totally be part of a happy ending!

THE HATE PROJECT

Chapter One

Once upon a time there was a grumpy old thirty-something called Jack and a tragically misunderstood (but younger) hermit called Oscar and they bickered so much that their friends told them to get a room, so on a particularly bad night they did. Stay tuned next week to see what happens to our hero (Oscar) and The Broker Who Pitied Him (Jack).

Not that I'd ever go on a show about relationships and neither would Jack. It's one of the few things we have in common. And before you say no one would do that in real life, one of my closest friends found the *cough, gag* love of his life on a YouTube advice show. He actually fell for the advice-giver, which should be against the rules, but apparently isn't.

Anyway, this thing with me and Jack started out as a

one-off after yet another cutesy gathering hosted by Dec and Sidney, my "YouTube brought us together *aww*" friends. For two people who didn't technically cohabitate they co-hosted a lot of crap, and this particular event was in my honor.

Or rather, in honor of me being laid off and falling into a pit of despair. I know pits of despair are about as clichéd as bell jars, but if the metaphor works, why screw around?

First I should say this: I hated my job. Hated-hated it. Hated it so much that there were days when I seriously considered driving into the cement barriers on the side of the freeway because the thought of literally dying sounded better than going to work for another nine hours of sitting in a cubicle taking customer service calls. And I'm not saying that like it's a joke to me; I've had intense anxiety all my life and thinking, *Death would be better than this excruciating (mundane) situation I must now force myself to endure* isn't actually all that rare.

I try not to let it get to the point where I'm fantasizing about the impact of my vehicle hitting a solid object, but I had nightmares about my job. Nightmares during which customers yelled at me for sending them a pillow in the wrong shade of periwinkle blue, or tried to return things because this blanket didn't feel soft as a baby's bottom (was that a common blanket-softness standard? and if it was: *creepy*), or that picture frame was *white* not *white-washed* like the description on the website.

Those are actual situations that happened, which became nightmares later. Or does that make them flashbacks? Whatever they were, I'd wake up sweating and nauseous like the customer was still on the phone demanding I go back in time and psychically intuit that when they clicked "twin size" on the Thomas Kincaid knockoff duvet cover they were ordering, they really meant "king size." *Shudder.*

I was sitting at my desk in my cubicle ("my" in a loose sense—we were not permitted to "personalize" our "workspaces" in any way) on a Friday afternoon when an email popped up from my direct supervisor, Brad. He'd been my supervisor for about three weeks and he was *such* a Brad. He had that non-threatening straight guy thing going for him that seemed statistically likely to mean he was a serial killer.

Or, okay, not really, but serial killers were statistically likely to seem non-threatening, right? And Brads are, by their nature, a non-threatening branch of the human tree. He was the everydude.

Brad, being a supervisor, had a very small office. More of an upright coffin for a very large person. The chair he invited me to sit in had to be moved to the side in order to close the door and then, uncomfortably, it blocked the door when moved back into position.

"This seems like a fire hazard," I said as I sat down.

"A…what?"

"A fire hazard. As in, if there was a fire it would be hard for us to get out of this room."

"Why would there be a fire?" he asked. As if *I* was the idiot.

"I think most fires in office buildings are unplanned." I thought I'd mostly managed to keep the *you idiot* addendum from my tone, but maybe I hadn't.

"I don't think we have to worry about a fire right now, Oscar."

I shrugged. "I'm sure that's what nearly anyone would say right before burning to a crisp in a fire, but okay. We won't worry about it." Obviously I'd already mentally rehearsed how I'd stand, turn, push the chair aside, swing the door open, and bolt for the stairs, but since everyone else would also be bolting for the stairs *and* they'd have the advantage of not having to escape from an upright coffin, I doubted my chances.

It should probably be noted that I was never A) athletic or B) of a particularly spry build, but even if I was both of those things, I'd still be seriously screwed by the misfortune of being wedged in Brad's office.

At which point I realized he was looking at me a bit too intently. "Did you hear what I said? About the papers?"

"Uhh. Papers? No, sorry." *Too busy thinking about where they'd find my remains, but I'm pretty sure they'd find yours right here in your office.*

"I know this is a difficult time—wait, I think I said that already—"

A difficult time? I should have been paying closer attention. "Can you start over?" I asked as he ran one finger with stumpy, straight-guy nails down an actual script.

This did not bode well. There couldn't be too many difficult times your supervisor needed a script for.

"We're in a very challenging position right now," he said earnestly. "The economy being what it is, and consumers not buying as many home goods, you understand our position in the market has been challenging."

It was like a slow-motion train derailment; I knew what was coming, but I couldn't help hoping that at the last moment something would change and the train would stay on the tracks.

"Which is why I need to tell you that—" quick check of the script "—your time here has come to an end."

I stared at him for a long moment. "I think I would have preferred the fire."

I drove home in a daze, trying to figure out what this meant. It was a terrible job, a job I wasn't suited for, that had given me panic attacks on a near-daily basis for the first three months I'd worked there. Which would have probably sent me looking for another job if it wasn't for two things: my loathing for and increased anxiety about job hunting, and the lack of assurance I had that the next place wouldn't be equally bad.

There are people who have a lot of anxiety and can also go to work like normals. (And yes, blah internalized blah blah, but I don't mean "normal" like it's better than being an anxiety-ridden wreck. I *like* being an anxiety-ridden wreck. Wouldn't have myself any other way.) My friend Dec has a certain type of anxiety and you wouldn't know it to look at him. But me?

Let's just say if you saw a round, soft, eye-contact-avoiding guy walking down the street, hands in his pockets, head down, skirting to the edge of the sidewalk to not get too close to people, you might think to yourself, *Hey, that guy looks anxious.* And if that guy was me, you'd be right. Or you'd think, *Hey, that guy might be a serial killer*, in which case you'd be wrong because they usually look normal, like Brad.

You see what I mean about not wanting to be one of the normals?

All that to say this: I hated my job. If ever there was a job that a regular person would *want* to be laid off from, it was this job. Which I hated. And yet all I could think about as I was driving home was how terrible it would be to look for a new job—I'd have to go to interviews, shake hands with people I didn't know and then sit there trying not to be distracted by the fact that I'd just touched some random and their skin flora was now co-mingling with my skin flora like an invasive species of plant, out of my control and changing things that didn't need to be changed.

Shaking hands is one of the worst forms of "politeness" ever invented. What is the point, other than the gratuitous touching of strangers? Saying "Hi, good to meet you" isn't enough, you gotta add some unnecessary physical interaction in there? You realize that even if the person you're shaking hands with washed after taking a shit, the other eight hundred people who also touched that bathroom door today didn't 100% comply with the signs, and even if most of them *did*, there are actual procedures to that sort of thing, soap coverage and friction and duration and…

Why is shaking hands even a thing? I don't want to touch your hands. No offense. And you can't say that at a job interview. "Thanks for interviewing me; I don't want to touch your hands."

Something else you can't say at job interviews: "Occasionally I take an extra-long bathroom break because I can't breathe, but don't worry, I'll be fine in a few minutes." I mean, I guess I've never actually tried to say that, but I just assume it's a bad idea, given I live in a country that routinely mocks all manner of physical, mental, and psychological challenges.

When I got back to my apartment after discovering that my time with my job had come to an end I sat very still on my couch for a long time. It was that or make a cake and then eat the whole thing. I know it's a cliché for a person of average-but-more-than-television-girth to stress eat, but I've been stress eating since I was five and my kindergarten teacher, sympathetic to slow eaters, would let me sit in the corner to finish my lunch if I took too long eating. I'd stuff extra food in my lunch so I could take a really long time and thus spare myself over half of the "sustained silent reading" period.

Sustained silent reading is hell for kids who hate (and/or are shitty at) silent reading. I got my extended lunch down to a science until I was just packed up and pulling out a book when it was time to move on to the next subject.

So, cliché or not, it's ingrained in me to spend my time eating when I am in a state of fear or anxiety. Losing my job induced both.

I did manage to text Ronnie, because it's what my former therapist, who moved and was never replaced, would have told me to do. Ronnie was my emotional contact person in times of trouble, if you will, and when she had times of trouble I was hers, though now she and Mia were married so I guess I'd been replaced in the old emotional support human role.

The system we had worked out was that I would text with whatever was happening and a green/yellow/red light for how welcoming I was to the idea of being contacted back. I sent: *Laid off. Mostly numb. Hate job hunting. Yellow.* Which basically indicated that she could reply but shouldn't worry if I didn't engage in a conversation.

She sent back: *Fuck those fucking fuckers* and a heart emoji.

You know your friends love you when they have a million questions they want to ask and they're super worried about you and they distill all of those things down to one non-demanding, high-curse-word-load sentence.

And a heart emoji.

As a rule I hate emojis because they're overused and I don't always know what they mean. But the heart emoji was…well, even I knew how to interpret a heart from my oldest friend.

After sending my text—doing my "self-care due diligence," my old therapist used to say before she moved to Portland and abandoned me—I resumed staring into space until my phone vibrated sometime later.

Dec: *Throwing you a pity party. Making pizzas. Tomorrow at six.*

The advantage to my particular friend group—the Motherfuckers—was that I wouldn't need to tell anyone else; now they all knew I'd been laid off. The disadvantage was they'd now try to show their love in different ways, and Declan's was food and parties. On the other hand, he made great pizza, I had nothing better to do, and I would be safe with my people. Better to be at his place than out in the world somewhere.

Still, it was a bit presumptuous that he just assumed I wanted to be part of a social gathering, so I punished him by not responding.

Within twenty minutes I got *See you tomorrow!* heart emoji messages from both Mason and Mia. That was the entire OG Motherfuckers crew reporting for duty. And yeah, okay, I was pretty numb from the low buzz of looming fucked-upedness, but it wasn't a bad thing, knowing my friends were thinking about me.

At least, that's what I thought until I was up all night imagining horrific job interview scenarios, trying to figure out what I'd do if I couldn't find work, and picturing what it would be like living in the guest bedroom at Ronnie's. The way my friends would eventually turn against me because I couldn't support myself, how I'd become this embarrassing hanger-on at drinks whom they couldn't disinvite, but who also couldn't pay his own way...

I woke up (that's a fancy phrase for what was essentially just regaining a muggy sense of consciousness without any accompanying alertness) around ten the next morning feeling unable to see anyone, including my friends. Possibly ever again.

Anxiety has different faces for everyone, and this is probably the most messed-up feature of mine: telling me again and again, persuasively, that the Motherfuckers—the first people who ever accepted and loved me for who I was—are on the verge of disowning me. No matter how much I know it's not true, it still seems real.

Since my friends had been at war with that voice for years, all of them checked in throughout the day, even when I didn't respond. Which led to a whole other round of "I'm not good enough to have wonderful friends like these," so by the time I was forcing myself to drive over for the Oscar's Laid Off Gathering, I'd been yo-yoing between extremes of "they're too good for me and I should be thankful" and "they secretly hate me and I should move to another country and change my name" all day long.

But then I got to Declan's and couldn't make eye contact with anyone and they sat me in a corner with a bottle of sparkling water, making noise around but not at me. I really, really didn't deserve them.

I'd never had friends until college. And even then, I wouldn't have had friends except that Ronnie and I were freshman year roommates (before she transitioned, obviously), and she was friends with Dec and Mase and Mia, and they came around a lot and just sort of looped me in. It happened slowly over that first year and suddenly I had… friends.

What's that thing with snake poison, where you take it in small doses every day to grow your immunity to it? That's what happened with the Motherfuckers. Eventually I built up a tolerance to their, like, happiness and friendliness and optimism. Now my brain just recognizes them as a part of me. The same thing probably happened to them: eventually they built up a tolerance to my moods and freak-outs.

The most important thing you need to know about my friends is that they're all way better people than I am. You can tell because they threw me a pity party. There's the aforementioned Declan and Sidney, who got together during the commission of a video series called *The Love Study* on Sidney's YouTube channel. Then there's Mia and Ronnie, disgustingly married to each other. And the last of the official Motherfuckers is Mason, who once tried to get married (to Dec) and was left at the altar (by Dec). Which was awkward for a while, but now it's fine. Though of all of us Mase is the one who wants a white picket fence and 2.5 kids.

Sounds fucking awful to me, but to each his own, I don't judge, whatever floats your life raft, et cetera.

Since I didn't want to get my impotent rage-slash-panic germs on anyone, I took up a seat in the corner and didn't leave it except to use the bathroom and acquire victuals. By which I mean vegan, gluten-free, cauliflower-based pizza that turned out to be delicious. It used to be that my friends had an informal rotation for who'd sit with me, trading off for the duration of the social event, but that was before Jack. Jack was new to the group. Dec had collected him from work, and for reasons I didn't understand (I would have suspected sexual favors if I didn't know better), he kept mostly showing up to drinks with the Motherfuckers. And was now also on the invite list for ad hoc gatherings to celebrate catastrophic job loss.

Jack and I had no other setting with each other than arguing. Since neither of us was all that nice (and everyone else in the Motherfuckers was very nice), it worked out. He thinks he knows everything, I definitely know everything, and even though for the most part we would arrive at the same point from different angles, we spent most of our fights poking at each other's angles to prove they were incorrect.

I probably shouldn't have been surprised when it turned out bickering was actually foreplay.

Since the party was in my honor I was obligated to stay through dinner, and I did. In my corner. Weathering the well-intended reassurances of my friends was hard enough, but when Dec brought out one of those quirky adult card games where kittens exploded I had to get the hell out of there. Too much goodness on a bad day.

Jack apparently had a similar thought. It wasn't the first time we'd made our escape at the same moment. This time, instead of parting ways on the sidewalk with a lukewarm *we know each other through friends* wave, both of us stopped.

He stopped a second before I did, which I immediately decided made him more desperate. It wasn't charitable, but I believe in keeping track of who has the advantage in any encounter. Even a one-off.

"I live ten minutes away," he said.

"Good for you."

His lips twisted a little, from not-smile to not-impressed. "This is a pity fuck, Oscar. Take it or leave it." With that he turned and made for a black two-door something-something on the other side of the street.

I hesitated. For about five seconds. But following up a pity party with a pity fuck sounded about right. "Just to clarify," I called as I caught up with him, "I don't do relationships."

He hit a button that unlocked his car. "Just to clarify, I'm not offering one."

Chapter Two

Jack's lips thinned into a very straight, very unyielding line, visible even in the low light of the car. "We've known each other long enough to share a fuck after a party if we want to, but you can say no anytime if you have better things to do."

"I could always do laundry."

"Laundry or me, your choice."

When he put it that way. "I'll do you. This time."

"Great. I'm not interested in anal sex, but I'm into most other things. My safeword is lollipop."

I couldn't help making an undignified not-giggle sound, the type of noise you make when you start to giggle, realize it's undignified, attempt to swallow it, and end up choking on the giggle you'd originally tried to tame.

"Bad form to mock a man's safeword, Oscar." But his voice sounded grudgingly amused.

Enough that I could elect not to bite his head off about it. "Lollipop, though. Is there a story there? Please tell me there's a story there and once you tell me I can text the Motherfuckers thread with it."

"No. And no. And how the hell do I get off that? I tried removing myself but I'm somehow still on it."

"'Somehow still on it' translates to 'Dec added you back because he can't imagine anyone not wanting to be on the Motherfuckers thread.' The only thing you can do is block him, I think. Or grow a pair of reproductive organs of your choice and tell him you want off."

Jack paused on that one. "Is he likely to look at me like I ran over his puppy if I do that?"

"Probably."

"Pass." He pulled into a driveway. An actual driveway of an actual house. I would have sworn he'd be in one of those glass-and-steel industrial loft-style apartments where it's one big room, some concrete pillars, and a single sliding door hiding the bathroom, but this was a house.

A house that might be falling down. "Is this place haunted? Because poltergeists are a hard limit for me."

"It's not haunted, it's poorly maintained, there's a difference."

"Oh-h, well then." I could feel myself getting more uncomfortable as we got out of the car. Now would be a nonideal time for a panic attack. People were so much less likely to fuck you when they'd just seen you hyperventilate with tears dripping from your eyes while you tried to convince yourself you weren't about to die.

I could take a pill, but then I wouldn't be able to fuck anyway.

"Where are we?" I asked, my voice rising alarmingly.

"My house. Or I guess my grandmother's house, but she's in care now, so I've been living here. Mind the hallway, it's dangerous."

Which was apparently Jack's way of saying it was a tunnel through boxes and stacks of… "*Rolling Stone*? Curve ball. Your grandparents are really into rock music?"

Up ahead he flicked a light on, which at least helped with navigating the final part of the hallway/tunnel. "Those are mine. Were mine. When I lived here." He leaned into the pool of light, looking, briefly, less like a combative dick and more like…well, just a man. The context of his grandmother's house (and apparent hoarding) softened Jack's edges somehow.

"We're not having sex in the hallway," he said.

For a second, anyway.

"Thanks for the note. I'm totally not fucking in your grammy and grampy's bed, by the way."

He glared at me, nose wrinkling in what would have been ugly on an older man or comedic on a younger one. "Fuck you, and no, obviously. Don't be disgusting." He straightened up. "You coming?"

I wanted to make a cheap joke about his choice of words (the Motherfuckers would never pass up the opportunity for a cheap joke, though Jack was new to our ranks, and may not understand), but in the end I couldn't think of anything clever or funny enough so I simply followed. The hall-cave came to a natural end at a doorway into a darkened room I took to be a living room. On the other side of that was more hall, the only thing interrupting it a couple of doors and a framed cross-stitch sampler that read, *Remember the secret.* Whatever that meant.

We reached the first door, at which point I paused, trying to read whatever it said in the pale light from the distant ceiling fixture. "Jack Attack Lives Here? Is that you?"

"Dammit." Instead of using words to express his displeasure, Jack began angrily pulling off his clothes. "I told you—" coat flung into a closet "—I grew up here—" shirt on top of it "—so yeah—" zipper yanked down "—I wrote that when I was twelve." He stood there, shirtless, hair mussed, lips dark red, slacks peeled open but still on his hips. "Problem?"

"Not yet." I hadn't expected him to be quite so…fit. I both lusted after and resented fit gay men. Lusted after because I'd been conditioned to want them (maybe more accurately to want them to want me). Resented because I was not that. Could not be that. And fuck them for shoving it in my face.

Unless they were actually shoving it in my face. To which I objected markedly less.

"The traditional thing to do when you've agreed to have sex and the other person has removed their clothes is to also remove your clothes." As if to spite me he pulled his slacks all the way off. "Christ, I have to stop going to those parties. You're all too young."

"You're thirty-five. It's not like you're half dead." Upon

reflection, given the house we were standing in and its absent owners, I might have skipped over the *half dead* comment. Thankfully, it didn't seem to faze him.

"I'm six years older than Declan, and every time I spend more than twenty minutes with him that gap feels longer."

I shrugged. "That's just Dec. We're the same age and he makes me feel old too. It's because he's too nice."

"Well then. As pleasant as this trip down 'make vaguely damning faintly praising observations about mutual acquaintances' lane has been, I'd appreciate it if we got on with this. I'll need to drive you back to your car and it may as well be sooner than later." His eyebrow twitched. "Unless you were planning to stay the night."

Not *planning* as much as *assuming and hoping it would be worth the lack of rest to get laid*, but there was no need to mention it. And fuck, what a relief. "No. I need my own space."

"With you one hundred percent. So?" He gestured. Toward me. Or maybe my clothes.

"Right."

My body doesn't fill me with endless self-loathing or anything (just the regular amount of self-loathing), but I do have the crummiest body image in the Motherfuckers. It used to be exhausting when they were trying to fix me. Now they've given up and mostly let me have my low self-esteem, except in extreme moments when they hump me in public to show how much they disapprove of my low self-esteem.

Still, it's not like you have to reveal that kind of thing when you're screwing your good friend's sometime-friend. I undressed with an air of defiance, like I was daring him to say anything shitty.

He didn't. For the first time all night. He looked at me up and down, eyes slightly narrow, and said, "I had no idea you were such a bear cub. Fuck me." He met my gaze. "Really, Oscar. Fuck me."

Something about the way he said it got under my skin. A little like he didn't think I would, or maybe like he didn't have much hope. It had been longer than I'd freely admit since the last time I'd done more than a hurried hand job with a guy from Grindr, but I wasn't about to be underestimated by this jerk.

I pushed him over onto the bed and shuffled with a complete lack of grace over his body until I was straddling his chest. He looked surprised but still haughty about it, as if this was a joke to him, which only pissed me off. "Open your fucking mouth."

"Aren't you coming on str—"

It's a tricky move, shoving your dick in someone's mouth when they're talking. But Jack, for all his douchebag posturing, apparently didn't want to actually hurt me. At least not yet.

His hands clamped down on my ass as he took me in, lifting his head, and wow, that's what his mouth was good for, I knew there had to be something.

"Oh fuck." I braced on the headboard, letting him do all the work, practically fucking his own throat on my dick. I was conscious of his hands gripping my flesh, but I didn't have time to worry about it because Jack was an exceptional cocksucker.

I wondered if he'd like to hear me say that. Then I wondered why I suddenly gave a shit what he'd like. Sex endorphins or whatever. A biochemical thing affecting my brain. His tongue did some kind of magical shit and I threw my head back, pulling away. "Stop—fuck—you have to stop or I'll come."

He stopped without fanfare or finesse. "Isn't that your goal? I assumed that was what we were doing here."

"Yeah, I just—" *didn't want to blow my load without even touching you first.* "Fine. Suck me off."

"Oh, well, if you put it that way." He rolled his eyes and went back to work, his fingers biting into my ass a little bit more sharply than they had before. I thought. Or I just felt like an inadequate one-off and was making it up.

The part of me that was a little annoyed by Jack's—whatever—casualness was quickly drowned out by the part of me that wanted to come with increasing need. My dick nudged the back of his throat and I could have restrained myself, but given the eye-roll I decided not to, thrusting a little bit deeper.

Fuck, fuck, it felt good, so good I had to bite my tongue to keep from telling him that. I was vaguely worried I might suffocate him if I thrust in much more and I didn't think we'd actually had a conversation that made "please choke on my cock" an acceptable sex act at this juncture, but he didn't seem to be choking, and he was definitely egging me on, digging his nails into my ass like that.

Screw it. "I'm gonna come." It was more aspirational than anything when I said it, but then Jack was looking up at me, eyes fiery now, almost like he was daring me, or challenging me, or messing with me, and it didn't take much to grab hold of his hair with one hand and pump myself into him.

As far as orgasms went, it was a little on the short-and-blunted side. Still an orgasm, but it hadn't blown my mind or anything. My balls felt a little let down by the experience.

Probably Jack's fault.

"I can't deep throat like that," I said as I awkwardly swung my leg over and knelt beside him. "So if that's what you're looking for, you'll be disappointed."

"Way to sell yourself." He gave his—okay, thick, mouth-watering—dick a few tugs. "I don't deep throat for guys, I do it for me. I like the loss of control. And getting a man off without using my hands is a rush."

I swallowed, a little bit bowled over by his directness. "Oh." Only a little, though. "What do you want?"

"A side hustle I find emotionally fulfilling, a fuck buddy who doesn't need me to be his sole support person in life, and a raise." His eyes widened dramatically. "Oh, you meant *tonight*. In *sex*. To get *off*. Lie back."

"I'm not deep—"

"Yeah, yeah, I know, just fucking do it, Jesus. I'm not looking for a blow job."

"Fine." I lay back where he'd been, but a little more up-right, to make sure he got the point.

"Why do you wear such baggy shirts?" One of his hands grazed over my chest, fingertips trailing through the dark hair that had hit so early on in puberty I was still a little nervous about it, as if someone might realize that manly chest hair did not belong on…a non-manly man like me.

"Because I'm comfortable in them."

"You're *hiding* in them. No one's really comfortable in shapeless, potato sack clothes." He shifted closer, one hand on his dick, one hand curling into my chest hair and tugging in a way that made it hard for me to respond.

Fuck you, you don't know me.

Go to hell, you arrogant prick.

Can I blow you, though?

Wait, where did that last one come from? Dammit.

"You'd look amazing in leather." He pinched one of my nipples until it responded, the treacherous thing. "You should come as a leather daddy to Declan's next costume party."

I snorted. "Oh, and provide joke fodder for my friends to laugh at for the rest of my life? No thanks."

His eyes caught mine like they were snares my casual glance just happened to wander into. "Why the fuck would they do that?"

"Jesus, look at me."

"I am, you idiot."

"If you can't work it out, I'm not explaining it to you." And upon consideration *I'm not as skinny as my friends are wahhhhhhh* isn't exactly a great look on anyone.

He sighed. Heavily. "Someday I really have to stop finding insecurity such a turn-on. It's inconvenient and does not bode well for my future happiness."

"Your future happiness fucking people you don't care about and meeting all of your emotional needs through your hobbies?"

"*Side hustle.* There's no point to a hobby if you're not getting paid."

I threw up my hands. Well, sort of. My hands did an impatient jump, flopping back onto the bed. "I think that's the literal point of a hobby. You have missed the *entire* point."

"Whatever. I'd like to come soon so I can drive you back to your car and go to bed." His hand began to move more quickly on his (still thick, still hard) dick like fighting might actually turn him on.

It would have been a lot easier to derisively point that out if my own body wasn't unfairly starting to respond to his relentless touching. It was the touching, obviously. Not the fighting.

"Oh, for fuck's sake, let me—" I reached out, putting my hand over his. "You're gonna fucking chafe if you don't have lotion or something."

"Lotion, what're you, fifteen?"

"Shut up, Jack." His name snapped off the tip of my tongue like a sprung trap. I maneuvered closer and knelt up, my hand forcing his into a different rhythm. Hadn't he mentioned liking to lose control?

"Shit. Yes." His voice hadn't exactly gone breathy, but it was a hell of a lot less insistent. And he was now almost kneading my chest, occasionally brushing down to my thigh and back up.

The sensation was oddly pleasant. I ignored it.

I gripped the junction of his neck and shoulder with my non-penis hand to steady us both and he made a low sort of keening sound. "You like me holding you in place?"

"Fucking get me *off* already."

I forced his hand to slow down but increased the pressure. "You didn't say the magic word."

"Don't be such a shit."

Now I was basically just forcing his fingers to squeeze his dick. I waited.

He gritted his teeth. "Fine. *Please* get me fucking off already."

"You're such a catch."

"Bite me."

It was awkward and clumsy and shouldn't have worked, not to get him fucking off already, but apparently Jack had an awkward-and-clumsy-hand-job kink. Between my hand on his throat (it had apparently migrated while I had my mind on other matters) and the way I was now ruthlessly propelling him to jerk himself off, his body managed a few lurching thrusts and he came. Just like that. Mostly on me.

We detached, ejaculate stretching between our dick hands for an extended moment of weirdness.

He laughed, this brief burst of hilarity that was gone before I had a chance to decide if it was beneath me to join in. "Gross. Here." He passed me a box of tissues, though my first thought hadn't been *Gross* as much as *Next time in my mouth.* No reason to mention that.

No reason to think there'd be a next time.

"I'm gonna wash up. There's another bathroom but it's upstairs and I have no idea what state it's in, so you may as well wait for this one."

"Okay."

So, there I was, in Jack's bedroom. His childhood bedroom? At least I wasn't surrounded by posters of—whoever Jack would have found hot as a teenager. Leonardo DiCaprio? He was a thing back then, right?

Nothing on the walls at all. Grown-up dresser levered in between a kid dresser and a kid desk. The desk had a sleek laptop on it and nothing else. In fact, the whole room felt bare. I might not have been that far off with imagining him in a sterile industrial loft; the only things on his bed-side table were a lamp and a wireless phone charger, like a hotel room he was only spending one night in.

By the time he got back I'd pulled on my clothes and inspected the thick layer of dust under the bed. Still no… nothing. No evidence of a personality. No lingering traces of teenage Jack.

"Bathroom's yours."

"Thanks."

The bathroom had seen some upgrades, and some still seemed to be in progress. A few tiles were leaning against the wall beside the bathtub. The shower curtain appeared to be a ship caught by an octopus, which seemed not-Jack-like. Then again, maybe death at sea was totally Jack-like.

I cleaned up and returned to find him sitting on his perfectly made unmussed bed, put entirely back together, with even his hair looking like he hadn't so much as felt a stiff wind today, let alone deep throated me while pressed against a mattress.

"Let's go." His voice was unreadable. In a way that I thought meant he wasn't experiencing feelings. Not in a way that indicated I should be trying to read his voice.

Maybe.

We were silent in the car, which was unsettling, given that we usually ended up sniping at each other. But usu-ally we were surrounded by people or—at least earlier—

on our way to have sex. Now that the sex had been had I guess we were left with…this. Nothing. Silence. Whatever.

He pulled up beside my car instead of parking, which was probably for the best. "Thanks for the ride," I said.

"Sure."

I got out.

He pulled away.

I didn't wave. He didn't look back.

So that was that, then.

My phone went off. Okay, maybe that wasn't that, then.

Except it wasn't from Jack. It was from Dec. *Was that JACK who just dropped you off in front of the house? OMG.* Followed by five shocked emojis.

I cringed. Probably should have remembered the extraordinarily long conversation about his landlords installing home security cameras that pinged his phone every time there was movement outside.

I sent back: *No. Don't you have anything better to do than stare at cameras, creeper?*

OMG IT WAS YOU

I'M LOOKING AT YOU RIGHT NOW

HAHAHAHAHAHAHAHAHAHAHAHAHA

This night was going swell but I was ready for it to be over now. I turned slowly and flipped the house off. Then I got in my car and drove home.

Chapter Three

It turned out that I sort of needed the structure of the hated job, or maybe just the structure provided by the hating of my job, because two days into looking for a new one I was a complete mess. I'd started three projects in my apartment that I'd been "meaning to get around to"—and not even gotten halfway into them before quitting. That was on the first day. During which I spent about twenty minutes looking at job listings before I needed a Xanax and a nap.

I kind of hate Xanax. Also it's the only thing that keeps me from having a panic attack. I think that means I should be grateful to it, and I guess I am, but I hate the way it makes me feel, all mush-brained and slow.

Ronnie, on the other hand, can take one and still be a

functional human being. Brain chemistry being a freaking epic mystery and all that.

I vowed, through my mush-brain, that day two would be the first day of the rest of whatever. I would get up and make a healthy breakfast, something I never had time to do when I was running to get to work. I would load up a playlist and do one of those internet workouts with all the push-ups and squats. I would, after doing all that, sit down at my kitchen table with my computer and a notebook and take stock of the jobs for which I was qualified, making a list, recording which ones I could just send resumes to, and which ones I needed to fill out applications for. In this fantasy I pictured the table all cleared off, not full of junk from the stuff I'd started "reorganizing" yesterday, so apparently fairies were going to show up and magic everything away overnight. And you know, that'd be a much better use for Santa or the Easter Bunny—if a supernatural being can magic into your house while you're asleep, it should at least be *contributing* something, right?

After that productive morning I would eat a healthy lunch, finish with the job applications in the afternoon, eat a healthy dinner, and go to bed, sleeping the deep, hard-earned sleep of the righteous.

Whenever I make grand plans like this ("It's the New Year! I'll be motivated to change my life!"

"It's my birthday! I'm thirty now, and thirty is old enough to change my life!"

"It's spring/summer/fall/a new moon/a new month/a new haircut/a new pair of shoes and this will change my life!"), the plans always rely on that elusive quality: waking up with the same motivation in the morning.

On day two I was even less motivated than I had been on day one. I ate instant oatmeal and drank a whole pot of coffee. When I was miserably buzzing from the coffee I *almost* got off the couch to do a single knee push-up. Thought hard about it. Pictured myself doing it. Closed my eyes and really tried to imagine what it'd feel like.

Which is where it fell apart, because one knee push-up would probably make me feel like a loser for only being able to do one push-up, and only a knee one at that, so I'd end up more depressed than doing nothing which meant clearly the right way to go about this was to do nothing instead. The whole "visualize yourself being successful and you'll be successful" thing is such BS. I've visualized myself doing a lot of things. Y'know. From my couch. Where I visualized and basked in my visualization and then managed to not do any of those things.

Is it considered "taking a nap" if you're so lethargic you can't keep your eyes open? Yes, right? Naps are supposed to make you live longer. Hashtag healthy.

Ronnie waited until seven p.m. to text me, which showed a lot of self-control. I'd told her my plans and she'd been *such* a downer about them...by predicting that deciding to change everything in one day was maybe, possibly, a recipe for changing nothing at all and also (my oldest friends can really twist the knife) just an excuse to hate myself for not fulfilling my own unrealistic expectations.

She would have been totally justified by texting: *Told you so.* Since obviously if I'd filled out a million job applications I would be all over the Motherfuckers thread demanding credit.

Instead she texted: *I'm picking up Korean food, clear a space for me on the couch.*

I surveyed the aforementioned couch and wrinkled my nose. I didn't text back. I did shove my collection of pillows, dirty coffee cups, crumpled up snack wrappers (it's only 100 calories if you limit yourself to just *one*, by the way), and tangled charging cables over the back of the couch so there was room for both of us to camp in my depression nest of blankets.

The blankets were staying. That was the skeleton of any good depression nest: a collection of soft blankets of various weights.

Ronnie handed over the food and went to wash her hands, returning with a dubious expression. "So your kitchen has exploded."

"Reorganizing."

"Ah." She glanced at the TV cabinet thing. "Reorganizing that too?"

"Yeah."

"Right. I'm going to open a couple of windows. And the curtains."

"It's nighttime," I argued.

"It's August, it's warm, and this apartment smells like the freaking bell jar."

See? What'd I tell you about good clichés?

I started eating while she let in a bunch of fresh air and street noise I didn't particularly want. "Didn't need a Xanax today," I mumbled.

"That's good! What with the way they make it so you don't get out of bed all day."

I laughed a little too harshly. "Don't need Xanax for that, do I?"

Ronnie sighed and leaned in to kiss the side of my forehead. "You know, you weren't doing so hot on your meds before now. You think maybe it might be time to switch them up?"

"Uh, right after I lost my job? Not really." Transitioning antidepressants was pretty much the worst possible thing on earth. Aside from famine and genocide and shit like that.

"Oh, true, yeah, it probably would have been better to do it six months ago. Hmm, what does that make me think of? Oh yeah, when I first brought it up and you were like, 'It's still too cold, it's not a good time.' And then when I brought it up again and you were like, 'Work sucks, not now.' And oh right, the third time, when you said, 'I just flunked a potential relationship, can't change meds too.' You notice a theme here, mister?"

I pretended to think. "Our conversations are super repetitive?"

She laughed. "Shut up. Seriously. There is no right time to fuck with meds, keep it in mind. Speaking of fucking with things—you and Jack, huh?"

"Me and Jack nothing, there's *nothing* between us. What'd Dec do? Put it out on the family thread?"

"Actually, he had an idea he wasn't sure he should bring up since you and Jack *nothinged* the other night."

I gestured threateningly with a dumpling. "I have *nothinged* a lot of men. So what?"

"Well." She turned all of her attention to her food. Definite warning sign. "You know how your schedule's pretty open at the moment?"

"Yesssss?"

"Jack needs help with his house because his grandmother's selling it, right?"

I frowned. "Uh. She is?"

"Wow, you were super tuned out at your pity party. Yeah. He said she's wanted to sell it since she moved, but now she's given him a legit deadline to get it cleared out. And I guess she told him to have some service come in and throw everything away but he doesn't want to, which I get, because there's probably good furniture and stuff."

"Uh." He hadn't explained about the hoarding, then. "Yeah, furniture." The tunnel in the back hallway. A pile of *Rolling Stone*. A cross-stitch sampler. Jack Attack Lives Here. Not that I was attached to the guy, but he had a lot of history in that house. It made sense that he didn't particularly want a crew of people to come in and take everything apart. "So what's Dec's idea?"

"That maybe you could help Jack with his house. He was saying he has to hire people anyway."

"That's a terrible idea. Jack and I can't stand each other."

She shook her head. "But that's why it's brilliant. He can order a dumpster for stuff that needs to be thrown away and one of those storage units they drop off at the house for stuff he wants to keep. All you have to do is move things into one or the other, right? And make a donate pile, probably. But that's just one more pile. Jack doesn't even have to be there as long as he takes you through and tells you what goes where."

"Huh." It was still a terrible idea, but also, fuck, I didn't want to look for a job. And the sex had been decent. Maybe it'd be possible to fuck buddy this arrangement into something a little consistent.

Because sex is good for the mood. It's like exercise, but with orgasms.

"This is still a terrible idea," I said.

"It might be," she conceded. "But neither one of you has all that much to lose. Why not try it?"

"I doubt you'd get Jack to agree. Even Dec isn't that much of a miracle worker."

"You underestimate our boy. He already got Jack to agree—at least to everyone going over on Saturday to get started."

"And Jack said okay to that?"

She paused. "I *think* he did? But I guess I wouldn't put it past Dec to just have everyone show up. I mean. He wouldn't. Right?"

"If he thought he was doing it for Jack's own good he might."

We stared at each other.

I pulled out my phone. "Mase will know." A minute later Mase's face was peering out from the screen.

"Oh, I see how it is, eating Korean without me. You jerks."

"This is pity takeout," I explained. "Because I am so pathetic Ronnie's worried I won't feed myself anything but frosting."

"In my defense, I saw two empty frosting containers in the garbage." She gave me a Look he could definitely see over the video.

"Oh man, that's rough. Okay, then. Still could have invited me but whatever." He wasn't actually hurt. You could always tell with Mase. There was a huge gulf between his teasing voice and his injured voice.

"What do you know about Dec's thing with Jack's house?" I asked.

"More than I know about your thing with Jack's something."

"There is nothing with Jack's anything. Literally. It was *no thing.* Ronnie says there's a house cleaning plan?"

"Yeah, Saturday."

"But Jack knows about it? Because it doesn't sound like something he'd consent to."

"I guess you'd know better than we would, hot stuff. Wink wink." And he actually winked, like his trolling-me energy was too much for just words.

I rubbed my eyes. "Shut. Up."

"I will. But only 'cause you're fragile. And I guess Jack wasn't super thrilled about it, but Dec was persuasive, the way Dec is, so that's the scoop."

"'That's the scoop' is not a thing people say," I retorted.

"And yet! I gotta go prep for my date tonight. Bye-ee!"

"Have a good date!" Ronnie called.

"You know I will, honey."

I slumped back in the couch. "Weird that Jack's okay with everyone going to his place."

"Is it? I mean, I know he's…him. But he does seem to need help. And we are, like, his friends."

Did he think of the Motherfuckers as his friends? He must after months of hanging out with us, though I'd never gotten the impression Jack was all that into friendship as a concept. "Uh, yeah. I guess."

She raised her eyebrows. "Dec didn't tell Jack to hire you yet. He wanted to make sure you didn't hate the idea first."

"Wow, that's so sweet and considerate of him."

"I know!"

"There's no way Jack hires me for anything. But I'll come on Saturday since I've got nothing better to do."

"Well also because—" her eyes flickered to the rest of my apartment "—usually you're super good at cleaning and organizing stuff."

I threw a napkin at her, which fluttered harmlessly over the back of the couch. I wasn't quick enough to protest before she'd leaned over and seen all the crap I'd tossed back there in advance of her arrival.

"Oh wow. Yeah. Cleaning not exactly your strong suit right now, baby?"

"Shut up."

"Sure, sure. How about we do a tiny bit of straightening before I leave, huh?"

I grumbled the whole time about how I didn't need help, but on the other hand, Ronnie and I had lived together in super messy dorm rooms. Of all the people in my life to embarrass myself in front of by not having done dishes in three days, she was probably the most forgiving. Or the least embarrassing. Or something.

By the time Ronnie went home my kitchen looked livable and the stuff behind the couch was cleaned up. She hadn't touched my blanket nest though. Ronnie knew to respect the blanket nest. Hashtag friends forever or some crap.

Chapter Four

And then there was the endless week. The week of jobless jobhunt jobhate. Time had no meaning. Sleep wake eat sleep wake eat sleep wake eat poop. Basically. In a nutshell.

To be honest, part of me was looking forward to Saturday. To the prospect of *doing* something. Accomplishing something.

I did manage to apply to three jobs. Sort of. I sent in my resume to them, anyway. With the same lackluster cover letter on each, with only the job title changed. *To whom it may concern, I am very interested in your position of blah-blah-blah…*

Needless to say, I did not hear back.

Hours passed in my blanket nest. Empty mugs piled up until I was out of mugs and had to wash one to use one.

So I picked my favorite and kept washing it and using it. I watched so many YouTube videos that I think the algorithm shorted out and suddenly it was showing me random stuff like woodturning (dudes putting logs on machines that spin them really fucking fast and then like chiseling them as they spin*) (*unofficial definition) and ticklish camels (though you have to wonder if it's laughing or just doing that horrible thing where it can't control itself but honestly hates being tickled).

I broke YouTube is the point. It no longer understood me. A single week of unemployment, at times round-the-clock video watching, moods that spanned from serious (-ly depressing) documentaries to the one with the ferret mom showing off her babies, and I'd managed to stump even Google's search-and-recommendation engine until I watched whatever it told me to watch. Which was everything.

By the time I showed up at Jack's on Saturday morning I was a shell of a man. A shell of a chubby, over-caffeinated, under-nourished, sleep-deprived man.

His first words upon seeing me: "Jesus, Oscar, you look deceased."

"Eighty percent deceased," I mumbled. "I need more coffee." I didn't need more coffee. I needed something in my body to absorb the coffee I'd already had. Like an entire baguette, maybe. "Also I need a baguette."

"Coffee's in the kitchen. I don't have a baguette but I could probably pull off toast."

"Toast. Yes. Please. Thanks." The kitchen was clearly a space he used—it bore no resemblance to the back hallway at all and was a strange mashup of things that fit in the house (the stove looked like it was straight out of the seventies) and things that had no business in the same era as the house (if that was an espresso machine it was restaurant-grade, and if it wasn't, it was a device for time travel).

I beelined for the coffeepot, which was not the gleaming spaceship you'd expect from a guy like him with *that* espresso machine, but an ancient Mr. Coffee with part of the plastic cracked and a chip out of the pour spout in the glass carafe. "Is this coffeepot from this millennia or—?"

"No." He aggressively thumbed the lever on an equally ancient toaster. "Look, today is basically my nightmare and I've regretted it for every second since I agreed to it. Is there any possible way you can make Declan take it back?"

I glanced at my watch. I was early. Not by much, but given the rest of the Motherfuckers were always late I didn't expect them for another fifteen minutes. "Uh, no. That ship has sailed. Why *did* you agree? I almost didn't believe it except Dec doesn't lie."

He slumped into a chair at the table and, after a slight hesitation, I carried my coffee (the mug had been precleaned and handily located above the coffee machine) to sit across from him.

"Well?" I asked.

"He threatened me. The little bastard."

That made…zero sense. "Threatened to what? Cry if you didn't let him help you?"

"Threatened to tell a mutual acquaintance of ours if I didn't let him help me. And then *she* would have come over, and that is—I can't deal with that."

"So you agreed to this instead? She must be terrifying."

"Oh, she is."

The toast popped up. For an awkward moment we both just sat there. Then he stood, effortlessly turning back into super competent Jack, who buttered toast and plated it and dropped it on the table in front of me.

"Thanks."

He waved a hand.

"Okay, well." It was almost difficult to think about someone else's problems after a week of straight-up self-pity, but I made the effort. "By the end of today at least some stuff will be…improved. The Motherfuckers work hard. We could…" I stopped myself before I said something offensive, like *We could turn the back tunnel into a hallway.* "…work on the back hallway, which might be helpful."

He grimaced. "Yes. Because what I want most in the world is everyone looking at the disgusting mess my grandfather made of the place and thinking about how weird he must have been, and judging him, and Grandmother, and me—"

"Yeah, okay, shut up." When he looked about ready to bite me, I added, "That's not their way. I'm the judgmental one. The rest of them are *good people.*" And despite the almost biting me, I thought he at least knew what I meant when I said that. "And for the record I didn't judge. So maybe, you know, back off."

After a very long look, as if he was trying to decide how truthful I was, he finally shrugged. "It was a secret. Always. No one ever made it past the living room, which used to be clear of stuff. Then, once I moved out, his collections grew and I think out of self-defense, Grandmother stopped fighting him on it."

I thought I understood a little. Not that I'm a hoarder. But I get taking comfort in things that aren't directly comforting. Like too much food or too much YouTube. Or staying holed up in my apartment with the curtains closed all week. Not actually good for me, but I knew that if I surrounded myself with familiar sensations, my brain would tell me I was safe.

It seemed like hoarding was driven by similar instincts. Not that I was going to ask.

"Fuck." He ran both hands into his hair, making his arms look incredibly hot in his white T-shirt, the asshole. "Forget I mentioned it. I just hate every part of this."

The doorbell rang and he cursed again then went to answer it, leaving me sitting there, at his ancient Formica table, drinking from a mug that must have been a free gift from a long-defunct bank, thinking about Jack like an actual human being, not a jerk who couldn't let anything go.

It was uncomfortable and I didn't like it so I ate my toast and distracted myself by strategizing about how best to haul a million pounds of paper out to the dumpster, and whether there was a recycling option.

Dec, of course, had taken care of it.

The thing about seeing him in a different context—about seeing any of them in a different context—was that no matter how well I knew my friends, they still somehow managed to surprise me. I knew Dec as a sweet guy with a ready laugh and a hard-on for cooking. To Jack he was a project manager with questionable references, though once they'd worked together for a few months he said he'd decided Dec wasn't that bad.

And the way Dec glowed when Jack said that, you'd think "not that bad" was code for "wildly amazing" in Jack-speak. For all I knew, maybe it was.

Point being, there was a huge bin for trash, a huge bin for recyclables (we're talking big metal containers that have to be lifted by machines, not regular garbage cans), a section in the front yard where we could put things that were to be donated for a later pickup, and—here Jack balked, but Declan won—space in the garage where we could put everything that he wanted to save because the pod storage thing wasn't going to arrive until Tuesday, an arrangement Dec was definitely taking personally.

"How can it take *ten entire days* for something like that to be delivered? It's outrageous!"

Ronnie, Mase and I all looked at each other. *Outrageous*, Ronnie mouthed. We cracked up.

"Okay, okay, it's fine." Dec, flushing slightly, turned to Jack. "There's still a lot we can do. Let's get started sorting things."

The group, currently gathered in the front yard, hadn't been inside yet. And for a second it looked like Jack really was going to call the whole thing off and send them all away.

Then, like I was watching the word "resignation" physically manifest itself, his shoulders rounded, his forehead creased. "My grandfather was a hoarder. That's a lot of what I need help clearing out. It's unpleasant, but that's what it is."

Only in that moment did I realize I could have warned them and avoided their surprise-masked-with-over-compensating-smiles.

"We're totally ready!" Dec said cheerfully. "Aren't we totally ready?"

Sidney, at his side, nodded. "I am totally ready to move some things into bins."

"All right."

And we all trooped into the house. Where we stood. In the clearing of the living room. Clustered between the coffee table and the armchair. Jack looked around. "I guess we're starting in here." He gestured vaguely and began to haphazardly dictate where things should go.

"Hey," Dec interrupted. "Maybe we start with quadrants? Leave the area by the stairs for now since you said no one goes up there and the stairs themselves will be a whole other thing. You and Oscar take the area between the kitchen door and the hall door, Sidney and I will take the front door side, and Mase and Ronnie can take the corner."

"Sounds good," Ronnie said, rubbing her hands.

"Great! Let's go!" Dec's enthusiasm for projects was unparalleled, and work began in silence. Dead silence. Just shoes shuffling and paper shifting and an occasional low-voiced question. I kept my distance from Jack, who was hauling things to the trash bin with a disturbing sense of urgency as if the whole house could be finished in a day if we only went fast enough.

The next time he went outside Dec said, "Oscar—you

think you can distract him for a few minutes? I'm worried he's, uh, not handling this well?"

"Distract him how? And if you say sex—"

"Obviously not. I mean unless—"

"*No.*"

He grinned. "Just start in on the kitchen maybe? Or take him out for lunch or something. Anything to like…make it less terrible in here."

I rolled my eyes and was about to say something in reply when Jack came back in, so we went back to work. And it's not like it was my responsibility to do anything about it, since I wasn't even really friends with Jack, and the "clearing out Jack's house" idea was Declan's in the first place. Except now that he'd pointed it out, I kind of couldn't stop paying attention to how oppressive Jack's presence was in the room. His semi-furious movements were a lot to take and the feeling that he was just about to explode was inescapable.

Dec made eyeballs at me and I sighed. You have sex with a man one freaking time and suddenly you're in charge of corralling him forever.

"Uh." What was I supposed to say now? "Can I see you? In the…bedroom?" I grimaced. "Not the bedroom. The hallway. The kitchen. Show me how to make more coffee or something."

"What the actual—"

I grabbed his arm. "Need to talk to you now."

He allowed me to drag him into the hallway, but once we were outside his door (*Jack Attack Lives Here*) refused to move. "What the fuck, Oscar? It's not really the time for a quickie."

"Oh, don't flatter yourself. You're being a prick to my friends, who are trying to be your friends, so fucking quit it."

"I didn't ask anyone to come here and do this!" he shot back.

"Because you suck at accepting help, good for you, join the club, but you obviously need it, so maybe stop being such a dick about it. *Or*—" I realized I was being Way Too Loud "—or call someone else to do this, but you can't do it yourself, asshole. You're gonna have to figure it out one way or another." I stood there, waiting for him to bite back at me.

He leaned against the wall instead, head down, ear practically brushing the framed crosswork sampler I'd seen the other night. *Remember the secret.* I wondered what the secret was, since the sampler for sure pre-dated the pop culture thing. Jack sighed. "My grandmother wants to come for dinner. I…misled her a bit about how much progress I'd made with the house and now she wants me to bring her over. But if she sees how I'm living…"

I had no idea what to do with dejected Jack. "Uh."

"Jesus, Oscar. Don't fucking try to be nice to me."

"I'm not! Like I'd bother."

He huffed a laugh. Or at least a huff. "I know everyone's trying to help. I'll work back here so they don't have to deal with my mood."

"Right. Good. Yeah. Okay then." Since there was nothing else for me to say I turned and went back to the living room. "Jack's going to spare us his dubious company," I said loudly enough for him to hear.

Dec shot me angry eyes, but in the hallway I heard another huff, this time more pronounced.

Most of the stuff we were hauling out fell into two categories: papers (newspapers, *TV Guide*, *Reader's Digest*, piles and piles of unopened junk mail, credit card offers, long expired coupons in little paper-clipped groups by subject, and boxes and boxes of receipts that we set aside to be shredded because some of them were really old and Sidney pointed out that they might have identifying information on them); and garbage.

Literal garbage. In small bags, some of them produce bags, some grocery store bags, some carefully sealed into battered Ziplocs. All dry, but some of it…dried. Leathery orange peels and powdery coffee grounds. What looked like the two sides of an avocado, but when I picked up the bag they crumpled, breaking apart.

It was a little surreal. And it took some juggling to get rid of them: gather up as many little bags as you could, try not to drop any as you walked, carry them out to the bin at the curb, and try to tip as many as possible inside. After a while there were a lot of "Man down!" shouts, as well as a few along the lines of "Watch your feet, I think there was glass in that one!"

And everything—everything—was dusty. We sneezed and we coughed and we made quiet comments about what might be living in the dust, with Sidney going on an impassioned (for them) monologue about dust mites getting a bad rap. Slowly, bit by bit, we made some space in the living room. It almost looked worse somehow, as if by dismantling the debris around the edges—which my brain had subtracted from my awareness—we'd ended up drawing attention to the fact that the room itself was small and old-fashioned, its wallpaper yellowed, its furniture worn. In eroding the piles we'd made the room appear more cluttered rather than less.

Dec called lunch around two and ordered pizza over an app, which was a thing I had to do more. I loved eating takeout, but I hated calling to order it. He'd stuck his head around to the hall to tell Jack we were eating, but Jack hadn't made an appearance. When the pizza arrived and he was still MIA, Dec nudged me to go tell him.

"Just as a reminder: Jack and I can't stand each other," I muttered, but I was already getting up from our impromptu front yard picnic. Maybe because Dec always won. Or maybe because part of me was a little bit intrigued by… welp, it sounded awful, but part of me was intrigued by Jack being vulnerable. He was the kind of guy who'd show up to drinks in a suit because that was what he happened to be wearing; it was hard not to feel intimidated. But this—him—less impenetrable…intriguing, yeah.

I found him surrounded by new piles. The tunnel effect was a little less than it had been, but the piles appeared to have crawled down the hall toward the bedroom. He looked at me, and maybe it was the effect of the dust or the old lighting or whatever, but he seemed a lot more pale than he had before. "You should eat some food."

"I have no appetite."

"And yet you should still eat some food." I hesitated.

"The living room…kind of looks worse, fair warning. You might go out through the garage."

So of course he went through the living room. "You weren't joking."

"My jokes are funnier than that."

"I hadn't noticed."

I rolled my eyes. "Anyway, there's pizza."

He reached out as I went to pass him, not quite touching my arm but I stopped walking anyway. "Do you think, if all of us work together, we can make this room presentable today? I want to be able to bring her home for dinner this week."

The place was wrecked. The pile of "we aren't sure what to do with this" was growing. And it was going to need a serious deep-clean before any immunocompromised old people sat in it. If I was a glass-half-full guy, I would have assured him we could do it.

I'm not a glass-half-full guy. "Not likely. I could come back tomorrow to do more, and probably Dec and Mase would too, though Sidney and Ronnie might be working."

"Damn."

There wasn't much else I could say to that, so I went outside to eat, and after a few minutes Jack followed.

He called me maybe an hour after I got home that night. Long enough for me to have taken a shower and put a frozen lasagna in the oven, but not long enough for it to have cooked all the way through.

I didn't answer. I never answer. Well, only if it's Ronnie or Declan, since both of them are capable of calling me back until I pick up, even if it takes an entire episode of *Buffy*. But, unlike them, Jack left a voicemail.

"It's Jack. Declan explained his master plan to me after the rest of you left, and if you want a job, I want to hire you. It's short term, and we'd have to discuss the money and scope, but I would pay you a lot just to save me those damn puppy dog eyes of his." Pause long enough that I thought he'd hung up. "And anyway, there's always the potential for more sex. Call me back if you're interested. Or text, whatever."

I probably wouldn't have done it if it wasn't to avoid Dec harassing me about it (his damn puppy dog eyes worked on me too, and he knew it).

I probably wouldn't have done it if it wasn't for the lukewarm offer of more sex, which I was lonely enough to find acceptable.

I probably wouldn't have done it if it wasn't for that last line, since I hate phone calls and would have never called him back.

I probably wouldn't have done it if it wasn't for that sampler in the back hallway: *Remember the secret.* What was the secret?

I texted: *As long as I get a bonus for dealing with your moods.*

He texted back: *The bonus is me not firing you for gross insubordination.*

And just like that, I kind of had a job.

Chapter Five

When you're looking for a job—even if "looking for a job" just means "feeling really guilty for not spending more time on websites where jobs live"—actually getting a job is the holy grail, the thing that once you get it, it'll fix your problems. It'll change your world.

And okay, I realize I only spent a week unemployed, but I have an impressively high gamer score for guilt.

We hammered out the details via email. It went something like this:

- I spend about three hours feeling sick and full of dread because I assume he'll lowball me and I'll have to negotiate for some reasonable payment. (I didn't know what "reasonable" was in this context, but I figured it'd take at least a week or two, so I was trying to gird my loins to demand a thousand dollars, even though I'd probably fold at seven hundred.)

- Email comes in from Jack (I'd been expecting a phone call). In it, he explains, "I've done some research and it looks like the range of prices for this type of job runs anywhere from five thousand dollars to twenty thousand dollars."
- I hyperventilate and have to pause for a glass of water.
- He further explains that given there are no pets involved, and the food involved is not wet or molding, he thinks seven is a fair place to start.
- Not *seven hundred* but *seven thousand.* Dollars. US dollars.
- He goes on to say he's open to renegotiating in the future should the job require it.
- I faint. Okay, not really. But I did have a moment of wooziness when I realized that was what I usually made in two and a half months and I wouldn't even have to talk to any people. Literally. I was being paid to do something that necessitated *not* talking to humans. Cue wooz.
- I send back a sedately worded email indicating that this arrangement is acceptable to me. Thank god for email. If he'd been able to hear my voice it would have gone up three registers in sheer relief.

- He sends back a sedately worded email to ask for my relevant employment information because of course Jack is the guy who even pays taxes on hiring a guy to clean a house. Or maybe because he's the guy who writes that off on his taxes. Or whatever.
- I send my information. And SCENE.

Which meant that details were hammered before I went to bed Saturday night. Achievement unlocked. Grail found. Whatever.

It became clear to me quickly on Monday morning that my problems were far from over.

"This should be easy enough to manage in a day," Jack said, looking (dubiously) at the mess he'd made of the back hallway.

"You worked on it literally all day on Saturday and made pretty much no progress."

He waved a hand, dismissing my very valid objection. "You will not be encumbered with my issues. Anyway, stay as long as you want. I just need this done."

I probably shouldn't have argued. Given he was paying me *seven. thousand. dollars* to carry some stuff to some bins. But not-arguing isn't exactly my forte. "And I'll get it done. But since it took five people to even begin to make a dent in the living room, I'm not committing to some crazy idea of yours that the back hallway will be done today. Also, what's the priority? If you're trying to bring your grandma over for dinner, what do you need to be ready for that?"

"That's not until Wednesday."

"*Wednesday*? Maybe you should blindfold her and take her directly into the kitchen."

"We eat in the living room." He said it so quickly it seemed to take him aback. "I mean we used to."

"So the priority is the living room."

He faltered. "I guess I could take her through the front door. Yes, all right, the priority is the living room."

The woman had lived in this house, in this state, for how many years? It wasn't like she'd be shocked, but whatever, not my family, not my dysfunction. "Got it. See you later."

He still didn't seem all that keen on leaving me in his house, but you know, what else was he going to do? Take a few weeks off to sit there staring at me?

I shuddered. And hoped, fervently, that he did not decide to take a few weeks off to stare at me while I cleared out his house.

"Okay. I guess help yourself to anything you want in the kitchen. If you want anything." He was still bringing a seriously uncomf vibe.

"Got it. Bye."

"Yeah. Bye, then."

And, finally, the door closed and I was alone. In Jack's grandparents' house. Surrounded by their/his things. It was an eerier sensation than I'd anticipated so I just stood there in the back hallway for a long moment, breathing in dust and the remnants of his morning coffee. Then I decided to take stock.

Since this was a paying job (and I felt like I should feel a lot more awkward about that, what with the sex thing, but I really didn't), I'd brought a notebook and a couple of pens with me. The back hall led down to a door that, once unlocked, revealed a backyard in dire straits. This might have been where the collecting started, or maybe it was where Jack's grandmother had first funneled it, but there were quite a few piles of debris, and they looked pretty old.

Jack's bedroom was on the backyard side of the downstairs bathroom. Strange location for a bedroom until I went back outside and realized it had been added on at some point, or maybe walled in from a porch off the kitchen, which would make more sense. Wall in the porch, extend it beyond the bathroom to meet up with the hallway.

Kitchen was fine. Nothing that required my attention there. Back hall was a mess. Living room needed a lot of help.

Since those seemed overwhelming, I contemplated the stairs instead. I thought I could make it up them if I was careful about moving the small appliances. Clearly there had been a walkable pathway here at some point in the not too distant past, because I could still see where the oldest clutter had been pushed up against the wall. A few steps still had enough space for a shoe close to the railing, some did not.

I navigated like a free climber. (No, of course I don't free climb, I'm not an idiot hipster with delusions of invincibility. I do engage in extreme documentary watching though; all the fun, much better bathroom facilities, a lot more snacks.) When I got to the top. I experienced a full minute of thinking the stairs were the worst of it.

That was before I saw the first bedroom. It was not enterable. I could wedge the door open, but beyond my body holding it there, everything else was stuff. Junk? It looked like junk, not at all like things that had meaning if you weren't keeping them because your brain told you to. But I could, once I slid my hand behind an ironing board held against the wall by a treadmill and found the light switch, see traces of pink wallpaper between mounds and piles of stuff, some of which looked like it belonged to a child.

Only one other room up here, plus a bathroom. Which might mean this room belonged to whichever of Jack's parents had been raised in this house. Maybe his mom, not to judge by the pink, but you know, that would make sense. Did that mean the kid stuff was Jack's?

I flicked the light off and closed the door, back to the way I found it, wondering about all the shows I'd seen on hoarding, and how tied in it was to emotions. Wondering what it must have been like to be raised in this house by grandparents who probably hadn't planned on having a little kid around again. Not that I knew much about it, only what Declan had said: Jack's grandparents raised him and he'd taken care of them the last few years until his grandfather got dementia badly. He'd died last spring, not long after they moved to the facility where his grandmother now lived.

Wow. That was...it. That was literally everything I knew about the man. Oh, that and he'd been divorced. He could probably get all of us thoughtful Christmas gifts based solely on what Dec had said about us, but he wasn't exactly a sharer, Jack.

The upstairs landing was dusty and there was a desk and a few odd items, but nothing that would raise alarm bells. I felt a bit like a creeper looking at the grandparents' room, but to my relief it was neat and tidy. Dusty and needed to be aired out, but neat.

The bathroom was somewhat gross, but he'd already told me he was going to have people come in to professionally clean the bathrooms and kitchen before he put it on the market, so that wasn't my job.

I retraced my precarious steps down to the living room and sat in the armchair to take a few notes. Sitting produced a nose-wrinkling smell of smoke and burnt polyester. I got immediately back up, nose wrinkling. Maybe the chair had been in a fire at some point? Not the best place to sit, anyway. I wound up in the kitchen, where the old Mr. Coffee had been cleaned and left on the dish rack to dry, the countertops were immaculate, and the gleaming espresso machine's little espresso cup had been rinsed and overturned on its gleaming metal tray.

So fucking Jack. I mean seriously.

The back hallway and the upstairs room were going to be the worst of it. And the backyard. He'd probably need a crew to come in and just haul everything back there away. Which is what he *said* he wanted inside the house as well, but he hadn't done it, had he? And it's not like Jack was wishy-washy when he knew what he wanted. See: deep throating. But maybe he just didn't want strangers touching his grandmother's stuff. Anyway, now he had me. Not quite a stranger, not quite a friend.

First up: the living room. I'd unearthed two vacuums, neither of which looked like it was from the current century. Was vacuuming in my purview? Probably not, but it would be satisfying to do after clearing things out. Assuming I made it to an "after" state. I rolled up my proverbial sleeves, opened the front door and all the downstairs windows, and started carrying some stuff to some bins.

The first two hours of actual work passed...peacefully? I'm not sure that's a valid way to talk about dismantling someone's late grandpa's hoarding cache, but since my usual work was sitting around in a state of low panic waiting for the phone to ring (cue: intense panic!) or sitting around on the phone with customers in a state of medium panic waiting for them to flip out on me (cue: intense panic!), even the grime and dust and muscle aches of carrying stuff from Point A to Point B was relaxing in comparison.

I took care of the easy stuff first. Garbage was obviously garbage, so out that went. Periodicals from a million years ago: garbage. Any papers that were not personalized—and damn, I didn't get the same TO RESIDENT crap in an apartment that my folks did in a residential house, but I'd never exactly felt grateful for that until I was clearing out all the junk that Jack's house received: garbage.

Once I'd dug through the first layers of stuff, I started hitting...well, more stuff, but less easy-to-toss-out stuff. Mail that was definitely junk, but *targeted* junk. What would a regular worker in my role do with this sort of thing? I knew Jack didn't want to see any of it. He hadn't exactly spelled it out, but my gut (and I had quite a gut *ba-ding-ching*) was that he'd feel best if the whole place was cleared out without any further involvement from himself.

Give the customer what he wants, right? I grabbed a box

from a collection of collapsed boxes, taped it back into its proper form with absolutely no pauses to scratch my head, or interludes set to a laugh track that would be featured in a montage about our hero not knowing how to do very basic things, and started putting anything I wasn't quite sure about in the box.

See, what they don't tell you about boxes is that boxes can be a slippery slope. Suddenly box one was halfway full of papers. Were they important papers? WHO KNEW?

Actually, a lot of people probably knew. I texted Ronnie, who had a mortgage and therefore must have the sacred knowledge of how long papers were supposed to be saved.

Ronnie: *I think seven years?*

Me: *So I should put anything older than that in the shred pile?*

Ronnie: *It's seven years from the tax year. Seven tax years. Not calendar years.*

Me: *Uh-huh. Um. Shred pile then?*

Ronnie: *You should probably run that by Jack and see what he wants to do, honestly.*

Me: *That is SO the wrong answer.*

She sent back a shrugging gif.

I knew she was right. But ugh. "Fine," I said petulantly to the empty house.

Me: *Hey, should I keep all the personal papers for you? Do you want me to throw anything of a certain year back in the shred box?*

Jack: *Keep the last ten years, shred everything else.*

And…that was it. Okay. Cool. Very clear.

I worked out what year was the cutoff, prepared another box, and went back to sorting papers. When I'd first assessed the living room, I'd thought that nearly all of it was garbage or recycling, and figured it would only take a few hours to sort into those two groups and deposit things in the appropriate bins.

But *so. many. piles* turned out to be personal papers I actually had to sort. And it was a little odd because for the most part it had seemed like the stuff being hoarded was of no practical value. But a lot of these papers clearly at least kinda mattered. So who'd been collecting them? And why?

In my family my mother was the one who kept all the important records, and my father was the one who moaned about how irritating it was to have her nagging him for his receipts for months. She had boxes meticulously ordered by year in the rafters of their garage and until I was sorting Jack's grandparents' stuff I'd never thought about it.

My mom's mom was a US citizen from Mexico and her dad was a Mexican citizen who'd been in the US since he was twelve and claimed he was a legal resident until the day he died, even though I guess everyone knew he wasn't. My mom had been pretty upset when she found out, but I got why he lied about it. And I got why other people covered for him. You spend most of your life in a place, pay your taxes, raise your family...by the end he really felt like an American.

And, depending on your definition, he *was.* A good American at that. But don't try to tell my mom. Something about the way they'd kept the secret from her messed up her head, so now Abuelito is one of the many things we never talk about.

Plus, she married my dad, this conservative white guy who was a proud Republican until, as he said, "The party went to the nutjobs." Poor guy. Must be rough to be abandoned by the people you assumed would always be there for you: other old white guys.

Anyway, Mom took care of the important things, like filing the taxes and tracking expenses. And Dad made more money and told himself that was the important part. And I was their too-round, too-gay, too-fussy son, with the anxiety problem they pretended didn't exist.

I was lost in thought—about families, and roles, and how things manifest from generation to generation, like would I be so caught up in protecting myself that I'd had the same four friends since college if I hadn't been raised by a woman who posthumously disowned her father for keeping an understandable secret from her?—when Jack got home. Lost in thought, and, it should be said, surrounded by piles of papers.

He stood in the doorway and blinked at me. "You're still here?"

I gestured to myself. And the hereness. "Yes."

"I didn't expect you to stay all day."

"It's a job. You're paying me."

"I think it looks worse than it did this morning."

I flipped him off. "It doesn't. That's an illusion. There's a lot of organization now and you're going to need more boxes."

"Okay. Have you eaten anything?"

"I *tried* to eat. But you have very little food. I think I ended up eating all the bananas and a can of beans."

His forehead creased in a way I would have taken for anger except I'd provoked him to anger before and this wasn't what it looked like. "I didn't realize I was meant to be feeding you as well as paying you. I'll try to be more prepared in the future."

Since it was a slightly shitty thing to say after telling me to help myself, I shot back, "And I didn't realize that every piece of mail this house has received in decades was all sitting right here in the living room, but you don't see me complaining."

His laughter came out a surprised bark. "Hell, Oscar. How awful was it today? You really did not need to stay this long."

"Could have been worse. And if you're bringing your grandmother over on Wednesday, I really *did* need to stay this long. There are way more important papers here than I realized when we were just pulling garbage out the other day."

His eyes scanned the floor around me. "She tried to put their affairs in order before things got bad. I think this might be the…remnants of that project."

I felt a little unsettled suddenly, like I was a sort of thief, stealing away his family's past. I stood up and brushed myself off. "Time for me to head home."

"If you want. It occurred to me that hiring you might make sex awkward."

I raised my eyebrows. "Not for me. Why? You think that's what you're paying for?"

"No! Not at all. If it's not awkward for you, then it's not awkward for me."

"Glad we got that out of the way."

We looked at each other for a long moment. A moment full of potential. A moment full of possibilities.

A moment full of variables I couldn't predict, which, despite my bravado about the sex thing, I wasn't actually ready to deal with. Jack's eyes did a roving, appreciative down-up, and when he met my gaze again, the invitation was clear as day.

Oh fuck. "Um, I need to...go. I have, uh, laundry or something."

"Laundry or something." He wasn't pissed. At least there was that.

I brushed myself off more aggressively than I had before to avoid looking at his face. "So yeah, sex again sometime, good call, see you tomorrow."

"Okaaay."

I escaped as quickly as I could, almost stumbling over one of my new piles in my haste to get to the front door.

Once I was safely in my car I could breathe again. And also curse myself for turning down sex. If that's what I'd done. *This is what happens when we don't rehearse, dammit. We lose out on sex opportunities. Sex potential. Sexpential sexportunities. Oh god, stop thinking before this gets worse.*

I began driving, already rehearsing possible alternative responses than "run for your life" just in case sex came up again. I could say, "On your knees, asshole." That might be a bit strong. Or "I'm always super down for getting it up, bro!" Yeah, no.

Or maybe the next time a guy—say, Jack—looked me up and down and back up like he was picturing me naked and turned on by the idea I could just…see where it went. Instead of claiming I had to do laundry.

Right, so, good plan. Next time: don't bring up laundry. Have sex instead. Seemed pretty simple. Do: have sex with Jack. Don't: make up excuses to not have sex with Jack. Mental note.

Wow, the night was a lot more boring when you knew that in some alternate timeline you were banging the hot, combative friend-of-a-friend who thought you were sexy. *Sigh.*

Chapter Six

I'd felt stable on Monday. Job had. Sex plan had. Problems taken care of.

On Tuesday I was a lethargic noodle in a dark study not at all improved by Jack haranguing me for being late.

"It's only ten minutes, for fuck's sake."

"Ten minutes in this commute is a lot," he snapped.

"Then make a spare key and you won't have to get your briefs in a twist waiting on me."

"Asking for a key to my house already, Oscar? We've only fucked once."

The idea was so monstrously unfair that I sputtered instead of replying and, clearly thinking he had the upper hand, he smirked and walked out.

The bastard.

I spent a good five minutes cursing him in absentia before I realized he was paying me by the job and I was only wasting my time. Then I went to the kitchen to put away the food I'd brought and ended up eating half a sandwich and—just to be an asshole—making a fresh pot of coffee in Jack's pristinely clean (if ancient) Mr. Coffee, with grand plans of leaving it no-longer-clean to make a point.

A voice in the back of my mind pointed out I was unlikely to actually leave the coffeepot dirty, not even to fuck with Jack, but if it was the thought that counted, I really *wanted* to.

After another cup of coffee, that was supposed to fix me but instead left me feeling simultaneously more heavy and unpleasantly head-buzzed, I went to my piles in the living room again. And sat down. Amid the piles. Pulling my knees up and propping my head on them.

Sighing may have been involved. Dramatic, hyperventilatey sighing.

I started work. Eventually. Even though I wanted to curl up on the floor in the fetal position for a nap. Except all the dust would probably have clogged my sinuses and my pores all at once and I would have come to hours later with my eyes streaming and my face broken out on whichever side was down.

Third paper in. I held it in my hand and stared down at it. Marriage certificate for John Bartholomew Phillips, dated thirteen years ago. Was Jack a nickname for John? I mean. It was, obviously, see: JFK. But I didn't know regular folks were allowed to do that.

Also, was Jack named after JFK? Because there was something I found weirdly endearing about the idea.

Thirteen years ago, Jack got married to some dude called Clyde Turner. I studied the name for a long time, trying to come up with a picture for the guy Jack had married and then divorced. Or maybe he'd divorced Jack. I didn't actually know. I shouldn't actually care, though it seemed like I was curious, judging by how long I'd spent looking at the paper. My head was starting to hurt. And I couldn't really imagine this…Clyde character.

If I was going to picture Jack in a wedding photo, he'd be tall and fine in a very nice suit, and his husband would also be tall (maybe slightly taller), also good-looking (though not quite as good-looking), with light hair to contrast with Jack's dark hair, and a more tan complexion to contrast with Jack's baby-powder-pale skin.

Hard to picture Jack smiling in that carefree, the-future-is-amazing way that Ronnie and Mia had smiled on their wedding day. Or that Mason had been smiling on the day he was supposed to marry Dec (before Dec took off).

I'd never smiled like that in my life. Not that you get to see your own smiles that often, but I could be sure I'd never smiled like that because I'd never *felt* like that. That gleam where people seem happy to be alive, to be living in that moment? I had never experienced that.

Not my thing. Not my wheelhouse. Not my…place. To be that happy.

I put the marriage certificate in the box of papers to save and picked up the next thing. Which was, drumroll please, a divorce settlement for Messrs. Phillips and Turner. Dated about a year and ten months after the marriage certificate. Yikes.

Divorce settlements for sure fell under "not okay to snoop through no matter how annoyed you are with the guy whose divorce settlement it was" and I virtuously put it on top of the box without looking at it.

At which point, having somehow "worked" for three hours and not managed to get half a pile of papers sorted—I hadn't even made a trip to the bins out front yet—I decided it was time for a snack and another cup of coffee.

The second I stood up I knew something had gone wrong. The smell coming out of the kitchen was no longer "fresh morning coffee." It had turned into "coffee-flavored sludge with high smoky notes and an undercurrent of tar."

Ancient Mr. Coffee machines apparently didn't have a timed shutoff. This one had baked my last cup of coffee away and kept cooking, leaving a pretty horrifying mess in the bottom of the carafe. I pulled it out, unprepared for how fucking hot even the screws holding the handle in were, and turned toward the sink.

Except my fingers were already on emergency alert and released before I could set it down properly.

Cue: *crash.*

Cue: *shatter.*

Cue: *rain of glass shards.*

Cue: "Oh *fuck.*"

I stood very still for a long moment waiting for this to be a bad dream. Waiting for a rewind that would mean I hadn't just broken Jack's grandmother's ancient Mr. Coffee. He'd probably grown up with it. He probably considered it a valued member of his family.

Also, it's not a bad idea to stand very still when you've just broken glass everywhere. Mostly, but not entirely, in the sink. As well as the counter and a bit on the floor.

Abruptly I was angry. What the fuck was wrong with me that I couldn't fucking place a carafe in a goddamn sink without breaking it? How had I even let it get this hot? It had probably been ruined anyway, but at least I could have tried to clean it out with some household science experiment including baking soda and vinegar and boiling water. But this? It was *shattered*. And there was no way I could find a carafe from this, what, early nineties-era Mr. Coffee? Amazon did not stock this item.

Rage boiled under my skin and I fought the urge to plunge my hands into the sink and pick up glass shards until I bled. Even though that kind of pointless drama was exactly suited to this kind of pointless rage.

But I didn't. I stood there, shaking, sweating, hating myself for being so stupid, hating myself for breaking Jack's coffeepot, and hating myself even more for caring that I had. Who kept a stupid coffee maker around after the casing cracked? Especially if Dec was right about how much money he made—and it was enough that he could afford to hand over seven grand for a contract job—why would he keep such a dumb old appliance anyway? I mean, who did that? How did that make sense?

It had to be because he was sentimental about it, but that was stupid too! What kind of idiot gets sentimental about a fucking coffeepot? Right? *Right?*

And oh fuck, I'd screwed up, I'd screwed up so badly.

***

The sensible thing to do was to start moving. Clean up. Carefully. Pick up the bigger shards of glass. Find some cardboard or something to lie them on for transport to the garbage if I couldn't find a bag. Or put them in the actual kitchen garbage and take that out to the bin. Or at least gather them together to keep them from hurting me while I cleaned the rest up.

Sweep the floor. Wipe off the counters—carefully, so as not to scratch them. Scoop out the shards left in the sink with a few layers of paper towels. Wipe everything down again. Hit the floor with some damp paper towels after the broom to pick up any slivers left.

I've broken glass before. I know how to clean it up. The whole plan rolled out in my head as I stood there, face numb, staring at the handle and remaining glass rim of what had been Jack's grandmother's Mr. Coffee carafe.

How had I done this? Shit. Fuck. How had I…fucked up this much in like point-three seconds? Was this some subconscious desire to hurt Jack because he'd been an ass about me being ten minutes late? No, right? I wasn't that big a dickhead.

Was I that big a dickhead? I didn't think so. But how would I know? I would. The Motherfuckers would tell me if I was a huge dick. Actually, sometimes they did, but only in a situational way, not in a general way. I thought. Hopefully? But no. Ronnie would say something. And Mase.

I didn't think I'd done it accidentally on purpose. This was purely accidental. Fueled by my panic that I'd let the coffee overboil. And I was back to how stupid I must be that I let the coffee overboil.

In my own house I would have floundered there infinitely, standing in a smattering of broken glass, locked in my own cycle of self-loathing.

But I was not in my own house.

I was in Jack's. Oh fuck. Jack's house. His grandmother's ancient Mr. Coffee…

I forced my hand into my pocket. I had to stop thinking. So I did the thing I rarely did, but this was an emergency. I phoned a friend. Thank god Ronnie answered.

Though she might have answered slightly differently than: "Oh my god, what happened? Are you okay?"

And fuck me, I started crying. "Why the fuck did you say that?" I blubbered. "I'm fine. Everything's *fine*."

"I'm right here. I'm not going anywhere."

Even though that was the only acceptable response—I never wanted to be told *everything was going to be okay* or to *take a deep breath* or any of those other so-called helpful things people feel the need to say if someone cries in their presence—it was hard to deal with the fact that I was so messed up in the head Ronnie had to feed me the lines I'd told her to feed me when I was messed up in the head.

"I fucked up," I said miserably, afraid to rub my eyes in case I'd gotten glass on my hands.

"Almost everything is fixable. Unless you murdered someone. Did you murder someone? Was it Jack? Just tell me you weren't fucking at the time, I don't think I can deal with that."

I sputtered a watery kind of laughter. "No. Fuck you. No one's dead."

We'd been friends since the day we moved in together freshman year, when I was a scared little gay boy, and she was a scared little trans girl, and both of us were terrified we'd been roomed with some big jock guy who'd want to kick our ass. We had years of jokes behind us. She waited a long moment before saying, "To be clear, I will totally help you hide the body. As long as it's clothed. Just guarantee me there will be no naked dead men."

"I didn't kill anyone!"

"If you're sure."

"Oh my god, I think I'd know."

"Okay. Because seriously, the last time you called me was like three years ago. You never call people on the phone. You hate the phone. I thought you must have committed a crime."

"As good as, I guess. I wish I only needed you to bail me out or something." I told her about the Mr. Coffee, and the glass everywhere, and the fact I'd gotten nothing done all day, and I'd been late, and Jack was already pissed at me, and I'd overboiled coffee, and now I'd fucked up this, like, family heirloom and there was no possible way I could replace it.

When I ran down Ronnie clucked her tongue at me and said, "There are a million replacement carafes online. See if you can find a model number and I'll order a new one, but maybe first you should clean up." Pause. "Do you want me to come over? I could help."

"No. It's fine. I mean, you're working and I don't need help, I just freaked out a little."

"Yeah. So. I'm going to say something you might not want to hear, but I just need to say it and then I'll drop it."

I clenched my jaw. "What?"

"Some of this is a meds thing. I'm pretty convinced. You don't have to change it up if you don't want to, but I think it might help. Other than that, put me on speaker while you clean and I'll tell you about the call I had this morning from the sweet old lady who couldn't remember her computer password and then couldn't remember what she wanted to do on her computer anyway. Like, ever. She couldn't think of one single thing she'd ever tried to do on her computer. It was sad-funny. To both of us."

And I wanted to not need moral support for cleaning up something I'd broken, but sometimes…it helped. To hear her voice as I swept the floor and gathered the glass and went over the counter and the sink a few times to make sure I'd gotten everything, then swept the floor again. At which point I figured I could probably cope with being alone, so I thanked Ronnie and got off the phone.

Everything still smelled like boiled coffee. I opened the windows and the front door, hoping like hell it would air out, though the day was hot and there was virtually no breeze. Typical. It was always breezy this close to the bay, if not downright windy, but on this day when I needed it to be, it wasn't.

It took way too long for me to find the right replacement carafe. Any labels or identifying characteristics of

Jack's machine had long since worn away, leaving only "Mr. Coffee" to help.

Not much help. There were roughly a gazillion and four different types of Mr. Coffee machines. Some of them weren't even coffee makers. By looking back and forth between the actual machine and a million images on Google I was pretty sure I'd found the right one. I ordered it, now exhausted, and decided I'd fucked up enough for one day and it was time to head home.

Except I couldn't just…leave a carafe-less coffeepot there. I rooted around for a good piece of scrap paper (envelope from a credit card offer circa 2008) and wrote:

Jack.

And then stared at it. At his name. Suddenly remembering the crack of the "k" when I'd had my hand over his, forcing him to touch his dick in the rhythm I dictated. How hot it had been. How…unsettlingly hot.

Jack.

What the hell was I supposed to say? *Sorry I broke your grammy's coffee maker, I'll come back when the new one gets here so we can pretend this never happened.*

But no. I was doing a job. And I'd wasted Tuesday being a basket case; I'd have to really kick ass tomorrow if he was going to bring her home for dinner. Not that I had any real strong reasons to care aside from whoever his grandmother was, she'd let him write *Jack Attack Lives Here* on his door when he was a kid, and I bet she'd kept things together for the grandfather too, before he died. Probably she was one of those sweet, omniscient-type old ladies. I wondered if she wore hats.

I shook my head and tapped the pen against the paper, trying to pick a way through my chaotic, unwieldy brain. I was in the middle of coming up with some fantastic way to say *Sorry I broke your coffeepot, hope it wasn't important to you, by the way, it'd be stupid if it was since it was just a coffee-pot and also it burned coffee so maybe I did you a favor* when the back door unlocked. And I froze like the proverbial deer in the proverbial headlights.

"You must really want to get laid, Oscar. You know you don't have to stay all day for me to blow you—" He faltered when he got to the kitchen and saw me standing there.

"I broke your coffeepot I'm so sorry," I said in a rush. "Not the pot. The carafe. And I already ordered a new one, but it's going to take like seven to ten business days to get here because expedited shipping cost the same amount as the carafe. Or I can buy you a new coffeepot if you'd rather. I didn't know what to do so I just bought the carafe. I'm sorry."

Put it like that, yeah, I definitely should have left a brief note and run away long before he was due home. Though in my defense the whole day had sort of melted into one sticky, tarry mess at the bottom of an overboiled pot of coffee and I hadn't realized it was so late.

He blinked at me, then at the sad, somehow naked Mr. Coffee. "Oh. Ah."

"I cleaned up." *Stop. Talking. Oscar.* "I mean, obviously."

"Yes."

"I'm really, really sorry."

"You said that already."

"Most of the time when you say that the other person says something like, 'It's okay.'"

The furrow in his brow deepened. "It's just a coffeepot."

"Oh. I thought. I guess I assumed it had been here a long time."

He set his briefcase on the table and began moving around as if everything was normal. "It had. Since I was young. But it's just a coffeepot."

Now I was confused. Because that was what you wanted to hear when you'd broken something: *No problem, it was just a thing.* So why wasn't that making me feel better?

"Sometimes stuff, like, has meaning," I offered.

"Well, this is a coffeepot. I can drive through Starbucks tomorrow. You don't have to replace the carafe, I can buy a more modern coffeepot." He shrugged, though he did it in the direction of the cupboard.

"Umm. Okay." Though it didn't seem like it was. "I guess I'll…go home then." Should I say I'd work extra hard tomorrow to get things ready for dinner? I was determined now, but not stupid enough to make promises. Plus, I'd screwed up in all the ways today, so claiming that I was going to do better tomorrow probably wouldn't hold much water.

"Good night," Jack said to the cupboard.

"Good night," I said to his broad, jacketed back.

I got in my car, noted the time, and spun my phone contacts until I reached the number for my psychiatric nurse. If I trap myself in a spontaneous forced-call (*You can't start the car until you've left this message*), sometimes I can trick myself into using the phone. I said aloud, "This is Oscar

Nelson and I'd like to make an appointment. My number is..." I hated phone calls, and it was annoying that Ronnie might be right, but also Ronnie might be right, so I should at least make an appointment. Or leave a message for an appointment to be made.

I hit the call thing and left the message. Points for me. Negative points for breaking a coffee carafe. Points for actually calling a friend when I needed support. Negative points for getting nothing done. The day was a draw.

"I'll do better tomorrow," I promised myself and drove home.

Chapter Seven

I did do better Wednesday. Mostly fueled by not wanting to pass another night of pure self-loathing. When I realized I couldn't possibly sort everything that needed sorting I took a page out of Jack's book and just shifted anything that wasn't trash or recyclable into the back hallway for later. At least by the time I left (I set an alarm to make sure I was out of there before he got home with his grandmother) I'd been able to vacuum and air out the living room as much as possible.

Drinks with the Motherfuckers was my reward for a day of hard work, dubious though it was. I got to the Hole a little before everyone else because the timing between me leaving Jack's and drinks beginning was slightly too awkward for me to go all the way home. In truth I'd always rather get there after someone else has grabbed the table. "Grabbing the table" seemed like such a straightforward thing, but I was never quite sure how to do it or if I looked like an asshole sitting alone at a table or if other people assumed I was probably waiting for my friends.

In short: I overthought grabbing the table until it was tempting to sit in my car and wait another half an hour until I was late, thus guaranteeing someone else would have grabbed the stupid table. Instead of doing that, largely to prove I was fine, everything was fine, I made myself go inside and take our second favorite table, sitting there alone with my beer, mindlessly trawling TikTok until the others showed up.

"Oscar!" Mase was first, sliding into the seat across from me. "Hey, you really cleaning Jack's place for money? That's perfect for you."

"Uh." I wasn't quite sure how to take that. "In what way?"

"In the way that you like cleaning and you like being able to pay your bills, so combining those things seems solid?"

"Oh. Yeah, I guess. It's weird. I think I found Jack's, like, wedding and divorce papers."

His eyes widened. "Oooooh. Tell me."

"That's it. I found papers saying he'd been married. And then papers saying he'd been divorced. Which we already knew anyway."

"How long did it last?"

We were interrupted by everyone else showing up at the same time, drinks being gotten, seating being rearranged.

At this point we'd settled into a regular Mase-Dec-Sidney on one side, me-Ronnie-Mia or me-Mia-Ronnie on the other side pattern. It was another hour before Mase remembered he'd asked me a question.

He filled the rest of them in on my discovery of Jack's personal papers, making me feel like a colossal dick for bringing it up in the first place.

"I know *nothing*," Dec said, leaning over the table.

"I didn't look at it," I mumbled, uncomfortable now. "Just saw that it existed and put it in a box. I don't think it'd be right if I went through his stuff."

Mia reached over to squeeze my hand. "Very ethical, Oscar. I think you did the right thing."

"Well, I think that's dumb," Mase said. "If you hire someone to go through your shit, you gotta figure they're gonna snoop."

Dec frowned. "That feels wrong but sounds right. I mean, I think I would assume that? Which is probably why I wouldn't want to ever hire someone to go through my shit."

"Oh my god." Mia glanced from Ronnie to Sidney. "No way. That's not right, is it? People wouldn't actually do that."

"It wouldn't be right, but I see their point," Ronnie said. "I would also assume that, even if I thought it was unethical."

Sidney hesitated. They never wanted to get involved in disagreements between us. Most of the time they still needed to be coaxed into conversations, though whether they just preferred participating by being present or because they were genuinely not sure what to say I didn't know.

"I don't know if I would *assume* that anyone would go through my things. Possibly because I'm not that interesting. But it might occur to me that they would have the opportunity."

"You are so diplomatic." Dec heart-eyesed at them disgustingly and they blushed.

"Diplomacy my ass, I want to know about this divorce." Mase stood up. "Oscar, you want another?"

I sort of did and sort of didn't, so I erred on the side of beer. "Please."

By the time he returned we were thankfully talking about other things, but I was still thinking about divorce settlements and marriages that only lasted a year and a half, and how Jack was only twenty-two when he tried out marriage, which was over a decade ago. Twenty-two was young. I couldn't have made a commitment like that back then.

What had happened? What had ended it? Not questions I could ask. More relevantly: why was I even interested?

Boredom. The weird state of temporary semi-employment. Uncertainty. Hell, maybe it was my stupid meds. Whatever it was, I pushed it out of my mind and drank another beer.

Jack and I had become a bit more terse since I, you know, broke his coffeepot. Then again, I was always right on time, and he was always right on his way out the door. I showed up Thursday, he let me in, I got to work, he left.

Since I was pretty exhausted by sorting papers, I'd decided to tackle the back hallway stuff I could easily dispose of. With some…sadness? Regret? I tossed all of Jack's *Rolling Stone* issues in the recycling bin (after googling "Can magazines be recycled?"). Some other collections could be disposed of just as easily. Out went a few other magazines I thought might be baby-Jack's, but I balked at tossing a few years' worth of *National Geographic* and put it aside with the complete *World Book Encyclopedia* (dated 1978) to be donated.

After the first day, I'd started prioritizing presentation. Instead of doing the thing that got the most done technically, I did the thing that was the best balance between "getting shit done" and "making it look like shit has been done." Like maybe in a perfect project management world you'd Marie Kondo it and sort stuff thematically, but my first attempt to do that had resulted in the living room looking much worse than it had when I started.

Okay. New plan. Watch me roll with change.

The hall ran the length of the house between the garage and the living area, so I spread out. Personal Jack papers in a box near his room, personal grandparents' papers next to that, anything I thought might be relevant to him that wasn't actually his (stuff about the house mostly) in a much smaller pile next to that. Things I thought needed to be shredded but didn't feel secure enough to make a call about in a box next to that.

Then there were…mementos? Keepsakes? A birthday card he'd made his grandmother when he was a kid. A picture of a kid and an older man at a baseball game, wincing against the sun in their eyes, both of them with ball caps on. Was the kid Jack? I wasn't great at faces. It might have been him, smiling into the sun.

Christmas cards and photographs. They seemed almost random. Only a few cards, only a few pictures. Nothing obvious connecting why *these* cards and pictures. A half-finished hat, knitting needles still stuck in the ball of yarn. An old packet of yellowing rolling papers which should almost certainly be thrown out but…what if they were his grandfather's? What if, when you opened the bag, they still smelled vaguely of tobacco (or, y'know, whatever Jack's grandpa had smoked)?

I set all those things aside as well.

Then I remembered I'd had this whole plan where I wanted things to look *better* when Jack got home. So far they looked way, way worse. Fuck me.

Getting rid of what I could recycle or throw away from the back hallway was taking…longer than I expected it to take. I don't know why I didn't realize it was going to take half of forever, since my first thought about the house after *Is it haunted?* was *Is this a tunnel of trash?*

I paused to take stock of the job. Piles were now spread up and down the hall. Lower piles! Markedly lower piles. But shit, it was a mess. I'd completely lost track of time and forgotten to eat anything, which might be part of why I was having a harder time focusing. I was standing there staring around when the garage door motor ground to life.

What the hell? It was quarter to five. Jack shouldn't even be off work yet.

Also: *fuck*. I was counting on having another hour to make things look…less terrible. Not that I was going to wait for him or whatever. Just if I happened to still be there I had some questions about stuff, and I wanted to know what the plan for upstairs was, and if he happened to be in the mood to get laid, well, I could also be in that mood.

I'd just swept three piles back from the door when I heard voices. A podcast? But no. Voices. Human voices. As in more than one. *Double fuck.*

I had no idea what to do. Run into the bathroom and hide? Run out the front door and drive away? Except Jack would have already seen my car. Not that I cared what he thought, exactly, but since we'd see each other again the next time he came to a Motherfuckers gathering, I didn't want to do anything too nutty. I could run to the kitchen, but it was a dead end—

Thus I was standing there, like some non-proverbial non-deer in headlights, when Jack walked in. With, it could only be, his grandmother. Who was supposed to come over for dinner yesterday. Did I get the day wrong? How was this happening?

She was much shorter than I'd imagined, her head only to the top of his shoulders, and she was leaning on his arm, but there was nothing in the least diminutive about the way she looked around at the mess, then straight at me. "It's time to fire the help, Jack."

My mouth unhinged. Oh. My. God. Um. I mean.

"*Grandmother.*" He shook his head. "This is Oscar, *who I told you about.* Oscar, this is my grandmother, Evelyn."

She grinned at me, her eyes still sharp. "Was that in poor taste? Jack's always telling me my sense of humor is gauche."

"Your sense of humor is inconsiderate."

"What? Surely the boy can take a joke." She stepped forward and held out her hand. "I know you're a friend of my grandson's. Don't mind me. Old ladies have very little to do aside from annoy the few sad sacks left who remember our names."

Slightly in awe, I shook her hand. "Good to meet you. Sorry about the mess."

"Young man, please don't be modest. We both know you found this place in a worse way than it is now. Though when Jack told me a friend was helping him with the house I did anticipate it looking...somewhat more helped than this, but I'm sure you have a plan."

"I do." Had she just called me Jack's friend? Twice? I glanced at him. "I...didn't expect you home this soon. And, uh, I thought you brought your grandmother over yesterday, so... Not that you have to tell me when you're bringing someone to your own house. But it would have looked better if you had because I kind of gave up yesterday, but I could have...made it, uh, better than this."

He opened his mouth as if he was about to say something—reassuring? cutting?—then didn't.

"Show me the rest," Evelyn said, voice firm. "I can take it."

Jack slipped sideways past her and I moved back to give him space. He held out his arm again to her and she accepted it with dignity, allowing him to support her into the living room. I found myself oddly tense, as if I was waiting for her verdict.

She didn't deliver one. "Why don't you ask your friend to stay for dinner? He's clearly been working hard."

"To be fair, he's been working for four days." The unspoken judgement of my (lack of) progress made me flush, mostly because I agreed.

"Mm hmm." Evelyn didn't look over at him. "And you've been at this for five months."

"I do have a job, you realize."

"Yes, dear. I realize. You work very long hours, have very little social life, and you're a very busy man."

If my parents thought I worked long hours, had no social life, was very busy, and made the money Jack did, they'd probably be proud of me. That might be stretching it, but at least I was certain they would say it in a different tone than Evelyn had, as if he was doing something obviously wrong, but she didn't think there was any point in mentioning it.

"I'll get started on dinner," he mumbled.

"I'll keep you company. And give me something to do, I'm not dead yet. Myrtle was telling me that they used to have cooking nights at The Meadows until some old bag cut her pinky off and now all of us have to get by on rations."

"They do not serve you *rations*. I've seen the food you eat."

"Oh, they serve better stuff when we have company." The two emerged back into the hallway, where I apparently still was.

Definitely having a blood sugar issue. I needed a banana or something.

Evelyn raised her eyebrows and despite obvious differences, she reminded me so much of Jack as she did it. "Staying for dinner, Oscar? My grandson is making a curry."

"An American-style curry anyway," he amended. "Nothing particularly difficult about it."

"I was giving you credit for making a meal. I'm sure Oscar finds a young man who can cook appetizing. Don't you?"

Before I could reply (not that I knew what to say when asked if I found Jack *appetizing*), he said, "You don't have to stay. You're a grown man. You can do what you want."

"Thanks, for a minute I forgot." Probably shouldn't snipe at him with his grandma right there. I toned myself down. "I like curry."

"Fine. Stay, don't stay, do whatever." He huffed off to the kitchen, leaving me alone with Evelyn, who winked.

"It's because he never relaxes. For a while he was at that other job, you know, and I thought maybe he could find a way to—But never mind. Tell me what horrors you've been unearthing in the archeological dig here. I told him to get rid of everything that's not nailed down, but I'm sure he won't."

"Well, he can't, I don't think? For, um, reasons about taxes or something."

She laughed and held out her arm. "I'm glad someone's managing this estate at long last."

I took it, awkwardly, feeling anxiety sweat spring out on my temples and in my armpits. "I'm just trying to sort some things…"

And that's how I had dinner with Jack and his grandmother. The first time, anyway.

★ ★ ★

Evelyn fascinated me. She was nothing like I thought grandparents should be, nothing at all like my own. She teased Jack about things my grandparents—my parents—would never bring up, asking him if he'd had any gentleman callers around lately, or if he'd made plans for what he'd do with his inheritance when she "popped off."

"I told you, I'm not talking about this." He glanced at me across the coffee table from where he was sitting on the couch (I'd insisted on the floor). "She does this just to annoy me."

She looked at me from the armchair, which still smelled smoky, but either I'd gotten used to it or airing the downstairs out had helped, because it wasn't nearly as strong now. "He's in denial about my imminent death."

"I'm not—you aren't—" He broke off and she laughed in triumph.

"You see? Even in trying to deny it he can't help admitting it."

"I simply don't see why you insist on discussing it," he said through gritted teeth. "If you're going to die at any moment, I'll deal with it when it happens."

"But how will you know what song I want sung at my funeral? It'll have to be one of those dire religious things that makes everyone feel terrible, like God's just about to smite them dead."

"I'm *not* playing a dire religious song at your funeral."

"Then play something fun. What's it, the one with the dancing? Play that."

"I'm also not playing the *Macarena* at your funeral."

She appealed to me. "Wouldn't a funeral with dancing be better than one without dancing? Tell me that, Oscar."

I blinked, having pretty much faded into the background while eating and listening to them. "Oh. Well." I caught his eye—and glower—and said, "Not the *Macarena*, it's too old. You want something more recent than that. Maybe *Gangnam Style*. That would be lively for a funeral."

She snapped and pointed at Jack. "Write that down. I want the song Oscar's talking about for my funeral."

"You're not actually that close to dying, sorry to say. There will probably be a more popular dance song by then."

"When it happens, ask Oscar. Let him pick. I'm sure he goes dancing more than you do."

I choked. "Um."

And Jack, smirking, turned an in-no-way-innocent expression at me. "How often *do* you go dancing, Oscar?"

"I don't dance," I began.

"Nonsense, everyone can dance." And to my horror, Jack's octogenarian grandmother stood up and held out her hand to me.

"Oh, no, I really can't—" And I really couldn't. Obviously this would be the moment in the heartwarming movie where I'd discover that, against all odds, I really *could* dance, that an argumentative old lady trying to prove a point could magically make my legs learn the steps and suddenly I'd be like a celebrity in week seven of *Strictly Come Dancing*, but my heart was pounding and my legs were heavy and immobile.

She snapped, this time at me. "Come on, then."

"Grandmother, you can't invite a guest over for dinner and then force him to dance at your whim, that's impolite."

She turned on him. "I have heaved my old body out of that nasty chair and now I will dance. Stand up, young man."

"I'm in the middle of dinner."

She stared at him.

He stared at her.

And then, after a tense pause in which I desperately wished I'd said no to dinner, Jack set his plate down and stood up.

"I taught him to dance when he was a boy," Evelyn said to me as she fitted her hand to his shoulder. "He loved it, though now he says he didn't."

"I didn't have much of a choice," he grumbled. "Since you forced me to do it."

"Oh, it's a tragic saga of dancing with your grandmother, the readers wept. Now come, you remember the steps."

He sighed. "Of course."

And they danced. Jack and his grandmother, in their living room, in the space now cleared by my/our efforts. He even twirled her, though there was no music. If you know how to dance, do you hear the music in your head? Were both of them hearing the same thing right now, the same echo of whatever they'd listened to when Jack was a kid?

All I could hear was their footsteps, the friction of cloth, their breaths, Evelyn's murmured cues.

Jack. In his work clothes, sleeves rolled up, tie off, top buttons undone, back straight, shoulders square. Dancing.

They came to some conclusion I didn't catch and stopped.

She kissed his cheek. "That's a good boy, humoring an old relic."

"You're not a *relic*, and again, you didn't give me much of a choice." Still, he seemed pleased as he sat down, cheeks flushed. "Can we finish dinner now?"

"I need to use the powder room. I may as well, since I'm upright. Next time you'll have to lever me out of that chair, Jack, no doubt." She disappeared down the hall, humming a tune that might have been a waltz. Not that I know shit about waltzes.

Leaving us in a slightly awkward silence behind her. I began eating the last of the food on my plate, my spoon scraping. He continued eating his. After a moment he said, as if he couldn't bear the silence any more than I could, "Sorry. This is probably not what you were expecting to do tonight, but I appreciate you staying." He cleared his throat. "For her. She loves company, and she didn't get to entertain the last few years because of the house."

"No problem." And it wasn't.

"Thanks."

Awkward silence resumed.

"Now, boys, we could watch a film before I go back to The Place. What about a Dirk Bogarde? He was the biggest gay, and he never admitted it, no matter what people said to him about it."

"That's depressing, Grandmother," Jack objected.

She paused. "Is it? I suppose it is, now that I think about it. No matter. We could watch a John Wayne. *He* was one of those violently anti-gay types you just knew had unsettling dreams sometimes and didn't know what to do about them."

"Let's watch something that has nothing to do with being gay," he suggested.

"No need to be *boring*, Jack."

"That's not—" He caught me trying not to smile and let it drop. "You're right. Everything that's not gay is boring."

She patted his arm. "As usual, I know you're humoring me, and I don't mind in the least."

Sensing my chance to run away—though I'd enjoyed dinner with them more than was reasonable—I made my excuses and left. I'd reached my limit of human interaction.

And maybe more than that, I had a lot to think about. Like Jack. In his work shirt gone casual. Dancing with his grandmother. That he could be intensely buttoned-up one moment and somehow playful the next probably shouldn't have been surprising to me, but it was the…sweetness of it. The way he'd smiled at her. The way they'd been so in sync with each other. She had pushed him into it, but he'd clearly enjoyed himself.

I couldn't get the image out of my head the rest of the night.

Chapter Eight

"I want to hear the whole story," Ronnie said, voice crackling as I drove into the parking structure of the medical center. "But after the appointment."

"Fine, I'll call you."

She said something else, but the call cut out.

She'd called right as I was getting off the freeway and I'd accidentally answered when I was trying to skip songs. Now I'd somehow accidentally mentioned dinner with Evelyn. Which meant five minutes from now it'd be all over the Motherfuckers.

For some reason that made me uncomfortable, but since I was on my way in to have my meds changed I didn't have a lot of energy for other forms of discomfort so I pushed it aside.

Ah, the unholy ritual of changing meds. Will the psych nurse ask too many questions? Will she put me on something that makes me feel worse? How long will it take before I know the effects are the new med, not the transition? Will I be back here in two months having a panic attack because my moods went from "super shitty" to "active danger to self and others"?

TUNE IN NEXT WEEK TO FIND OUT.

The appointment was relatively painless. Shelly-the-psych-nurse asked the usual questions, listened to my (rehearsed) speech, and did the thing I'd asked her to do: sent in a new prescription. And the second it was done I was completely horrified, the meds version of buyer's remorse: *what have I done?* The devil I knew was a jerk—Ronnie was right, I'd been feeling less stable for a while—but what if the devil I didn't know was so much *worse*?

Not that meds are the devil. I resent them (always) but I also remember that life before I got to college (and started trying to address the anxiety instead of hoping it would go away) was so, so much more excruciating. The cool kids in high school skipped class to have sex and/or do drugs; I skipped school to freak out in my car. At the time I was angry at myself for freaking out "for no reason." Later, in therapy, I would learn that anxiety was not in my control, and neither was freaking out.

And then I'd start meds, and it was easier to shift just far enough away from panic to breathe through it. Most of the time anyway.

At least, when the meds were working. But that precious buffer of breath between me and losing my shit had eroded away. Hence why I was here. Getting a new med. That I sent to Mia, who was the keeper of my medical records-slash-the person I called when I thought I was having a crazy side effect because if I looked on the internet for side effects I would inevitably have, like, all of them.

She messaged back: *Come over for dinner? We're having salad. And meat.*

Home-cooked meals I didn't have to cook twice in one week? *I'm in. You had me at MEAT.*

She sent back a happy face.

Now I just had to go pick up the new thing, which was similar enough to the old thing that I could start taking it tomorrow morning without doing any complicated tapering.

Fuck. Right. No big deal. Ugh. Meds.

Dinner was amazing and early. I like eating early when I go out so I can, y'know, go home. Home was safe. Second to home was probably Ronnie and Mia's place, but I was still happy that dinner was early.

Mia answered the door by saying, "There's nothing I'm particularly worried about on the new med research front. You do you and I hope it makes you feel better." Then she kissed my cheek and shouted, "Ronnie! Oscar's here!"

"Is it really necessary to herald my presence like you guys have a manor house and she might not have already heard us talking?"

"Um, let me think about it." She pretended to think about it. "Yep, it's necessary." Then she raised her voice again and shouted, "We'll be in the kitchen!"

"Because she might not be able to find us?" I clarified.

"Well, we could have gone to the living room."

"Not if salad is in the kitchen."

"You make a fair point," she said gravely.

"Oh, well, thanks so much."

"Ronnie, we'll be eating salad in the kitchen!"

I cringed. "Oh my god."

Salads with the Motherfuckers were a whole thing. I'd shown up at college thinking I hated salad. That was before Mia and Declan got ahold of me. Between them, they'd expanded my conception of "salad" into whole new realms of saladom. I showed up thinking salad was lettuce, a few bits of tomato, and ranch dressing. Suddenly my salads had nuts and fruits and bits of meat or beans or even tofu, which I disliked on principle, but Declan made this marinated, grilled tofu that tasted good in a salad when you surrounded it with other delicious stuff.

"Spill! And tell me why you didn't eat all day yesterday," Ronnie said, coming into the kitchen as Mia and I finished assembling the salad of dreams. They'd even picked up the candied walnuts that were my dirty little unhealthy salad secret.

"I can't keep doing this," I told her, voicing the thing I kept thinking but hadn't fully articulated to myself. "I can't keep *leaning* on you like this all the time, like you're my emotional support animal. Especially now that you—" I waved a hand. "Now I can't actually reciprocate anymore."

Mia did a wide-eyed head-shake sputter. "Excuse me? Who's she going to complain to when we have marital problems, then?"

"Like you're going to have marital problems!"

"Okay, okay." Ronnie turned to her wife. "First: we are *not* going to have marital problems and if we did I'd obviously talk to you about them since that's the only thing that makes sense." She spun to me. "And *you* can shut right the fuck up. I cried on you for weeks and months when my hormones were a mess and I was early transition and I didn't think anyone would ever see me or love me if they did, so shut up, Oscar." She pointed directly at my face. "Got it?"

"Um. It still doesn't seem fair, though. That was…" I didn't know how to say what I meant.

She kept staring at me, all unimpressed eyebrows and pursed lips.

"You shouldn't have had to deal with that shit. It should have just been…okay. It wasn't your fault."

"And you having anxiety is your fault? Explain how that makes sense."

"No, I mean—" I rolled my eyes. "You had this thing that you didn't even get to start dealing with until college and then you did, and you got over it, and now you don't need to cry on me all the time anymore. But I just keep… having the same stupid shit come up all the time."

"Okay, first, I can have big fuck-all trans breakdowns whenever I want, there's no statute of limitations on those, so don't go thinking you've escaped them. Second, what I hear you saying is that if you were the trans one and I was the anxious one you'd cut me off and tell me to stop leaning on you?"

"No! Oh my god."

"Why would I do that then?"

"I didn't say you did, but..." The Therapist That Got Away would tell me to share my feelings because Ronnie was my safe person. "Fuck, I don't know, I just hate being this guy."

Mia raised her hand. "Is this the thing about how you're going to somehow piss all of us off and we're going to abandon you? Because you know Mase says there's nothing stopping us from abandoning you all the times you pissed us off before, so why would we start now?"

"Maybe I'm becoming more of an asshole in my old age," I suggested.

"Oh, maybe!" she said with rather disturbing enthusiasm. "Like suddenly you become addicted to foie gras, and not the ethically manufactured stuff, but the seriously messed up stuff, resulting in the force-feeding of lots of innocent ducks to meet your demand?"

"Oh my god, no, I do not eat freaking *foie gras*."

She made a face. "Okay, fine. Maybe you're secretly a hipster and you've been too afraid to tell us because you thought we'd abandon you, but we can probably accept you even if you are a hipster." She seemed slightly doubtful about that.

"Um, fuck you? And no."

"Or..." She nudged Ronnie. "Help me out, babe, what else can Oscar do to make him more of an asshole so we'll abandon him?"

At least Ronnie had to think about it before assigning me the role of duck-force-feeder or, god forbid, hipster. "Okay, what if it turns out all this time Oscar's secretly been a spy for a powerful fundamentalist church and he was put into college as a covert operative in order to infiltrate the gay agenda and send back updates about how we were planning to queerify the world and he has a whole secret life where he's married to a woman and has five children because they're not allowed to use birth control and he's actually a super charismatic crusader for traditional values with a cult favorite syndicated radio show where they keep his identity a secret and call him The Undercover Avenger." She paused for breath and I opened my mouth to say—something? anything? but then she was talking again and my mouth just hung open in horror/awe/bewilderment. "Then the FBI sends their own undercover agent into the church to investigate it for being a hate group and Oscar's wife takes the kids and flees to the feds because she doesn't want to be in the cult anymore but they'll only take her if she gives up Oscar so one night when we're all at drinks the FBI raid the place and arrest him under his real name and we're all like, 'Oscar, what the fuck?' and he's like, 'This is who I really am, I've been straight all along!' and cackles evilly and we're all appalled and we just stare around at each other until someone—probably Mase—is like, 'That's it, Oscar is officially out of the Motherfuckers, no one have contact with him ever again,' and the rest of us agree, and poof, it's like he never existed. Would that do it?"

We both stared at her. I managed to close my mouth, since I had no freaking idea what to even say. Mia made a sort of helpless noise. "Um. Did you see that on a show or something?"

Ronnie beamed. "Nope. Made it all up on the spot. I'm a creative genius, right?"

"Um."

"No!" I said. "I—I'm not—I wouldn't—Ronnie!"

"Yeah, that's what I thought." She reached out to fuck with my hair and I dodged away. "See? That's how extreme you'd have to get for us to even think about abandoning you. So maybe shut the fuck up about it, hmm?"

I just gaped at her. "You're the literal worst."

"What? I'm not. I'm *supportive*. Now get over yourself and tell me about Jack's grandma."

Since it was hard to feel guilty about leaning on the emotional *support* of anyone who could troll me like that, I relented. "She's basically the coolest old lady I've ever met."

"Oooooh. Tell us more!"

"Jack apparently told her I was his friend." I wasn't sure why I mentioned that immediately, but I did, and they exchanged a look. "What?"

"We already knew you and Jack were friends," Mia explained. "You didn't?"

"I don't think of us as *friends*. I mean. We know each other."

"So you're acquaintances?"

Ronnie nodded. "Sure, sure, 'acquaintances with benefits,' all the kids are doing it these days."

"That's not what I meant, just." What did I mean? "Anyway, she said she knew we were friends. And then she invited-slash-forced me to stay for dinner. And then Jack made actual food. Like in his kitchen."

"Where else would he make it?" Mia asked.

"What food did he make?" Ronnie demanded.

"He called it 'American-style curry' and it was surprisingly good."

Mia sighed. "Surprisingly because you didn't think your acquaintance Jack could make a curry?"

"Uh. I mean. I can't make a curry, so."

"Of course you can make a curry! Anyone can make a curry. It's like garlic, ginger, onion in a pan, add coconut milk, spices and garbanzos, done."

Ronnie patted Mia's arm. "As frustrating as I know we find Oscar's insecurities, let's not be too quick to dismiss them. Remember the mac and cheese incident."

She giggled, because going from outraged to giggling was the emotional range Mia had. "Oh no, I forgot about that! But that wasn't a cooking fail, that was a like… Grindr-related cooking inattention issue."

"It was burnt mac and cheese all over our stove."

"I cleaned it up!" I protested, flushing. "Plus, he was hot. You would have burned your mac and cheese too if you'd been getting the pictures I was getting." When both of them gave me *Uh, no* looks, I added, "Or, you know, the lady equivalent of those pictures."

Mia started to shake her head, then stopped and turned to Ronnie. "Actually, he might be right. Sometimes you send me *very* distracting pictures. I might burn my mac and cheese too."

I stuck out my tongue. "Okay, thanks, that's enough—"

"True, there was that one time you forgot your boss was on hold," Ronnie said, grinning.

"Only for a few minutes! Then I remembered." Mia

went pink. "Gosh, that would have been so embarrassing. Um. Anyway."

"Yes. *Anyway.* Then Jack danced with his grandma and I went home, the end."

"Jack danced?" Mia asked.

"With his grandma?" Ronnie added.

"Yes, he danced with his grandma and then I went home." I stared at my salad, not sure why I'd told them about the dancing, also kind of picturing it again in my head.

"Jack doesn't strike me as a dancer." Ronnie reached for her glass of juice, almost knocking over Mia's. "Oh crumb, sorry—"

In the slight disturbance that followed I managed to change the subject to starting new meds, which was successful. Changing the subject was successful. Starting new meds was a cluster that remained to be fucked.

Chapter Nine

One of the borderline unhealthy ways I handle tricky transitions is by sleeping. Sometimes depression helps me out and I can do it naturally. Sometimes I dose myself with pills just to limit my conscious-and-therefore-thinking time during the day. Friday passed all right, at least in part because I kept telling myself I couldn't possibly be feeling the new medication yet.

Saturday I felt a little lethargic, so I slept a lot.

Sunday I felt mopey and sad with the occasional burst of white-hot rage. I took a pill so I could sleep most of the day, then took another one so I could sleep most of the night.

By Monday I was a bit screwed up in the head, whether from too much sleeping or too much coffee or the meds,

I didn't know. And it didn't matter. I got to Jack's, barely said good morning, and started going through papers.

Except I didn't care. Not about the papers, or about the job, or about anything else.

But it *was* a job, and I've been down this road often enough to know *I don't give a fuck about anything* was the prelude to *I care too much about everything.* Even though I was fucking fed up in the moment, I didn't allow myself to leave the house. Or send a scathing text message telling Jack to burn everything if he didn't want it.

Or have a random from Grindr over for the purposes of copulation, which was another facet of my not giving a fuck. I was horny. Specifically horny to get off without complications, possibly without names.

Instead I ate a spoonful of Jack's peanut butter, which was, not surprisingly, some kind of all-natural shit that I had to stir first. Then I had a piece of toast with peanut butter on it. Then a banana. I considered having a piece of toast with peanut butter and a banana on it, but those all-natural jars are small and I was in danger of making a conspicuous dent.

I reheated the coffee I'd brought over from the morning and added some of Jack's organic almond milk to it.

Aside from the bananas on the first day, I'd tried not to disturb any of his stuff. You know, except his coffeepot, though the replacement carafe had come in, and had fit, and was now clean and upside down in the dish rack as if it was the original. I'd definitely started bringing my own coffee.

Today, though, in the name of not giving a fuck, I used a little more almond milk and stood at the back hallway door, staring into the dreary yard, wondering if it had been cleaner when he was a kid, if he'd played back there. Not that I cared. Obviously.

I spent the rest of the afternoon working on the stairs because I couldn't face the stacks of things in the hall. Didn't get very far. Didn't give a fuck.

When I heard the garage door open I stood up, and there I was, standing at the foot of the stairs, when he came in on his way to the kitchen. He'd walk in, drop the mail on a corner of the counter, get himself a glass of water, and drink the whole thing. I'd seen him do it a few times now.

Today he walked in and stood very still, looking at me where I stood very still, looking at him.

"I'm horny, I don't want to bother with the apps, and I'm already here," I said, not moving.

He did not blink. "Deal."

I started to unzip my pants.

"Not here, we're in the living room." His voice had gone a little bit high.

"We're the only ones here."

"Yeah, but..."

The thing is, I'm not usually the guy who whips out his junk in the middle of someone's living room, but this restless sense of not being attached to my actions made me—not that guy, but me, in that guy's skin. I didn't exactly pull my dick out, but I did make a suggestive sort of motion in between my pants and my briefs. "Fine. You tell me where it is and is not acceptable to suck dick in your own home."

I was half-hard already, just knowing sex was imminent.

When he started striding across the room the sex engine in my brain went from tortoise to hare in seconds.

"Oh, fuck you, Oscar," he snapped, dropping to his knees in his nice suit and reaching for me.

If no man has ever knelt in front of you in a suit and taken your cock out to suck, you have *missed out.* It's an experience.

Then he slid one hand up over my…midsection. Stomach. Belly. Pick your word for the part of my body I try to never look at or think about. I pushed him away, but he looked up, my cock about to be in his mouth, and raised his eyebrows. "If I'm going to blow you, I'm going to enjoy your fucking body. Take it or leave it."

It was a deeply unfair ultimatum. I opened my mouth to protest this injustice when suddenly he swallowed my cock and like—fuck me. Not that I'd forgotten about his mad deep throating skills, yet he managed to surprise me all over again. I rocked forward, but his hands, one on my *torso* and one on my balls, kept me in place as his mouth and throat worked my cock.

Then he fucking pulled off again. Because he's a monster. "Sorry, I didn't hear your answer. Do I have consent to—" both hands slid to my chest, pushing my shirt up "—enjoy your sexy, hairy body? Or not?"

"You're a fucking asshole, you know that?"

He grinned. Like a regular person. Like a…friend. Who was fucking with me. And grinning about it.

"Oh, shut up, you smug jerk." I tried to pull his head back to my cock but he braced himself on my—on me.

"No, I need to hear your enthusiastic consent for me

running my hands all over you. Say the words like a good boy, Oscar."

"Seriously, you can shut the fuck up." But I couldn't deny that the way his fingers were kneading against my skin like a cat's paws was kind of turning me on. "Is this how you get off? Making me uncomfortable?"

He shrugged, one of his hands returning to my cock, stroking it in a far-too-leisurely way. "Seems like I'm not the only one getting off on you being uncomfortable."

I wanted to growl at him, but he was, y'know, stroking my cock. "Show me."

Eyebrows up again. "Show you what?"

"Show me how much this is turning you on. Since that's what you're claiming. I want to see."

If nothing else, it forced him to take his hand off my body.

Fuck me for being just slightly sad at its absence.

He undid his belt and opened his—okay, then. So. It *was* turning him on. He was mouthwateringly hard. I hadn't had him in my mouth, but now… "Fuck, Jack."

"That's what I'm trying to do, yes." Then he took me back in all the way down, my cock hitting the back of his throat, his hand on his own.

If you've never had a man in a suit suck your cock while literally *getting off* as he does it—

I groaned. "Fuck. Stop. Don't. You."

I think he laughed. Like. Around my cock. The jerk. I grabbed his head, he sucked harder, I cried out—

"Fuck, fuck, fuck, stop, I can't—hold on—"

Except he didn't want me to hold on and he won, the

orgasm tearing through me almost before I could fully enjoy it. He went to pull back but I held him there for an extra second just because I could and far from being pissed about it, his hand sped up on his cock.

"You fucking prick," I mumbled.

He met my eyes, his own crinkling, lips still around my shaft, hand working himself fast and hard.

"No, fuck you, stop it."

He didn't, of course, but I pulled back from him and tugged his hand away, and he let me. "What's the problem? I can finish myself off."

"Yeah, well, fuck you. Come on." And I walked off to his bedroom like I had a right to it.

Somewhat to my surprise, he followed. "The hell, Oscar?"

I shoved him back on the bed and planted my hand in the middle of his chest. "Shut your mouth. Lie down. Take it." I pushed his cock up and began sucking his balls, making his body jolt.

"Shit—" He moved to pull away, but I clamped down on his thighs. "Oscar, what—"

"You like it when I lose control, well fuck you."

What followed could generously be called a grapple. I tried to get my mouth on his cock, he tried to flip me over, I straddled him to keep him down, he ran his hands up my body again, pushing my shirt up, making appreciative noises.

"Stop that!" I snapped.

He managed to arch his neck, licking my…stomach.

"Why? You're hot. It turns me on that you're uncomfortable with your hotness."

"Why won't you just let me get you off? What is *wrong* with you?" I took hold of his cock and started sucking, using my hand like a good little gay boy who never learned to deep throat but gave pretty excellent head anyway. I'd intended to blow him away with my mad skills, but his arms came up over my ass and pulled me closer so he could…fuck, was he *nuzzling* me?

I pulled away, glaring at him. "Seriously, what's your issue?"

"I don't have an issue." He turned onto his side and began stroking himself again. "What's *your* issue?"

"I'm trying to blow you and you're being a dick?"

"Am I?" He gestured towards my—I hastily tucked myself more firmly away and did up my pants. "I think you like fighting with me, Oscar."

"Okay, I don't have a damn fighting kink, I just want to get laid."

"And you did. So?"

"No—I mean yes—" I frowned. "What the hell? You don't want me to blow you? You realize we've had sex before. I've gotten you off *before*."

"You've never practically attacked me before. Not that I'm complaining." He rolled onto his back again and like… kept touching himself. As if I wasn't even there. "It was hot. You being all intense and needy."

"I didn't—it wasn't *needy*—you're such an asshole, Jack."

He laughed. "I know. Sorry."

I hesitated, torn between getting up and…not doing that.

I finally lay down beside him, really looking around at his bedroom, the old, possibly-never-been-washed curtains, the way dust danced in the light still coming in between them. "Meds are fucking me up," I muttered. "I go from like wanting to throw myself off the Golden Gate Bridge to wanting to fuck anything that moves and is a dude, to like...blackout rage. In ten minutes. All day long."

"That sounds exhausting."

"Yeah."

"Is this...how you can tell the meds are working? Or not working?"

I sighed. "No. To both. They might be fine, they might be trash, the transition doesn't indicate anything either way. The transition just *sucks*."

"I'm sorry I gave you a hard time. You haven't blown me before and I wasn't prepared for you to do it tonight. And also it's fun to torture you."

"You're a monster. In a nice suit."

"That's the best way to be a monster." He reached out and pulled my hand to his cock, which was still very, very hard. "Hand jobs work for me."

"They don't...not work for me. Just, today I saw your cock and..." I turned my face away "...sort of wanted to taste it. Whatever. Never mind."

His cock did a little jump in my hand. "Shit. Oscar." He pressed my fingers against him, forcing mine into a different rhythm. "I like blowing you. I like having my hands all over you because it seems like it fucks with you, but some part of you wants it."

"No part of me wants that," I mumbled, letting him control my hand.

"Okay."

Never trust a man in a nice suit when he says, "Okay," like he's humoring you to shut you up.

"Will you take off your shirt if I promise I won't touch you? It turns me on."

I grimaced. "That makes no sense."

His fingers tightened over mine. "Your body image issues are not my business, but if you think I'd stoop to pretending I thought you were hot to make you uncomfortable, that's shitty."

"You're accusing *me* of being shitty right now?"

He laughed. It was blunt and huffy and in no way shared, but it was laughter. "Fair point. Fine. You don't have to."

Except he could go fuck himself. "Yeah, thanks, I'm aware I don't have to do anything I don't want to do, you prick." On any normal day it wouldn't have happened, but today I wanted to fuck with him back, and today I didn't care what it meant or what the consequences were. I pulled off my shirt and straddled his legs, reaching for his cock again. "Torture this, douchebag."

He grinned. "Okay."

See what I mean about the *Okay* thing?

He took over my rhythm on his cock and I braced, thinking the other hand would come up to touch the rest of me. Now that I was in this more upright position, I remembered why I hated it. Gravity was not forgiving when it acted on my middle lumpiness, and I tried to focus on his cock, his hand, over my hand, the glide of his foreskin, the seductively soft skin over the quite impressive hardness beneath.

"You're so fucking sexy when you're all pissed at me and trying to get me off." His other arm went back behind his head, propping him up so he could look at me, at our hands, at everything more easily.

I flushed. "Shut up."

"With that furry chest, your little nipples poking out like they want attention."

It was really hard to concentrate on finishing him off. "They fucking don't."

His hand tightened over mine and started moving faster. "I love the curve of your stomach, the way your dick looks when it's hard, jutting out like it's begging—"

"—oh my fucking—"

His hips were moving in short jerks against my legs. "—like it's begging for my mouth, like it needs to feel my lips around it."

The bastard was having an effect on me. I redoubled my efforts, trying to force his hand faster on his cock, but he kept up exactly what he wanted, not allowing me to push him over. "You fucking sonofa—"

"You're the one having sex with me."

"Error in judgement, clearly."

"It must be hard pretending you aren't hot for me talking shit."

"I'm fucking *not*." I knelt up to—to do something—to get more leverage, to get control, to feel taller even though he was already lying down—but it just gave him the space he needed to make his move, toppling me to the side and flipping me over until he was on top, kneeling over my body and relentlessly dragging my hand back to his cock.

"I'm fucking close," he said, a little breathlessly.

As much as I didn't want him to get his way, I couldn't deny how hot he looked, still dressed, sweat gleaming on his face, golden in the bits of light coming in through the windows, and hard as hell, looking down at me. "Come already, you fucking asshole."

He grinned and leaned forward to brace beside me, forcing my hand faster, groaning, balls brushing my stomach. "Oh, fuck, Oscar—"

I wanted to hate him, but hearing my name in that I'm-just-about-to-come voice made it impossible.

He, *we*, jerked him off all over my chest, and the low sounds of his pleasure made me thrust involuntarily against him before going rigid in horror at having done so.

He took a few shuddering breaths, still leaning over me, hair disheveled, shirt no longer perfectly in order. His fingers still tangled with mine on his cock.

Then, as if a bubble had popped, he pulled away, completely, hand and cock and body, leaving me lying there with jizz in my chest hair, feeling ridiculous.

"Here." He settled a box of tissues next to me. "I need to—" Hand wave at the hallway.

I mopped up as best I could in his absence and pulled my shirt over myself, crossing my arms, then uncrossing them, standing up, then sitting down. Fuck, I hadn't even taken off my shoes, though his were at the side of the bed as if he'd kicked them off at some point and I hadn't noticed.

"You can stay for dinner if you want!" he called from the bathroom.

Yeah, fuck that. "I have to go!" I called back. And I did. Real fast. Post haste. Immediately. The toilet flushed and I damn near scrambled for the front door, opening it right as I heard him emerge from the bathroom.

I didn't start to relax until I was three stop lights away and able to focus on relevant details like pedestrians and the idiot blasting Sublime in the car next to me.

Good. Focus on other things. Not Jack. Not the pressure of his fingers. Not the way he'd said my name. Not his jizz on my skin.

Not the way all of it had made me half-hard again.

Dammit. You think you're just going to fuck your sometime-friend and at least you won't be horny anymore, and then he goes and screws it up by...by fucking you and then making you horny again. Asshole.

I definitely should not jerk off when I get home to the thought of Jack being such a total prick. Nope nope. Bad idea.

Not that it mattered anyway; by the time I got home the wheel of fortune controlling my mood had swung back to *go to bed for days and hide from the world*, so I did that instead.

Chapter Ten

Motherfuckers gathering at Declan's in honor of Sidney being *very slightly* (their emphasis) promoted. I sat in my usual corner after saying hello and telling them congratulations. I liked Sidney. As far as a partner brought in from the outside went, they were my ideal: didn't care if we were friends, clever enough to follow jokes, made no demands on me as a person.

I guess in a way that's my ideal human in any context. I was pondering that when Jack walked in. Things had been…very neutral between us since I, y'know, walked out when he was in the bathroom after sort of demanding he have sex with me.

Which was…totally a normal thing to do. Shit, no, it wasn't. I'd panicked. And then run like hell. And then panicked more. And then pretended it hadn't happened. And so had he.

"Oscar," he said, sitting next to me in the corner of Dec's living room. Apparently I was still Jack's port in a storm of Motherfuckers, even with the awkwardness.

"Jack. Didn't know you were going to be here." I had no idea what to say to him.

"Declan," he said in explanation.

"All those good intentions?"

"Yes."

The awkward silence was almost certainly my fault, right? Still, he was sitting next to me. Like. That meant. Something? I didn't know, and I was sure I wasn't supposed to care. I was the one who'd walked out, ergo I should…not give a fuck. Unfortunately now that the meds were beginning to level out I was capable of feeling embarrassed by my actions.

But I hadn't said anything all week and neither had he, so here we both were. Sitting together at Dec's party in honor of his incredibly introverted partner's work promotion.

"I arranged to have the to-be-shredded stuff picked up Monday. I told them you'd be there if they knocked." He paused. "Is that okay? Are you comfortable opening the door and showing them where the boxes are?"

My brain had a very fine filtering mechanism for condescension and it usually hit a lot of peaks when I was talking to Jack, but as hard as I tried, I couldn't hear anything assholeish in his voice. "I'm good with that. And thanks, the…piles of piles are beginning to feel insurmountable. Like no progress is being made."

"Well, it is. Some days more than others, but." He shrugged. "I'm just happy to be getting rid of stuff."

I didn't think the corner of Dec's living room was really the best place for me to bring up his mom's room, but once I was done with the hallway stacks, I'd have to start moving upstairs. And this was the most we'd talked all week. I felt weirdly invested in continuing our conversation. "I've been poking at the stuff on the stairs. Do you have any particular plan for the second floor?"

"Just to get rid of everything we can get rid of and put the rest in storage." His words were callous as hell, but his tone was unreadable. Callousness usually comes with a complementary tone; I wasn't quite sure what to think about the lack of alignment.

"And the…second bedroom? I think that will be the next big thing to tackle."

"Leave it to the end. Once the stairs are passable I'll have people come in and deep clean the bathrooms, so don't touch those. Everything in them should be thrown away anyway. The rest should be more of the same."

Referring to the bedrooms where his mother and grandparents had slept as "the rest" seemed…let's just say if I'd said that to my old therapist she would have called me out. Not that I was going to call Jack out. "Got it."

He looked at me, and it's not like he smiled straight-out, but his lips did a thing, a twitch-curve-relax thing that felt close to a smile. "You know the only time you're not fighting with me is when we talk about the house."

"Excuse me, I'm not single-handedly responsible for our fights. You're usually there too, you know."

"Only usually? Do you fight with me when I'm not there?"

The starkness of the question, which was meant in play, took me aback. I couldn't very well say, *Yes, and you're just as annoying when you're only in my head.* "Don't be stupid."

He laughed. "Anyway, Grandmother wants you to come to dinner again. She made me promise to ask you. Twice. She also told me to go easy on you about the house, even though I told her I was paying you, which seems good enough. I did tell her you probably wouldn't want to endure another dinner with us, but the idea that someone would dare resist the thing she wants them to do is pretty foreign to her."

"I didn't mind—I mean—I liked your grandmother." *Smooth, Oscar.* "I really liked your grandmother."

"That's true!" Mia called from where she was all too clearly eavesdropping in the kitchen. "Oscar said your grandma's the coolest old lady he's ever met."

I grimaced. "I'm not sure I said that exactly—"

"You did!" Ronnie chimed in, also all too clearly eavesdropping. "That's verbatim."

I twisted around and glared in the direction of…right, everyone but Sidney was eavesdropping. Sidney, bless their un-gossipy heart, was in a corner of the kitchen on their laptop. "Go away."

"What? Nothing!" Mia grabbed Mason's arm. "We're just hanging out in the kitchen!"

"Hell yeah we are," he agreed. "The kitchen. Also, like, one side of this large room that includes the living room, but it's not like sound travels and we can hear everything you're saying, that would be *preposterous*."

She shoved him towards Dec. "Yes, hush, moving right along, we'll be in the kitchen doing kitchen things!"

Ronnie grinned. "You should totally have dinner with Jack's grandma again, Oscar." After delivering that little bon mot, she went to fake-pretend she wasn't eavesdropping with the rest of them.

"Sorry," I mumbled. "They're the worst."

After a brief pause he said, "You really wouldn't mind having dinner again? I know she can be a handful." He didn't say it like, *I know she can be a handful and a burden.* He said it like, *I know she can be a handful and it's my favorite thing about her.* Which I respected. As someone who can also be a handful.

"I did like Evelyn. Though I'm totally not dancing with her."

"That's what you think. Give her time to wear you down and you probably will."

"I don't dance. Like ever." There was commotion behind me and I turned right in time to see Mason plaster his hand over Dec's mouth, and Mia and Ronnie close ranks behind him, like they were shielding the whole thing from view. "Oh my god," I muttered. "Fine, I danced *one time*. Because they told me I wouldn't know if I hated it unless I tried and I was young and let them talk me into it, but I hated it, okay?" Secretly, so secretly I'd never admitted it to anyone, I'd hoped maybe I wouldn't be terrible at dancing, that I was one of those people who shock everyone with their sudden ability to dance like Michael Jackson.

Spoiler alert: I did not dance like Michael Jackson.

"You fell for that old 'how do you know you don't like it unless you try it' thing?" He smirked, his tone falling between *affectionately teasing* and *kind of a jerk*. "Granted, I've never heard it applied to *dancing* before."

I shot him a sour look. "I wanted them to back off, and after they saw how bad I was, they did."

Another commotion behind me. This time I didn't turn around, figuring they'd stifle Declan, but instead it was Mase's voice. "No, come on, we can't—Oscar, you jackass, we didn't keep pushing you because you said you hated it. We thought you danced fine. Well, okay, not *fine*, you were awkward as fuck, but only because you weren't used to it. You would have been fine if you'd wanted to keep going dancing with us, but you freaked out so we backed off."

I still didn't look around, but I couldn't look at Jack either. I had the unsettling impression he was staring too all-seeingly at me so I focused instead on the window into the backyard, where the dog Dec pet-sat was yapping at a bug in the middle of the yard.

"He's right, babe." That was Ronnie. "We talked about it, but we didn't want to pressure you. I mean, more than we already had."

"And you did seem genuinely miserable," Mia added.

"Wait, *everyone* gets to talk but me?" Dec demanded.

It was hard to tell without looking, but I was pretty sure Mason rolled his eyes. "Well?"

"Uh, so, everything they already said. Is true. Like. Yeah. I was all for making you dance more, but—"

A thumping sound as all of them hit him at once.

I continued to ignore the entire thing and after another few tense seconds Mase called, “We’re going back to making food now, just FYI. You guys can talk again. In private. On the other side of the room. Where we definitely can’t hear—”

More thumps.

“I’ve never spent this much time with people who were so embroiled in each other’s lives,” Jack mused. “You can still come to dinner. Dancing is not required. Though for the record I like the idea of you dancing.”

I gritted my teeth and continued staring out the window. The dog had given up on whatever it had been attempting to snap out of midair and was now alternately sniffing and pawing at a hole in the ground.

“I’m thinking about having people in to paint once everything’s cleared out. Probably white, or off-white, whatever the most generic color is to appeal to the most generic home buyer.”

Paint the house? “Inside?”

“Interior and exterior. I think that makes the most sense in terms of selling.”

“I guess.” I didn’t feel good about it though. I’d gotten used to the—okay, dingy, but also homey—light yellow in the kitchen, the wallpaper in the living room, the blues in Jack’s room and bathroom.

“Don’t tell me you’re getting attached to the old place. I thought it was haunted?”

And god, was he…was he teasing me? I met his eyes again. Hard to say, but I thought he looked kind of amused.

“I’ve cleared the downstairs of ghosts,” I said, keeping

my tone even. “The upstairs might still be haunted. And I doubt the ghosts would like people painting.”

“Unless the ghosts can afford to buy it at market value, they don’t get a vote.”

“Dinner!” Dec called. Then an “Oops, sorry, Sid, didn’t mean to, like, shout in your ear.”

My eyes caught on Jack’s again, sharing a moment of *only Declan would accidentally shout in his partner’s ear.*

I looked away first. Then we went to dinner.

Chapter Eleven

The rhythm of cleaning changed. I'd do two hours in the morning sorting the papers in the back hallway, piles and piles which never seemed to go down now that I'd thrown out all the garbage and recycled all the recyclables. My dreams of just plowing through and clearing out the hall had vanished after a single day in which I got…about the same amount done in seven hours that I could do in two because after two my brain started shorting out and I went slower.

Much slower.

It didn't help that I'd gone back through the box I'd already "sorted" and actually sorted it. It probably wasn't in my job description, but if anyone ever went looking for any of this stuff, I didn't really want to leave it at "Here are a couple of boxes full of literally every potentially important paper, good luck."

Instead, I'd pulled the box into the living room, where there was more space, and begun organizing things. Evelyn's papers, Jack's, his grandfather's, anything related specifically to the house. That way if Jack needed to find something he'd at least have a shot at knowing which box to check.

Of course, then I had to assemble some boxes, label them, and find a place to put them where I could leave them undisturbed from day to day. I didn't want Jack to see them. It wasn't quite what I'd agreed to do and also… I suspected he'd tell me not to bother. But that would be stupid, since if he needed a mortgage statement or a tax form it'd be irritating to have to go through every single saved paper looking for it.

Best to keep it all tucked away. Since I'd cleared the stairs enough to walk up (I'd hauled all the books downstairs and boxed them neatly by the door in the place the to-shred stuff had been until the service had picked it up; get rid of one box, replace it with another, ad nauseam), I did my paper sorting on the upstairs landing, tucked out of sight.

After sweeping. And running the vacuum over the swept floor for good measure. And then damp-mopping it and opening all the windows because the second floor was dusty. I didn't have real severe dust allergies, but my eyes were itching by the time I'd set up my paper sorting system. And by "system" I mean "labeled boxes lined up against the wall into which to sort papers."

I soon decided it wasn't good enough. There was a solid

qualitative difference between a credit card statement from five years ago and a copy of last year's taxes. Thus evolved level two of the system: a row in front of the boxes for more important papers. Taxes, official documents, Jack's marriage and divorce stuff. I dug around in the desk on the landing until I found some large manila envelopes and left them with the important papers.

Then I surveyed my whole setup with pride for a minute before going back to work.

Still, even with my fun adventure in organizing, I could only sort papers for so long before my eyes started to cross. After which I'd eat something and move on to a different project.

Jack had texted that he had people coming in to do the bathrooms on Thursday, so I figured I'd at least poke around in them first to make sure there really weren't any personal items that needed to be kept. The main upstairs bathroom, which I'd only been in once to open the window, had the vague feeling of disuse that I associate with abandoned buildings. Stuffy, over-warm, the air still and unpleasant-smelling.

Aside from a sliver of soap beside the sink and maybe a quarter of a roll of toilet paper, there was nothing else, not even a worn hand towel or an unraveling bath mat. A crusty frosted glass sliding door shielded the tub and shower, but nothing inside, just emptiness and dust.

That was pretty straightforward. With some trepidation—and an uneasy sense of trespassing—I entered the room where Jack's grandparents had lived until they'd left for the facility where his grandfather died and Evelyn still resided.

The air was heavy and hot. I opened the window and averted my eyes from the rest of the room. It wasn't my place. Or. Okay. It was my place. Since I was literally being paid to work on it. But not today. Today I was just checking over the bathrooms before strangers came through to clean them.

Evelyn's bathroom was small, a cramped room with a toilet, a tiny sink, and a shower stall, all of which looked... in need of cleaning. But there were other things as well. A glass sitting beside the sink where someone had rinsed their mouth. A towel folded neatly in thirds the long way and hung in a ring on the wall. A slim vase on the windowsill with a single dried flower, brown and dusty now.

The window stuck and I had to flip the lock a few times and jiggle the frame to get it to open. The breeze flowing between all the windows I'd opened gave me the impression that old air was leaving the house, pushed out by sunlight and summer heat.

This bathroom had a medicine cabinet, and of course I looked in it. Who doesn't look into medicine cabinets? Aside from a roll of gauze, a few plastic razors, and some outlines in rust where other things had stood for a long time, there was nothing there. The shower, though, still had shampoo and the end of a bar of soap in it. I guess when she was moving, Evelyn had bought new stuff, which made sense, though looking at it gave me a chill. People had, y'know, showered there. Regularly. For years. I didn't have all the math, but they'd been in the house a long time, and if the room next door was Jack's mom's...his grandparents might have showered in this room even when they were Jack's age. Or mine.

I backed out, half tripping over the frayed-edged bath mat. "Fuck!" The sound of my own voice startled me and I stumbled out into the bedroom, creeped the fuck out.

The bed was made. Why was the bed made? Though I couldn't imagine a woman like Evelyn leaving a bare mattress, not if she knew Jack was still living in the house.

Did Jack have…guests? If he did, would he let them sleep in his grandparents' room? And why did that wig me out?

I went back through the room, accidentally brushing against the dresser and disrupting a line of dust. I closed the bedroom door behind me and told my heart to stop pounding. Sternly. I sternly lectured my heart to stop beating so quickly. And—thank fuck for meds—it did.

The house wasn't haunted. This was not a ghost story. Unless the ghosts were the projections of my imagination on this house where Jack grew up. Arguably that's what ghosts are most, if not all, of the time, but despite its appearance, I didn't sense any actual presences in the house.

I did decide that I'd go back to the stairs for the rest of the afternoon. Not because I was super creeped out or anything. Just because they needed to be done. Maybe I could at least finish that project before Evelyn came to dinner.

I usually left around six. Sometimes Jack was home by then, sometimes he wasn't. But I didn't want to fall into the trap of like *waiting* for him. That seemed like a bad idea. Especially after last week, and uh, the whole, the thing where I was crazy horny and then just crazy.

Again: used advisedly. It's the good-crazy when you have amazing sex with a guy you know. And, okay, low-key bad crazy when you fly out of the house after without saying goodbye, but whatever, we'd seen each other a bunch of times, we were fine, and I wasn't, like, hanging around hoping he'd show up and want to have amazing sex again. I had my dignity.

Question: when exactly had I started thinking of sex with Jack as "amazing"?

Answer: probably when he knelt at my feet in his damn suit and jacked himself off as he blew me. At a guess.

Anyway, it was necessity, not, like, lust, that convinced me to finish the stairs in one day even though that would take me past Jack-arriving-home o'clock. I wanted to make progress. With the house. If it also happened to mean we had sex, okay then. That was just where the cards fell. In no part due to me or any lust-related—uh—totally practical decisions I might make.

When he still wasn't home I made a related practical decision to vacuum the stairs as well. They were hardwood, but Jack had one of those vacuums that worked on hardwood. I did that, then the landing. As I was putting the vacuum away I finally heard the garage door open.

And, because I'm halfway crazy, I had the sudden urge to run out again and pretend I hadn't heard him. Like I'd been legitimately, intentionally not-waiting for him, but it was past time for him to have gotten home, so I knew it was possible. I could have avoided it. I hadn't. And now here he was and my first thought was *Maybe I can slip out the front door and he won't know I heard him.*

Which was ridiculous because he'd have seen my car.

As a consequence of my indecision I was still "putting away the vacuum" when he walked in. I heard his footsteps stop and for a moment I didn't turn. Like maybe he was a T-rex and couldn't see me if I didn't move. Except obviously that was not accurate so I looked over my shoulder and said, "Hey."

"Why are you in the closet?"

I shut the door. Firmly. "I'm not. Haven't been in the closet since I was eighteen."

Cue eyebrow-raise. "Eighteen?"

"Went to college, came out."

"Nice. Want to have sex? I had a fantastic day."

"And that makes you…want to have sex with me?"

He shrugged. "Unless you're going to disappear while I'm in the bathroom again. Admittedly, that was nonideal."

Pause while both of us waited to see what I'd say to that.

"Um. I…think I can commit to not doing that today." Which was weak sauce. "I won't. Do that. Um."

"Right, you give it some thought and I'll be right back."

Kitchen. Briefcase. Mail. Water. Jack's just-home-from-work routine.

Did I want to stay for sex? Yes. But I couldn't guarantee I'd handle it any better than last time. And I wasn't as horny. The old sex engine was revving from tortoise to about *deer that sees car coming but isn't particularly concerned, walking slowly off the road.*

Then again, he *was* in the suit.

"Well?" He reappeared. "Aren't you going to ask me about my day?"

"Um." *I thought we were maybe going to have sex?* "I don't usually. Not that we have a *usually*, but—"

He rolled his eyes, but even his eye-roll had a disturbingly playful quality. "It's a relatively typical response to someone saying they had a fantastic day. Person One: 'I had a fantastic day!' Person Two: 'What happened?' See how it works?"

"It's enlightening. You should come with me everywhere to tell me how humans behave."

"Who has the time for that? Anyway, I'll tell you, since you didn't ask: a project I've been working on just finished and the client is so thrilled they wrote an email about what a phenomenal asset I am to the company." He polished his nails on his lapel, like the biggest nerd who ever lived. "I'm high, that's what this is. I'm high right now."

"On your phenomenal-ness?"

"Yes!" He backed me up against the closet door. "So? Are you going to stay and have celebratory sex with me? It might be phenomenal. Because I have it on good authority that *I* am phenomenal."

His absurd enthusiasm should have been embarrassing, but I couldn't help but notice my sex drive had ramped up a bit. Not quite to hare, but definitely to the rabbit family. And his hand on my chest was—felt—something.

I shoved him back. "Fine. I wouldn't want you to visit this disgusting mood on some unsuspecting schmuck on Grindr."

"That would be tragic. I'm sure your sacrifice brings you honor." He rounded behind me and started—there was no other word for it—*herding* me toward the bedroom. "Take off your clothes, Oscar. Seriously. I want to see every bit of your bear cub body right now. I'm hard just thinking about it."

"Umm." I ducked out from under his grasp and turned so I could hold a hand to his forehead. "Are you sick or something?"

His grin was a bit feral. "Why?"

"Because you don't usually talk this way." I'd fucked up and gotten in range of his hands, which now slid over my chest. When I tried to shift away, one of his hands clamped down on my shoulder while the other… "What the fuck are you doing?"

"Having sex with you. Why? Is it making you uncomfortable?" Except he didn't sound all that apologetic.

"Fuck off, Jack." I stepped away and started stripping off my clothes. "I'm not uncomfortable."

"Oh yeah?"

"Yeah." Now I was angry and irritated and, yes, also horny.

"Good, because I am really riled up right now." He paused with his hands on his buttons. He paused…to watch me undress.

I turned my back. "You're being ridiculous."

"At least it doesn't make you uncomfortable."

I swallowed the seven cutting things I wanted to say to that and ripped my socks off my feet. "Fine. I'm naked. I don't care about being naked."

"Lie down."

"Bossy tonight, aren't you?"

"I don't think you mind it, Oscar."

I rolled my eyes, but it probably wasn't all that successful, so it was good I was still facing the bed. An unsuccessful eye-roll is the most embarrassing kind. I decided to keep up the act that I didn't give a fuck about anything and sat myself down against the headboard, pulling my feet up, locking my hands behind my head. There. That was a good *I'm not uncomfortable at all right now, nope, not at all* pose. A real *power* pose.

"Hell yes," he said, eyes roaming over my skin. He shoved his pants down and climbed up over me.

"Absolutely not. Take your socks off."

He stopped, his expression comically confused. "What?"

I crossed my arms in front of me now. Uh. So that was less a "power" pose and more a "disapproving matron" pose. "Take your damn socks off. I'm not having sex with you unless you take off your socks."

"Some guys are into socks."

I stared at him.

He laughed. "Fuck, I really needed this tonight. What will you do if I refuse?"

"Refuse to what?"

"Refuse to remove my unoffensive footwear."

"Then I—" If I told him I wasn't going to fuck him with his socks on there was every chance he might actually call my bluff. I couldn't possibly walk out right now, like this, without coming. I pushed him back. "Do it."

"Make me."

"The actual fuck—" was all I got out before he leaned forward and sucked my cock into his mouth. I couldn't control the instinctive thrust up into the warmth, but I did manage to lightly push at his head. "You're such a prick."

He pulled off. "I know. C'mere."

"What—"

He kissed the tip of my nose, cutting off the words and grinning. "Play with me, you grumpy bastard." Then he coaxed me up, pulling at my hands until both of us were kneeling. "Closer."

I felt—so many contradictory things. Still irritated, and awkward, and uncertain, and uncomfortable with all of the above, but fuck it, I couldn't let Jack get the better of me. I grabbed the back of his head and pulled his hair. "The fuck has gotten into you?"

"I'm high, I told you."

Then he was kissing down my neck—kissing! my neck!—but it was more like we were in some sort of battle. I tried to pull his hair hard enough to jerk him away, but he did some—some—some*thing* with his tongue and teeth and I may have let go accidentally. I wouldn't have said "play" but maybe that fit as well as any other word.

He slid closer to me, one of his knees slipping between mine, and began stroking my cock with one hand while curling the other around my neck to, like, keep me in kissing range. My neck. To keep my *neck* in kissing range.

Not to be outdone, I mirrored him, grabbing his neck a little bit harder, stroking his cock a little bit faster. He leaned in close, so close I couldn't stop looking at his lips, waiting for them to make contact with mine. But they didn't. They curved up sharply. "Bring it, Oscar, fucking *bring it*."

After that things got very chaotic. Were we fucking each other? Teasing each other? Was anyone winning? It didn't seem like anyone was losing. His hand and my hand and I locked my teeth on some patch of his flesh—his shoulder?—until he gave way and I was on top of him, but clumsily, bracing for him to force me off, but he didn't. He laughed.

His legs came around my ass and while I had to hold myself up, he was free to dispatch his hands wherever he wanted: my chest, my nipples, my stomach. I didn't remember feeling so…so stuck in place before, but then, kissing hadn't been involved before. Which…was that weird? It might have been weird. I couldn't decide.

And at least he hadn't come for my face. That would have been, you know, too much something. Too serious.

But this was playful battle including lips on non-lip skin, which was totally not serious at all. The intensity of non-lip-kissing playful Jack was…well, it wasn't unpleasant, anyway. I kept doing it, even when his legs trapped me in place, even when one of his wandering hands came into contact with my cock, and then he sort of wiggled until his cock was also there and he was…stroking both of us together in this way that didn't feel like a fumbled hand job in the back corner of a college party.

The pressure—his fingers, the firm and warm presence of his cock—combined with his teeth nibbling at my jaw did…something to me. A sort of…quiver? A quiver of pleasure shot through me, my balls, my spine, my lips, my tongue, even my brain seemed more than usually invested in this endeavor until I closed my eyes and just fucking *felt* it.

Jack thrust up, his heels digging into my ass for leverage, thrusting against my cock and into his hand, and again that thrill went through me.

I moaned. Legitimately. Without meaning to.

My eyes shot open and I was ready to pull away, to say something sharp, but his eyes had slid shut and… I don't know. I kind of just looked at him in that moment, when he was vulnerable and undefended, expression soft with pleasure. It was…a little disturbing, a little compelling.

A little hot, to be honest. Seeing him like that.

I shuddered against him, stopping my thoughts so I could just enjoy the fucking. *Enjoy the fucking, Oscar, stop overthinking everything.* In a miraculous turn, I could. Eyes squeezed shut, physical awareness sky-high, the sound of our skin, our breaths, the taste of…of Jack. The smell of him. The feel of him everywhere.

It was enough to push me over the edge and I came with another embarrassing moan, rendered less embarrassing moments later when he followed, uttering a much louder, and okay, much deeper groan.

"Fuck, Oscar. That was…"

"I prefer my sex acts to go unreviewed," I mumbled.

He sighed contentedly. "I'm good with that."

I awkwardly extracted myself from our mess and passed him the tissues. "Sorry. Um."

"Apology not accepted. Thank you for humoring me."

"I…wasn't." I felt a bit ridiculous and pulled my shirt on, ignoring the bits of…wetness I'd missed cleaning up. "You never kissed me before. My, uh, neck. Any part of me. Before."

He didn't say anything for a long moment. "I'm not proposing we make out the next time Declan has a party. But in this context it seemed like an interesting idea and I wanted to surprise you."

"Fine. In this context."

"Glad we agree."

I glanced at him. "Are you humoring *me* now?"

He smiled. "Maybe. Only a little. You want dinner?"

"Uh. I think I have some at home. But thanks."

"Sure."

And that's how we left it. I didn't run away this time. I... took my leave in a perfectly acceptable manner.

Chapter Twelve

When I got sick of paperwork on Wednesday I did something I'd never planned to do: instead of moving on to another part of my actual job, I...cleaned.

It was accidental at first. I'd tracked back and forth through the living room enough times to feel like I should sweep before Evelyn came over for dinner. So I swept the main area. Since I couldn't picture Jack moving furniture around to clean, I shifted the couch, chair, and coffee table to do a more thorough job of it, disrupting enough dust in the process that I had to open the front door and kitchen window to try to blow it all out.

Then I needed to dust just to clean up after my previous cleaning efforts.

Jack had insisted we get rid of the furniture we found

under the piles of stuff because "If no one's seen it in five years, it can't be necessary," so what was left was the couch, chair, coffee table, and a credenza-thing with the TV on it. I'd already gathered up the old VHS tapes and old VCR into a box to be donated somewhere, but I hadn't started on the framed pictures that lined the top.

Except once I had taken them all down the room looked…vacant. Furniture and a TV were fine, but the pictures had made it feel like a home. Jack with his grandparents at various ages, Jack graduating from high school, Jack graduating from college, teenage Jack in a bathing suit grinning at the camera with a backdrop of…a swim meet or something? Holding up medals. Well, one medal, but multiple pictures of Jack with a medal. Not like he had all of them in one picture. There was a collection.

Thou shalt not ogle one's fuck buddy's teenage photos was a commandment I never knew I needed. Still, there were enough pictures at pools to indicate that Jack had been a swimmer, and had done it well enough to grin at the camera repeatedly.

After taking all the pictures down and dusting the credenza I put all the pictures back up, cursing myself for not taking the precaution of a before picture so I could replace them correctly. Dammit.

Dusted was better than not-dusted, though. I ran through with the vacuum on its wood floors setting and ran that over the couch and chair for good measure.

At which point I realized I'd just spent a couple of literal hours cleaning Jack's living room in the hopes that Evelyn would…what? Feel impressed? Pleased? Ugh. I did not want to care about anyone being pleased with me, but Evelyn was an old lady, so maybe it wasn't that bad a thing to want.

And I liked her. I looked forward to seeing her later. That, also: pretty fucking weird.

This time her first words were, "Young man, have you been disrupting my mementos? These pictures were in a very specific order, I'll have you know."

She said it so sternly that I was about to stammer some kind of reply before Jack cut in. "They were not, Grandmother. Stop trolling Oscar, he's only here because he inexplicably likes your company."

Evelyn raised her eyebrows at me, eerily similar to the way Jack did it. "Oh, I'd be surprised if that were the *only* reason he's here."

Ugh, was she trying to imply something?

"You're paying him, aren't you?"

I glanced at Jack, who opened his mouth, then shut it, then opened it again. "Not to have dinner! Oh my god."

I didn't know which was worse: being suspected of being paid to have sex with Jack or being paid to have dinner with a snarky old woman. Since that was unsolvable (and I definitely had the impression from the gleam in her eye that she'd find a way to turn any response against me), I changed the subject. "Sorry about the pictures. I'm leaving them for last. Speaking of which, I had a question about the picture in the hallway. Or I guess it's some kind of craft thing."

She smiled. "My only attempt at cross-stitch and I was

terrible at it, but Jack's grandfather didn't seem to mind. Yes? What's the question?"

"Well, it says *Remember the secret.* So I guess I was wondering…what's the secret?"

Evelyn's smile deepened. "That's the sort of wisdom I can only pass on to you when I think you're ready for it, dear boy. Now show me what you've been up to while my grandson works on dinner."

I wasn't super comfortable with the arrangement and half hoped she wouldn't be able to go up the stairs—until I realized *I hope this little old lady is too infirm to climb stairs* was a super fucked-up thought. And Evelyn was not infirm. She took the now-clear stairs with ease and surveyed my landing organizing system with satisfaction.

"Very good. When Robin died, we had a hell of a time tracking down everything we needed. You would be shocked by the sheer amount of bureaucracy involved in death." She nodded at my piles. "I suppose it might have been an opportunity to organize things then, but I had other concerns. Sometimes, dear, you think you're ready for a death, but it still knocks the wind right out of you. Still does, some days, going on months afterward. Anyway."

I didn't say anything. Because I had no idea what to say. Thankfully, she didn't require participation.

"Jack tells me he has cleaners coming in for the upstairs." She pressed the bathroom door open slightly with her fingertips and made a face. "A sound idea. I wouldn't want you to have to do this job, and in any case, he's paying a reasonable price."

I just bet she'd asked, too. "I wouldn't mind, but I think

he wants a real…final job. I'm sure they'll have steam wands and special detergents or something."

"I'm sure they will." She passed right over the upstairs bedroom I'd identified as potentially Jack's mom's and went into her own old bedroom. "Terrible smell in here. Did he not pay to have this cleaned as well? He should. It may be possible to add it to the job." She went over to the window I'd opened before I'd gotten creeped out the other day (which Jack must have closed). "How can you stand working in this house, child?"

"It doesn't bother me, I guess?" I was doing that reflexive question-at-the-end-of-a-statement thing more with Evelyn than I usually did. It was a habit I'd picked up from Dec and it bugged me. "It really doesn't bother me." There. Statement. No question mark.

"I suppose it's different if it's not your home, isn't it?" She stood at the window and looked around. "I didn't realize I'd left this room so shabby. How *embarrassing.* Well, I would say to keep some of these linens—the sheets are garbage, but this quilt was made by my aunt when I was a child—but I'm sure Jack plans to get rid of everything." Stepping toward the bed, she reached out, her hand hovering over it.

"I'll put it in a box for storage," I promised. Rashly. "He'll never know."

Evelyn smiled but shook her head. "Ah, but then it defeats the purpose of keeping it. This quilt was meant to be used, not stuffed away in a box. Well, maybe he can donate it to someone who can use it. Will you see to that, Oscar?"

"Of course." I vowed to save it. If I had to bring it home

myself, the quilt would not be going to some random thrift store. Maybe Ronnie and Mia would want it. They were quilt-types.

"Thank you, dear. Everything else should go. Including the bed, for goodness' sake, we've had this since before Jack was born. The one I sleep on now has a remote control to raise and lower it, much less fluffing of pillows to do. The furniture as well—all cheap stuff Robin kept fixing all those years. Refused to let us buy anything better even when we could have afforded it. 'Why buy when you can fix?' he'd say with the silliest smile on his face." She shook her head. "It's funny, Jack is a mix of both of us. He picked up Robin's desire to never let anything go, except with him it's all up here." She tapped her head. "He and I always agreed that the best thing to do was clean house."

I was so unprepared for that kind of personal information that it must have shown on my face, but she shrugged and moved on, only looking into the bathroom for a moment before going back out to the hallway. This time she pressed her hand briefly against the closed door to the other bedroom.

"Anything in here can be done away with." She retracted her hand like it was landing gear and walked off down the stairs, not looking back.

All families probably had stories, secrets, doors they never wanted to open again. But Jack's family had all that in a physical manifestation, almost as if the house itself was a dying member of the family and no one was quite sure where to look when it tried to tell its tales.

I followed Evelyn to the living room and found them setting up dinner.

"My grandson has, against my advice, decided to grace us with his lasagna." She eyed the offending dish on the coffee table with distrust.

"Don't listen to her, I make excellent lasagna."

"*Alfredo* does not belong in lasagna."

He sighed. A comfortable, long-suffering sigh. "I like a creamier lasagna than you do, Grandmother. I think it's time we moved on."

"Of course you do. You think it's normal to add sauces into dishes where they're neither needed nor wanted."

Jack looked at me. "It was the first recipe I ever made where I altered it from the original and she's never gotten over my impertinence."

"The original was just fine on its own without you going all over the internet trying to find ways to screw it up!"

As if to prove I had no understanding of family dynamics, he kissed her cheek, and she immediately relented. Like. Weren't they fighting a second ago? It seemed like they were about to be fighting *more*, except now the fight had evaporated.

"It's not the worst thing I've ever tasted," she said grudgingly after taking a bite.

"Oh, well, thanks *so much* for that, Grandmother."

"You're welcome. Oscar and I have been talking a bit, Jack, and we think you should get this cleaning service of yours to do the whole house."

I blinked. "Um."

"It's quite dusty, you know. And I assume you're going to have painters come in as well?"

I glanced from one to the other. Jack was studiously eating his food. "Um."

"We agreed that it would be best to get started on those projects sooner rather than later. Didn't we, Oscar?" And the way she looked at me made me wonder if maybe we had actually said all that and I'd somehow missed it.

"Um."

"Don't let her tell you what you think," Jack advised.

"He entirely agrees with me."

"I do?"

She beamed. "Of course you do, dear." Turning to Jack, she added, "Oscar's a very nice young man."

"I know, Grandmother."

"I like him quite a bit," she continued, but I wasn't tracking because I was staring at Jack. He *knew* I was a "nice young man"? What did that mean?

"I know where this is heading and I already—"

"Oscar," she said, ignoring him. "I have an unfortunate gap in my schedule next week and I was wondering if you'd humor an old woman and visit me where I live."

"Grandmother!"

"My usual companion is on vacation and it helps so much to have a young person around for a couple of hours, you know, to liven things up—"

"—I *asked* you not to—"

She beamed at me. "We could play checkers. Do you play checkers? I never got into chess—too fussy—but checkers is just my speed." With raised eyebrows she glanced at Jack. "What was it, dear?"

"It—I—" He shook his head, looking genuinely annoyed. "Oscar has better things to do than—"

"Spend time with a boring old woman?"

"You're not *boring*, but—"

"I don't," I said. "Have better things to do." Not that I'd ever thought I was suited to hang out with old people, but Evelyn was no ordinary old person. Plus, it seemed to bother Jack, which made it worth doing regardless. "I mean, aside from being here, my schedule is pretty open."

"Excellent! I'll get your phone number from Jack and we'll set it up."

Fuck. I hated phone calls. "Um. Do you text?"

"Text? I *can* text. If it's necessary." She raised a quizzical eyebrow.

"Um." *Hi, I'm crazy and can't talk on the phone without losing my shit.* "Texting would be better."

"All right, then. How about this: I'll call you and leave a voice message about when I'm available and you can reply by text message? That way we're both comfortable with our communications?"

I swallowed hard, my eyes darting toward Jack to see what he thought of my awkwardness, but he was still looking at Evelyn. "Um," I mumbled. "Yeah, that works. Thank you."

"You're absolutely welcome. Now, Jack, was there something you wanted to say?"

"Nothing I haven't already said, not that you paid any attention. Oscar, I'm having a beer, would you like one?"

Yes, and *It would be irresponsible since I don't know how beer interacts with these meds yet* and *Oh god if you guys are going to fight with each other I really need one.* "Um. No thanks. I should…not. I should probably go soon."

"You're not done with dinner!" Evelyn said, seeming genuinely crestfallen.

"Going out on a limb here, but it's possible Oscar doesn't want to be used as a pawn in a fight we were already having."

"Oh, Jack, you know I don't play chess."

He rolled his eyes. "Your 'I'm just a silly old woman' act doesn't work on me, Grandmother."

"More's the pity. It's the prerogative of the young to make the old more comfortable."

"And that means I should let you get away with being rotten to my friends?"

There was that word again.

"I wasn't! Oscar, tell my grandson that I was not at all rotten to you."

I took the noble-slash-coward's way out. "I…don't think I want to get in the middle of this, honestly. Um. I should go home. Can I bring the dishes up?"

Neither of them seemed all that invested in the dishes, but I felt unaccountably like *I'd* done something wrong. When I hadn't. I was relatively certain.

I was just dropping the dinner plates in the sink when I felt a presence behind me.

"I'm sorry about that," Jack said. "You aren't obligated to go hang out with my grandmother. She can get through a couple of days without her normal caregiver."

"I don't feel obligated." I leaned back against the counter and looked at him. "The only other thing I have going is this big cleaning job, but my hours are flexible."

"And your boss is forgiving?"

"Wouldn't go that far."

He shifted from one foot to the other. "It makes me uncomfortable."

I shrugged. "Sounds like a personal problem."

"Fair enough. And exactly what she'll say to me the second you leave. You don't have to, you know. We have brownies for dessert if you want one. With ice cream."

God, brownies, heated in a microwave, ice cream melting on them…

At which point the body-shaming devil on one shoulder went to war with the sweets-loving devil on the other shoulder in yet another in a lifetime of epic battles for my virtue. The worst part was that neither of them was all wrong, but that each was right for the wrong reasons, leaving me basically losing whatever way I chose to go.

Devil #1: Do you want to get *fatter*? Is that what you want? To be even less attractive than you are now? Then eat all the brownies and ice cream you want, buddy boy, and poke another hole in all your belts!

Devil #2: Don't listen to him, have dessert! One night of brownies and ice cream isn't going to make a bit of difference in the long run and you've *earned* it! You deserve to enjoy yourself!

Obnoxiously, there were good points to be made on each side. Eating all that sugar would probably spin me out all night. But then again, sharing dessert with Jack and Evelyn wasn't some epic failure of willpower, *or* a reward I'd earned. It was just…eating dessert with Jack and Evelyn. Totally value neutral.

You were supposed to be able to eat whatever your body told you it wanted and eventually you'd be eating like salads and vegetables or whatever. My eat-whatever-you-want failsafe was broken. My road to extreme bodily discomfort was paved with thoughts like *One more's not gonna kill me* and *If a man can't have another handful of M&M's, what's the point of any of this?*

"Oscar."

I came back to myself standing in Jack's kitchen, and Jack was a lot closer than he had been before. Really close. "Sorry."

"It's no problem. Dessert?"

If I said yes, was I saying it because I was desperate for brownies and ice cream? Because I was spitting in the eye of my internalized fat phobia?

Because I wanted to spend more time with… Evelyn. Probably that. The Evelyn thing. Not, like, any other thing about spending more time with anyone who wasn't Evelyn.

I slipped to the side. "Yeah. Do you heat them before putting on ice cream?"

"Obviously."

"Is it vanilla?"

"Caramel swirl. Vanilla goes well with pie, but caramel swirl goes better with brownies."

"Okay, now I'm definitely staying."

"Here." He passed me a gallon of ice cream (normal

people ice cream, nothing fancy) and a scoop. "You get ready, we have to ice cream them fast."

So Jack cut brownies, zapped them in the microwave, and passed them to me. I put two scoops on each and he added forks. We returned to the living room like we'd invented the combination of ice cream and baked goods.

And Evelyn clapped her hands, as if she was just that impressed. "Oh, lovely, boys. Absolutely lovely. I'll take the biggest one, please."

"You always taught me to let guests choose first." But Jack's tone had reverted to his usual warm banter with her.

She winked at me. "I'm sure Oscar would let a sad little old lady have the biggest brownie. Wouldn't you, dear?"

"Um…"

Jack sighed. "You're really the worst, Grandmother."

"Thank you, darling. Now dig in."

Warm brownies with caramel swirl ice cream is the food of the gods. Make a note.

Chapter Thirteen

Weekends left me rootless. Especially *cough* after sex with Jack on Friday. Unlike our usual getting-off-as-fast-as-possible, on Friday we seemed to be in a competition to make the other get off first, prolonging things by…quite a margin. It was fully dark and I was aching in some not wholly unpleasant ways by the time I drove home.

I still couldn't deep throat, but since he still didn't seem to care, I worried less and just enjoyed blowing him. Torturously. For *a while*. A favor he returned until I had to bite down hard on my tongue to keep from begging. Jack was still an asshole. But an asshole with mad sex skills, as Dec would say (and not pull it off) and Mase would say (and totally pull it off).

But then it was that weekend stretch when reality became a little unmoored and time blurred into video game loading screens and a vague sense that I'd eaten too much (yet simultaneously not enough) while trying to escape the inevitable truth that eventually there would be no more house to clear out, which meant no more sex competitions with Jack, which further meant no more income.

Seven thousand dollars felt like a lot of money, and it was, but it wasn't *save me from job hunting indefinitely* money.

Thoughts like that led to more loading screens and shit, did I eat…that whole bag of Ruffles? No. Right? Except I did remember opening one…was that this morning? Yesterday? Tracing back my snacking didn't help either on the acquiring reality level or the morale level. I abandoned the effort and ate a banana.

There. Nutrition unlocked. Now more shooting strangers on the internet.

Evelyn left me a message requesting my company on Tuesday and Thursday in the afternoon "around two." I never know what people mean when they say "around" a specific time. Is that a polite way of saying "at" two? Is it indicating a certain amount of flexibility, and if so, how much? Does "around" mean ten minutes on either side is fine? Twenty? Arriving ten minutes later is acceptable, but not before?

I decided to aim for two o'clock and dismiss the whole "around" thing. I texted her back that I'd see her Tuesday at two, already having second thoughts about the whole thing. I'd agreed largely to mess with Jack, and now I was actually going to…you know, hang out with his grandmother.

What if we had nothing to say to each other? What if I

bored her? What if I was bored? What if the whole thing was excruciating and then I had to go again on Thursday?

Fuck it, less thinking, more shooting.

I was looking forward to Monday. Work. Having something to do. Something to achieve. I was nearly done with the paper sorting, enough that I could carry the rest up to the landing and sweep the back hallway. Some of the older piles had been back there for a long time and I'd unearthed a small bookcase and two stools. When I moved everything there were actual dust outlines on the walls.

I mixed some water and white vinegar and wiped the walls down, as well as the stools and bookcase, which I brought out to the garage. Jack had managed to have a truck pick up the rest of the furniture we'd gathered so far, but after the upstairs, he'd definitely need to have them stop by again.

My second impression of the house—after thinking it was haunted—was this hallway, piled with things, feeling more like a tunnel than a hall in a residential home. And now it was...clear. Clean, even, and empty but for Evelyn's enigmatic cross-stitch on the wall. God help me, I was actually proud of it. So proud that I lost my head momentarily and sent a picture to Jack.

He sent back *Impressive.*

Which was a very Jack reply and brought me back down to earth. And: back to work.

I'd been looking forward to, for lack of a better word, fucking later, but about halfway through the day I realized my brilliant plan to have sex with Jack when he got home from work was destined for disappointment. A quick check of my sex drive revealed that systems were offline.

Fucking meds fuck fuck fuck fucking meds.

Back.

To.

Work.

Goddammit.

I wasn't ready to tackle the upstairs extra bedroom, but I checked in on the bathrooms (now sparkly clean and sanitized) and wiped down the furniture in Evelyn's old room so we could move it downstairs whenever…that was a thing. I also threw her aunt's quilt in the washing machine on gentle. Fuck it, I'd bring it home with me. I wasn't donating it.

I kept busy, hoping my cock would magically perk up, but no luck. Jack got home at the usual time and waved hello on his way to the kitchen as I was putting away the vacuum again. This was getting to be a routine: me finding ways to extend cleaning past six, him arriving home unsurprised to see me still there. This was the moment I'd been dreading for the last few hours, since I abandoned all hope of my libido picking up.

"Well?" He gestured to the hallway. "After you."

"I…" …had a few options. I could try to will myself hard, to paraphrase Ani DiFranco. (Never talk to Ronnie about Ani DiFranco; her Ani phase was *eternal*.) Which didn't have a real high probability of working, but sometimes I got lucky. I could make up a stupid excuse, which Jack would know was a stupid excuse, and then things would be awkward again.

I could…tell the truth? I hadn't tried that before in this context. "Uh… I can't…right now. The meds sorta…fuck with me." Vague hand movement, which I stifled by shoving both hands in my pockets. "In the libido area."

Understanding dawned and his *come hither* turned into *never mind then*. "Oh. That seems like an extremely poor side effect for something designed to make you less depressed."

"Yeah. I guess they figure in a straight-up choice between death and not getting laid, the rational choice is not getting laid."

"That doesn't seem all that rational to me."

I shrugged. "Me neither. But I keep choosing it, so."

"Is it… I mean, does that go away, or…?"

"It's not real consistent, but it's never been permanent. Don't worry, I'll be able to service your sexual needs again soon, boss."

"I guess you can keep your job, then," he sniped back. "But no, I meant is that how it always is?"

"No. Sometimes. It's off and on. I guess I feel like the meds slightly lower my, whatever, sex drive in general, but on the other hand without them I have a hard time leaving my house or talking to humans. Definitely not getting laid if you can't do those things. At least, not in person. But this is a new batch of crap in my system and it's only been two weeks. Long enough so I feel it, maybe not long enough to discount the transition." *Please, please let this be part of the transition*. "Anyway, today I'd have to force myself and I probably wouldn't get hard. I could still get you off. If you wanted."

"Hmm. No, I think if I was going to torture you by coming when you can't I'd want you to be bound with your hands behind your back or something, not medically unable to access arousal."

"Oh my god, 'medically unable to access arousal,' what are you, a prescription drug ad?"

"It beats 'dicked over by the medicine that's supposed to make you feel better.'"

"I don't think it's supposed to make me feel *better.* It's just supposed to make me able to go to work and buy groceries."

"I think not being able to do those things would likely feel *worse*, so indirectly it's making you feel *better.*"

I rolled my eyes. "Thanks for letting me know. Do you want me to blow you, or—" I did the universal motion for *hand job*, which is the same as the universal motion for *jerking off*, whether used literally or metaphorically.

"No, Oscar. Maybe if you were hard and desperate for it. Not when you can't get hard at all."

"Lollipop, you asshole."

He grinned spontaneously, the expression breaking apart all the snark. "You remember."

"I don't forget a man's safeword, no matter how ludicrous it is." But a disturbing sense of warmth moved through my chest, as if I was…pleased that he was pleased. "To return to the point, you will absolutely not be tying my hands behind my back so you can torture me, thanks very fucking much."

"But I'm allowed to tie your hands behind your back for other reasons?"

"*Doubtful.*"

"That's not a no."

I pressed my lips into an unimpressed line.

"You do surprise me, Oscar. But stay anyway, I picked up sushi on the way home. There's enough for you if you want some."

Translation: he picked up sushi for us to share, because sushi's not exactly a food you get extra of to save for tomorrow.

That felt…awkward. I fidgeted with my keys, wondering if it was more or less of a commitment to stay when we weren't having sex. That was a reason. A point. A goal. This would just be…dinner.

Then again, it was sushi.

"I'm in. Did you get spider rolls? If so, dibs."

"You can't call dibs on an entire roll, you heathen."

"Watch me."

It was weird, being there with no actual excuse. No reason. Beyond habit, I suppose. Jack had bought dinner for me with the expectation I'd stay after work to fuck. I'd looked forward to having sex with him all weekend. Now here we were, with no sex, eating dinner together. And the weirdest part was probably that it felt like any other night.

It didn't feel relationship-y or anything. It just felt like having dinner with Jack.

By which I mean I made an offhand comment he latched onto and wouldn't let go of. Par for the course.

"Wait, you think I'm a *broker*?" The disbelief practically dripped from his words. "I'm not a broker."

To be honest, I didn't actually know what a broker was, I just thought that's what he did. Broker stuff. "Uh. Declan said you were, I think? Like the people on *Billions*?"

He closed his eyes and shook his head, like the stupidity of what I'd said was unfathomable. "Declan said. Of course he did. Because he has no idea what I do and just associated some scrap he picked up to the closest possible pop culture reference."

"Hey, *Billions* is good!" I protested.

"*Billions* in its most trash moment is better than a lot of shows ever get, but still, I am not a broker. Which I think is a sort of simplistic understanding of what they're doing on the show anyway."

"Oh. So…what do you do, then?"

He picked up a California roll and dipped it in way too much soy sauce. "Financial analysis."

"And that's…not what they do on *Billions*? Because it sure seems like it is what they do. On *Billions*."

"I sit at my computer and generate reports about what other people are doing with money. Sometimes, when I'm feeling lively, I use brighter-than-usual colors in my graphs." He looked at me as if daring me to mock his color-coding. Or otherwise disrespect his work.

"That sounds cool. Do you like it?"

"Yeah. Well. What I was doing before I met Declan was a lot more stressful. I worked for a big company and was in constant competition with my coworkers and worked ridiculous hours. So this is a lot better than that was."

It seemed like there was…more. More to say. I waited.

"If I'd been doing this when my grandfather was…less

impaired than he got in the last few years, maybe the house wouldn't be in the state it's in now. I used to get home at nine or ten at night sometimes and be out of here again by seven the next morning. I think they could have used more help than that." He explained quickly, "It's not like I never left home. I got married, and after the divorce I got a nice apartment I never saw except to sleep in. But my grandparents started needing more help and I didn't want to keep paying rent, so I came back here."

"I wasn't actually judging you for staying with your grandparents."

"And I pay all the property taxes and buy a lot of the food. I mean, I did. When they lived here."

"Jack, seriously, I don't think you were taking advantage of your grandparents. And I'm sure Evelyn loved having you here."

He grimaced. "When I was here, anyway. I should have done more for them back then. But it took me...a while to get over the divorce. Mostly because I'd decided I didn't want to think about it and worked sixty, seventy-hour weeks so I wouldn't have to."

This thing, where Jack almost seemed uneasy with the decisions his past self had made, left me feeling uncomfortable. Almost sympathetic. Naturally, I responded with sarcasm. "What, you took extreme measures to avoid your feelings? Can't relate to that *at all*."

That got me the wannest of smiles. "Such a cliché, I know. It wasn't just the divorce, either. I knew something was going on here—with Grandfather, with his 'collections'—but I didn't realize how serious it was. Which is probably hard to imagine since you've seen the house, but at the time it didn't seem like a big deal. Until it was."

I thought about the bookshelf in the back hallway. A bookshelf was so innocuous. "I can imagine it. And it's not like it was the whole house. The upstairs landing was clear. And your grandparents' room."

"Because Grandmother had rules, yes. I don't think she noticed when he started doing it because she'd never go into my mother's old bedroom. He filled that up and then his collections started to spread to other places." He shot a rueful glance toward the back of the house. "Though the yard's always been like that. There were definitely signs, even before they had me. But the hoarding intensified the older he got. And for a long time he was convinced—" He broke off for a moment and cleared his throat. "He was convinced my mother would come back. That she was just 'living her life' and then she'd decide she wanted me after all."

Holy shitballs. "Um. Was that… I mean…"

He shrugged. "They were old when they had her. She was young when she had me. She was here for two years before running off again."

So that was intense. I ate a piece of sushi, not sure if I wanted him to go on or stop or what. My own complaints about my parents—*vaguely present; pretend away anything they don't like*—seemed petty in comparison to, like, *Lasted two years then left me and never looked back.* "You don't remember her?"

"Oh, no, she came around sometimes. She didn't disappear. She just didn't want to be my mother. And now she's living with her new husband in Florida."

I blinked. "Hang on. Your mom knows all this is happening, with Evelyn and the house and everything, and she's…not helping? Like at all?"

"What would she help with? I have this handled. And Grandmother's fine. If she wanted to, she could move back here to the house, but she's got a rigorous social life at her apartment. She just wants the house sold and gone." There was a note to his voice I couldn't completely figure out. Grief about the house? Anger about his mom?

"Are you mad at her for leaving? Your mom, I mean. Not Evelyn."

"Mad at her? God no. There'd be no point. Plus, Grandmother more or less forgave her, and she was the one left picking up all the pieces. It wasn't my place to hold a grudge."

Something about this didn't seem quite right. "Are you…the pieces? In that analogy?"

"Yeah, okay. I just mean I had everything I needed and obviously my mother was not very good at mothering." Another shrug. "Anyway, I feel like I'm talking too much about my own weird family. Is yours less weird?"

"I don't really know. My dad's super conservative and my mom is second generation Mexican in America. Which is a little weird if you think about it too hard."

"Huh. What's the…attraction there?"

"I guess they fell in love? Or I think they fell for the solution the other one offered. My dad wanted a minor rebellion with a side of conformity, so he married a woman his family didn't think was good enough—or white enough—for him. My mom wanted to get away from the idea of being an immigrant's kid, so she found the whitest guy she could find and didn't let me take Spanish in high school."

"Holy shit. Seriously?"

"Yeah. I took French." I gestured around. "Because we have such a large French-speaking population in California, right? *Tellement stupide*," I added in my terrible French accent.

He smiled. "Say something else."

"Umm..." I squeezed my eyes shut. "*Chose* something? Or something *chose*? I think it's something *chose*."

"I took Spanish. Um. *¿Que es tu color favorito?*"

"What?"

"I asked you what your favorite color was, because for reasons beyond understanding that's one of the things we learned how to say in Spanish class."

"At least you retained some sentence structure. I retained, like, pointless vocabulary. I can do the months. And count to a hundred. Days of the week."

"You remember how to say something's stupid. And whatever the other thing was."

"Yeah." I tapped my head. "I remember how to say 'something.' Not sure how useful that is."

"It's bound to be more useful than 'What's your favorite color?' Seriously, under what circumstance in a Spanish-speaking country will I ever need to ask someone what their favorite color is? Have you literally ever asked anyone about their favorite color?"

"Maybe when I was five. *Maybe*." I paused. Dramatically. "Well? What's your favorite color, Jack?"

"Hmm." He leaned back on the couch and crossed his

legs out in front of him, looking longer and leaner than usual, quite the former high school swimmer. "Turquoise," he said finally. "My favorite color is turquoise."

"You sure? Do you want some extra time on that? Seems like a big decision."

"One's favorite color is not a *decision*. It's a *feeling*."

"A feeling," I repeated.

"Obviously." He was warming up to this now. "It's a *sensation* you feel when you see a certain color. That's how you know it's your favorite." He nudged my leg with his foot. "What's your favorite color? What color brings you life, Oscar? You know it when you see it. What color makes you *feel* something?"

"This conversation is disturbing."

Nudge. "What color makes you tingle, Oscar? What color turns you on?"

"No libido, remember?"

"Turns you on in the favorite color part of your brain, not the sex part."

I reached for the takeout bag. "Is there acid in this? Did you spike the sushi? That would be unusual, but I wouldn't put it past you."

"Why are you being so cagey about your favorite color? Is it embarrassing? Is it gold lame? Or leopard print?"

"Those aren't colors, they're fabrics. Or—or patterns. Or something."

"Ah-ha! It *is* gold lame."

This time I sniffed at the spider roll I was saving for last. "You're acting ridiculous. You have to be under the influence of something. Did you get high in the bathroom?"

"I'm an adult, of course I didn't get high in the bathroom. If I wanted to get high I would have done it in my car before coming in from the garage, like a grown man."

"Is the garage your man cave?"

"Hell yes it is. I meant to tell you, the back hallway looks really good. I mean. It still needs to be painted and the lights should be replaced and the bulb at the back door is still out, but I haven't seen it without junk crawling up the walls in years. So thank you."

The switch in tone threw me. "It's what you're paying me for," I mumbled, slightly uncomfortable.

"I'm paying you to help me clear things out. The organizing and the cleaning and the…care. That's more than I expected, and I appreciate it."

I had no idea what to say to that. "I accept bonuses in the form of sushi and blow jobs."

"Done."

We went back to eating while some small space in the back of my brain had opened up enough to register a *feeling* or a *sensation* that felt suspiciously ungrounded in fact. Factually, Jack was a fuck buddy I was having dinner with, nothing more than that. That he'd recognized how much effort I'd put into my work for him—the effort was for Evelyn, of course, but the job was for him since he was the one who'd hired me—triggered a vague sense of… feeling in me.

Just like a favorite color. You knew it when you saw it. This was a feeling. I didn't know *what* feeling, but I was experiencing a feeling. Shocking development, news at eleven.

Chapter Fourteen

The thing you don't take into consideration when you agree to hang out with someone's grandma mostly to annoy them is the inevitable moment when you're sitting in your car at said grandma's old people apartment complex trying to force yourself to go inside.

Just walk inside. It's easy. You can do this. You can do this without having a panic attack. Which was mostly made-up. Maybe I could do it, maybe I couldn't.

Revise: just walk inside. It's not actually that easy. You can do this. You can maybe do it without a panic attack. Focus on the doing it. Deal with the panic attack if it happened. Same as every other day of the week.

I'd been watching people go in. There seemed to be a lobby area with a desk, so probably my game plan was to go in and find someone being paid to entertain clueless visitors. Good plan, go team. Got this. Slow breaths. Not being hunted by lions, brain, back off. We're navigating some very basic small talk, ideally with a human making money to do exactly that. We have managed similar situations before and survived.

Seriously no lions. Let's just keep breathing.

When I'm really trying to talk myself down I become a splintered first person plural, like the rational part of my brain is trying to calm the *if I have to walk up to a stranger and talk to them right now I am literally going to die* part of my brain. I sat in my car and pluraled to my heart's content.

"Around" two, right. Get there on time, freak out in car.

Hand on handle. Open door. Keep breathing. Walk toward building. Keep breathing. Prior analysis confirms it's a Pull not a Push, approach door, scan for other life forms, confirm no other life forms on potential collision course.

No, no, we said *pull* not *push*. Recover. Pull. Open door. Step to the side to reassess.

I approached the desk area, rehearsing what I'd say—*Hi, I'm looking for a resident, her name is Evelyn*—

Evelyn…

What the hell was Jack's last name?

I'd seen probably hundreds of papers with their names, I had to be able to remember, even if he'd never actually said it, Evelyn Something, Evelyn Something, go through the alphabet, quick—

"Can I help you?"

Fuck, fuck, fuck, I was losing my grip. "Um. You know.

I think I'll. I should." I reached for my phone in panic. "Let me just text the person I'm here to see."

"Okay!" The woman behind the counter was younger and perkier than me. Good fit for the job. Terrible to encounter when panicking.

My hands were sweating, my fingers were tingling. Great. I carefully navigated to my thread with Evelyn and then stared at it. Uh. What did I say? I could tell her I'd arrived and didn't know how to find her. I could ask for her last name. I could text Jack to ask. I could text Dec, he'd probably know. I could—

"Oscar!"

Oh thank god.

"Oscar, dear, here you are. Hello, Jenny, how are you? This is Oscar, my grandson's young man."

I opened my mouth to say something—*Um, no, and you know it, lady*—but a quick pinch to my side and a corresponding grab of my arm to keep me from moving away shut me up.

"Such a nice boy, he's come to keep me company, isn't that lovely? See you around, dear." Evelyn guided/forced me away with her, not speaking until we were around the corner. "You don't mind if I tell people that, do you? It's just they're all so gossipy, and they do look at you differently when they think you've got young people looking after you. *Not* that I need looking-after, but that's the perception of a single woman at my age. In any case, I've arranged for us to eat lunch in the dining room, got us a table and everything."

Notice how she didn't actually wait to see if I minded?

Also, dear god, lunch, the dining room, whatever that was. Here I thought getting there at two would save me from a formal meal. "Um…"

It soon became clear that at least one of the reasons she'd asked me over was to…show me off. In a manner of speaking. And regardless of the fact that I wasn't dating Jack. She introduced me to so many people by the time food arrived that I was almost numb to it. Trial by fire. Exposure therapy. Something.

I'd strategically ordered a turkey sandwich, hoping the tryptophan might settle my nerves. I had no idea if that was how tryptophan worked, but it seemed like it was worth a shot. For most of lunch I was worried that Evelyn, whose social inclinations surpassed even Dec and Mia's, would invite one of her numerous friends to sit down with us, but to my relief, she didn't.

She insisted on paying (I wasn't alert enough to put up a good fight) and then led/dragged me up to her actual apartment. Where I slumped into a chair and accepted a Coke out of sheer desperation to regain my brain.

"Dear, you don't look so good."

"Um. No. I don't. I'm not." Long pull of sugar and caffeine. "I try not to be in intense social situations like that. They take a lot out of me."

She looked genuinely contrite. "My god, Oscar, why on earth didn't you say so?"

"I…" Deep breath. Eye contact. "Because I didn't have any time to before we were sitting at a table. You sort of dragged me in there before I totally realized what was happening."

"I did? I didn't mean to." And I believed that. "Here, would you like some chocolate? Chocolate makes everything better, just like they say in that funny movie about the boy wizard and the teacher with werewolf AIDS."

"Werewolf… AIDS?"

She waved a hand. "It was perfectly clear that was the corollary. Now then, some chocolate will fix you right up."

And while chocolate was not quite as evidence-based as Xanax, on the other hand I enjoyed the experience a lot more. "Thanks, Evelyn."

"No matter. Let's get your mind off all that. Checkers?"

"Uh, sure." At least it was a game I knew how to play.

"You're making excellent progress on the house." She pulled out a board and began sorting the pieces into red and black. "I'm looking forward to seeing the hallway when I come over for dinner next, Jack tells me it's entirely walkable now."

"Well, I mean, I mostly just moved things around."

"It's been a long time. I'm sure you wonder how I let it get that bad, but it happened slowly. That's no excuse, of course, but it's the only thing I can tell myself now about any of it." She pushed the reds across the board and started setting up the black pieces on her side.

"I don't think you need an excuse. That kind of thing happens."

"Not to me, mister. But to Robin…he was such a sweet man. I can't tell you how very, very sweet he was. Until the end. Even when the dementia grabbed him hard in the last couple of months, he never stopped being sweet, which was a blessing to him. It doesn't happen that way for everyone, you know."

I didn't, know. At least not personally. But from what I'd learned watching TV shows, dementia seemed to mindfuck everyone a little differently, so it made sense. "It sounds like that must have been hard on you guys. You and Jack." My pieces were in place.

She moved. "Hardest on Jack. A boy needs a man to look up to. And I don't mean that in some absurd 'boys without fathers will become criminals' way. It doesn't have to be a father or a grandfather or even a relative. But children need *people*. Who care about them." She glanced up at me as I studied the board unnecessarily intently (to keep from looking up at her). "Did you have that, Oscar?"

"Uh. I mean." I moved a piece. She moved a piece without paying any attention. My fingers hovered over another one. "My parents."

"They were good to you?"

"I guess so. They weren't *bad* to me."

"Sometimes that's the best we can do. I suspect, if you asked my daughter, she would say something equally lukewarm about Robin and myself. Jack, now, he had the best of us. We were less—" She waved a hand. "Suffice it to say that by the time we were surprised by Jack, we'd realized that most of the things we thought were important the first time around were utter bullshit. If you don't mind the language."

I didn't, and it didn't sound like she much cared if I did. "Like what? I mean, what were the things you thought were bullshit?"

"Oh, raising a responsible young person, raising a child we'd be proud of, telling our child what *we* thought they should do. I never stopped telling her what was *right*. I thought that was my job, you see. To guide her, to share my wisdom with her."

"I mean…wasn't it? Wasn't that your job?"

"No, boy. My job was to give her all the things she needed in order to figure those things out for herself. Oh, when they're very young, you help more. But at some point you *stop* helping unless they want it, and I—we—didn't. Then she popped up with our Jack and faded away as if…as if Jack was the only reason we'd had her in the first place." She jumped one of my pieces and I kinged her. "The only time I tried to impose my will on Jack, I lost, and he got married anyway."

Gulp. That didn't seem like something I should express interest in. Though I was curious. And it wasn't as if I was *really* his boyfriend, in which case being interested in his ex would be tacky. I was just playing at being his boyfriend, so it was a totally different thing. "You didn't think he should get married?"

"Well, I thought he was young for it, I admit, though Robin and I married young and made it work. But no, it was that I saw what he was doing, finding the most boring, dependable, *pleasant* man he could and immediately settling down with him. That was not going to be a good life for my grandson. And, as you know, it was not."

Don't ask what happened. Don't ask what happened. Don't ask what happened.

"What happened?"

You weren't supposed to ask what happened!

"He was desperately unhappy, wouldn't admit it, and was devastated when that nincompoop he married broke it off. The trouble is, he thinks he's let go of it, but I can tell he hasn't. Not a single steady boyfriend since then, no one he'd introduce me to, as if he can't bear to try again. Of course, if I mention it, he tells me he's simply decided he's better off this way." She clucked her tongue. "Can't let go of anything, that child. I hate to see it all repeat. But I'm sure he'd be very annoyed if he knew I was telling you about it."

"Probably. Annoying Jack is one of my favorite things to do." I wasn't totally sure why I'd said it—*favorite* was such a strong word, wasn't it?—but she grinned.

"I can see that. It's something he needs and hasn't always gotten for himself. The boy takes everything so seriously, it's good that you make him laugh."

There it was again, the strange impression that we inhabited different realities somehow, and in hers Jack and I were this cute gay couple who laughed a lot and were good for each other. In mine we were…what, exactly? Acerbic acquaintances who occasionally had sex? Fuck buddies where one of us happened to work for the other—and oh yeah, play checkers with his grandmother, because that was perfectly normal fuck buddy behavior. It was ludicrous.

So why did some part of me halfway wish I inhabited Evelyn's reality instead of mine?

Chapter Fifteen

On Wednesday I finished everything I'd been working on. The whole house.

Except Jack's mom's room.

Um.

Okay, like, *most* of the house. A lot of it. A huge amount.

The stairs were clear, the living room was clear, the back hallway was clear. I'd organized the savable papers into boxes and organized the boxes with all of the vital-seeming papers in envelopes on top, with names on both envelopes and boxes. Evelyn's bedroom had been cleared of all the stuff I could move, with only dressers and the bed left.

Her quilt had found its way, once clean, to my apartment. I hadn't mentioned that to anyone.

I'd also cleaned everything. Which was still not in my

job description? But continued to feel good to do, so I kept doing it.

I finished a little early and wasn't quite sure what to do with myself. I could leave. Probably should leave. What with tying up all the loose ends and not wanting to start in on the store-everything hoarding bedroom until Friday. Except I was pretty sure if I stayed I'd get to have sex with Jack.

You can always vacuum a couch, right? And an armchair. I sprinkled some baking soda on the chair and rubbed it in, then let it stay for like fifteen minutes before vacuuming it up. It didn't get all of the smoke smell out, but it may have helped a very small amount.

I was saved further time killing by Jack's arrival. We had sex. Yay, returned libido. Yay, sex. Yay, no-commitment fuck buddy.

Thursday I cleaned my own place before heading over to see Evelyn again. Thankfully she didn't propose lunch in the dining room, but she did feed me homemade nachos in her apartment. She trounced me three times in checkers (again, keeping tally in a tiny notebook beside her of all the times she kicked my butt and the one time I managed to eke out a win), and she introduced me to a dozen people who "just stopped by." ("*Such* gossips, I told you.")

And that was that. We hung out. Her caregiver person was coming back the following week. I expressed having enjoyed my time. She told me not to flatter an old woman.

Jack arrived. Wait, what?

"Grandmother. I hope you're behaving yourself."

"What? I made the boy nachos." She waved a hand. "I was being culturally sensitive."

He winced so hard I worried for his face muscles. "Oh my god."

"It's a *joke*, Jack. Oscar knows it's a joke, even if it is *gauche*."

"I don't mind," I said, mostly to annoy him.

"That's not the point."

I grinned. "I know."

"One of you is as bad as the other, I swear to god." He took what appeared to be a deep, steadying breath. "Are you ready to go? Did you invite Oscar?"

"I'll go get ready and leave you two young men to hash it out." She winked at me and disappeared into her bedroom.

"Why did Evelyn just wink in a totally suspicious manner?"

He shot me an *I'm barely amused and you might even be imagining that* look. "She's always being suspicious. And winky. Would you like to come to dinner with us? It's my grandfather's birthday, so we're celebrating by going out to a restaurant." He raised his voice. "The irony of which might actually be obscene!"

She laughed. "Oh hush, it's fine! He'd like us to enjoy ourselves!"

"Grandfather hated spending money," he explained. "Hated it a lot. He'd never go out to eat, and once I was older we were allowed to order takeout once a month. Only takeout, because then you don't have to tip your server."

I bit my lip to keep from smiling. "Sounds…um…"

"He wasn't cantankerous about it. He just hated spending money on pretty much anything."

"I think Evelyn's indicated as much. She seems happy to be able to have a new bed."

"The bed, oh my god, did you *see* their old bed? That mattress is the least comfortable thing on earth, and I swear it's fifty years old. It cannot be hygienic. We may need people to haul it out and burn it. Anyway, you want to come to dinner?" He raised his voice again. "Grandmother's buying!"

"You're damn right I am!" The door opened with a flourish. I don't know how that's a thing, but Evelyn definitely opened her door with a *flourish*. "Here I am! Ready to be escorted by two handsome gentlemen." She put her arms out. "Shall we?"

I'd thought she was delighted to show me through the halls, but it was nothing to having both of us there. "You remember my grandson Jack? This is his young man, Oscar..." The first time she said it Jack and I glanced at each other and then quickly away again, but by the time we'd reached the front doors both of us were practically immune to the claims.

"I wish you wouldn't act like Oscar and I are dating just so you can be the trendy grandma with the gay grandson. It's insulting."

"Surely it's not." She looked at me. "You're not insulted, are you?"

He rolled his eyes as he unlocked the passenger side door for her. "So if *I'm* insulted, it's irrelevant, but if Oscar is, you'll stop doing it?"

"I don't think I said that, mister. And I think I have the right to be insulted by the implication that I'm trying to be 'trendy.' I am not."

"Grandmother."

"What?" She got in the car and closed it with a decisive snap.

"Gah," he mumbled. His eyes caught on me. "Sorry, did you even decide to come with us or are we kidnapping you?"

"No. Um. I mean." What *was* this feeling? "I think I do want to come with you? Er, sorry. Should I drive myself?"

"You could, but why would you? I'm coming back here after anyway." He pulled the front seat up and gestured grandly to the back.

So, you know, I got in.

We went to an Italian restaurant and I ordered mushroom ravioli in a pesto sauce that was super garlicky and amazing. Also it wasn't that expensive, and I hated when people were buying my dinner because I felt obligated to get something cheap. This restaurant didn't have "cheap" entrees, but mushroom ravioli was on the not-terribly-expensive side of the menu.

Ways I knew my meds were doing something to alleviate my anxiety: I could sit in a restaurant with people and actually participate in a conversation (to the degree it was demanded, which, when out with Jack and Evelyn, wasn't all that much). When anxiety was high I could barely make it to drinks with the Motherfuckers, which was always the same tables at the same bar with the same people.

Yet there I was, sipping ice water, sweating uncomfortably, but otherwise all right. I sighted the restrooms so I knew where to hide if I had a panic attack, but it seemed like I…wasn't going to have a panic attack.

Until I started thinking too much about it. I forced myself to focus on what they were talking about (bickering over what color to paint the house, blue or green) and managed to reel myself in. Thank god.

Jack and I walked Evelyn back to her room ("Such gentlemen") and said good-night. I was more aware of him than usual on our way back through the halls of the building where Evelyn had told everyone we were in a, like, relationship. It felt like we had a sign over our heads. Or handcuffs.

"Thanks for spending time with her this week," he said as we neared my car. "She insists she doesn't need company, but she's so much happier when she has it."

"Is she ever without? It seems like she has a lot of friends."

"As I understand it there are a lot of social complexities that Grandmother pretends to be entirely above while not actually being entirely above them."

I leaned back against the door to my car, hesitant to let go of this odd moment under a streetlight, warm breeze blowing through. "Yeah, she talks a lot about how she's not into the gossip and drama, but I notice that she doesn't exactly turn away from it when people start talking either." Feeling like I was somehow being disloyal, I added, "I mean, none of it's malicious or anything. She falls on the fun side of gossip and drama."

He smiled and there was something soft about it. Maybe because of the lighting or the pleasant sensation of having gotten through dinner without being overwhelmed, or maybe it was the way Jack looked when he was talking about his beloved grandmother. "She's had some hard times in her life, you know? I'm glad she has these people around her, friends and neighbors, some of them she's even known for a long time and has rediscovered since moving there. It feels good that I can give her that, make sure she's taken care of."

The same thing she wanted for him—friends, loved ones, stability, security. "She loves you so much. You're basically all she talks about."

"Me and the gossip, you mean?" he…teased.

"You and the gossip. Though she's right, that Bernie is a real so-and-so."

He laughed. "He is. A real so-and-so."

Then, as if it was the most natural thing in the world, we kissed. Kissed for real. Kissed like two men who kissed often enough to know just the right pressure, to have a comfort with our angles of approach, with the subtle motion of lips and tongues. No clashing teeth, no accidental too-muches, no hesitant not-enoughs.

I stepped forward.

He touched my arm with one hand.

I reached for his waist.

His other hand went to my neck.

Circuits all over my body lit up with feedback—yes, more, there, good, please, oh, *oh*. I pressed in against him and somehow we were in each other's arms, still kissing, breathing easily, even though we weren't nearly as experienced at kissing each other as we were at blowing each other.

I don't know for how long. It progressed to something that was a lot more like making out than merely kissing, and I realized at some point that my fingers were gripping his shirt underneath the jacket, and his fingers were tangled in my hair and for whatever reason it felt all sorts of *yes* instead of the *oh fuck when will it end* I usually felt when people wanted to make out with me. Which was rare.

It was part of my pitch: *I'm not really interested in kissing.* But I hadn't said that to Jack because kissing hadn't even been on the table.

Now, apparently, it was. Until my back hit the car and both of us broke apart.

"Shit. Oscar." He ran his hands through his hair. "I'm glad you came to dinner with us."

"Me too." I wanted to wipe my mouth where my lips were tingling, but I didn't want him to think I was wiping him off. I wasn't. I didn't even want to.

"I'd ask you back to the house, but I have to go in early tomorrow, so."

"I'd rather go home anyway. Um." I frowned. "Not more than I want to have sex with you, but I have a routine, and I didn't plan to stay out, and—" I broke off. "Sorry. I'm pro-sex with you, for the record."

"And the…meds aren't messing with you today?"

I flushed. "No. Everything works. I just."

"It's completely okay, I didn't mean to make this awkward."

I laughed a little harshly.

"What?"

"Everything with me is awkward."

He stepped toward me again. "I don't find that to be true. Not to challenge your identity or anything."

"No, it's..." I didn't know what the hell it was.

He reached out and rested his fingertips lightly against my neck. "I'll see you in the morning. Or I could lend you my spare key if you can't make it early."

"Um. I mean. I guess I'm a little worried I'll make you late if I don't get there on time. But I'll set my alarm." Early. Very early. An hour and a half early. Two if necessary.

"Don't worry about it. And I won't either." He pulled out his keys and I watched the light glittering off metal as he twisted a key off the ring. "I'll lock up and you can get in and give me the key back after work. Or if you want to go home, you can leave it in the kitchen and lock the knob when you go." He held it out to me.

"Oh. Thanks." I took it, the heat from his hand seeming almost bright on my skin. "See you tomorrow."

"Yeah." He kissed me quickly and turned away, his footsteps sounding loud in my ears.

I stood there. Watching. For a long moment. Until my brain kicked in and prodded me into the car.

My lips were still tingling. Or maybe it was just the illusion of tingling because I could still remember what it felt like. His proximity. His fingers. The thrill of kissing him without thinking about it too much.

The weight of his key on my key chain felt heavy, but in a strange, unsettling way. Like trust.

Chapter Sixteen

Friday was the big day. The day I opened the bedroom upstairs and started cleaning. I expected it to be…a clusterfuck. And it was? But in a way, it was easier. Evelyn had said this was where the hoarding had started, and that made sense. It had the air of a room that hadn't been opened in years. I couldn't access the window because of all the stuff in front of it.

I looked at it like an archaeological dig, like I was seeing all the layers of what had happened in Robin's mind. He'd started at the far end of the room, I thought. In the corner. Then out from there. I did a little climbing and scouted a dresser, and maybe a bed, but it might have been a huge pile of blankets and clothing. I couldn't tell.

This room was an entirely different prospect than the

rest of the house. Instead of picking through the last few years of debris, this was much older stuff. Sets of dishes, kitchen appliances in various stages of disassembly, more piles of books, the kind you could get four for a buck in front of used bookstores: Grishams and Clancys and Kings, dog-eared, spine-creased paperbacks. More VHS tapes, three half-repaired VCRs. A staggering number of coat-racks, some of which were sort of wedged in, not even on the floor.

I started pulling it all out and sorting it. Coatracks to the garage with the furniture, books into boxes for donation, clothes into bags for donation, magazines into recycling. No personal papers of any kind (at least not yet, thought I'd only seen the top layer so far). By lunch I could open the door maybe halfway, which was a lot better than the *stick your head inside if you dare* amount I could open it before.

Then again, that just made it more obvious how much more work there was to do.

I was nervous about Jack getting home. I'd intentionally arrived a bit too late to see him in the morning, but unless I wanted to run and hide (and miss out on sex), I'd have to see him in the afternoon. Which was good. Fine. Something?

But what if he kissed me again? And what if it went bad for me? Kissing usually went bad for me. I couldn't take the intensity of it. Maybe it had worked out all right in the parking lot, in the dark, after a dinner during which I hadn't wigged out, but this was...daylight. No magic to it. I was dusty from cleaning. He'd be straight from his job. It would for sure go wrong for me today.

The second I heard the garage door open (my ears were now tuned directly into that sound) I extracted myself from the bedroom and closed the door. Sure, the landing was a staging area for stuff I hadn't gotten done, but whatever, needs must. I got downstairs just as he was walking in from the hallway, so I followed him to the kitchen. "Maybe don't go upstairs for the next few days."

"Uh. No?"

"It's chaos. But I swear it's *organized* chaos."

He plugged in his phone and washed his hands. "Got it. I won't worry about the chaos."

"How was work?"

"Decent, but I'm glad it's Friday." He grabbed a beer from the refrigerator and offered one to me.

I took it, slightly bemused. I'd expected something else after The Kissing. I'd expected to jump straight into bed. Or maybe I'd hoped to have the courage to drop to my knees for him right there in the kitchen, though I should have known I wouldn't. What if he didn't understand? What if he hadn't felt it? What if he laughed?

Instead here we were, drinking beer and shooting the shit.

"Do you have any idea how long this last bit will take?" he asked. "No pressure at all, I just need to schedule painters at some point."

"Painters?" He'd mentioned it before, but I'd sort of pushed the idea aside.

"Don't you think?"

Both of us glanced around the kitchen. I'd gotten used to the pale lemonade color of the walls, but if I looked too carefully I could see that it was scuffed in some parts and dirty in others. "I guess maybe."

"And the living room got touched up after the fire, but—"

"Wait, there was a fire? I *thought* I smelled smoke sometimes!"

"That's why I moved my grandparents out of the house. My grandfather fell asleep in his armchair and dropped a cigarette he wasn't supposed to be smoking in the house. Needless to say, Grandmother was *miffed*." He paused. "I think it also scared her that he could have burned the house down, especially with all the papers and *things* everywhere. So she became a sudden advocate for moving. Anyway, the house needs to be painted, interior and exterior, before we put it on the market."

"Right. Yeah. That makes sense." It did make sense. My idea that the house was haunted had faded since I'd been working, but it could use some sprucing up. "I guess it doesn't have much curb appeal right now."

He snorted. "Definitely not."

"I'm not sure how long the room upstairs will take. It has a few bigger pieces that will probably need the furniture donation people to come in again."

"We can arrange for that. Do you think two weeks is enough time?"

"Um." I had no idea. Mostly because I didn't know what I'd find underneath the top layer of stuff. "Two weeks is probably fine. It's hard to say."

"It is?" He wasn't asking it to be a prick, but I felt myself bristling anyway.

"Well, yeah. Because it's impossible to know what else is in there and how much time it'll require. If there ends up being a lot of paperwork or mementos or something else, then it'll take more time to sort out. If it's all stuff that can be donated or thrown away, then it will take less time. But I don't know yet."

He held up a hand. "I wasn't being critical."

"I'm not trying to drag out the job," I mumbled.

"You sure? Maybe you can't resist my dick."

Teasing. This was teasing. I *knew* this was teasing. "I think I really can. I should go, it was a long day." I put the beer down and stood. "Two weeks is probably fine. If it's not, I'll let you know."

He also stood. "You don't want to finish your beer?"

"I—no. I don't think so. I don't—" I swallowed, my eyes slipping around the room, skating over the familiarity of it, the carafe I'd broken then replaced, the table where I ate lunch, the two beers. "I don't do this. The like…the hanging out. Beers. Kissing. That kind of thing. I can't do it."

He frowned. "We're having beers after work. You can't have a beer after work? Your friends go to drinks once a week."

"Yeah, well, that's fucking different, isn't it?" My heart was beating faster. "*This*. I can't do this. I thought maybe sex, but this is too much. Last night was too much. I can't—I'm not—it's not just beers, Jack."

"It's literally just beers. I'm not proposing. What the fuck is your problem?"

"The fuck is yours? What do you want from me?"

His lips flattened into a line. "Nothing. I want nothing from you."

"That's not what it feels like." Sweat lined my temple. "What the fuck was last night?"

"What the fuck are you talking about?"

"This!" I gestured between us. "I thought we were just fucking."

"We are."

"Yeah, but now we're going out to dinner with your grandmother and we're kissing up against my car and—and beers and shit. I can't fucking do this." It sounded a teensy bit batshit when I said it out loud. "Look, I just can't."

"You can't drink a beer with me."

"All of it. I can't do all of it."

"You can't drink a beer with me. Or kiss me." His voice was so fucking dead. "But you can fuck me. As long as I don't invite you out to dinner with my grandmother. Right."

Somehow his pulling-away made me want to strike out at him, like how dare he talk to me with that dead voice right now when I was flipping the fuck out? "You know exactly what I'm fucking talking about, you asshole. It was sex. That's all it was. Then it was cleaning and more sex, and that was fine. But suddenly it's all this other shit too and that's not what I goddamn signed up for."

"If kissing was a hard limit for you, you might have mentioned it."

"I said *no relationships.*"

"Kissing's not a legal contract, Oscar, it's just kissing."

The—the unfairness of it—when he knew damn well it

wasn't "just" kissing—made me clench my fists until they shook. "It—you—*nothing* is 'just kissing' to me. Kissing is—I can't—" The words weren't coming, which made me all the more frustrated, and the frustration made it even harder to speak. "We never did it before! So, if it was *just* anything, why weren't we doing it all along?"

He shrugged. "I don't know. It wasn't a plan I had, to seduce you after going out to dinner with my grandmother and then not actually invite you home with me. All you had to say was 'no thanks' and it would have stopped happening. It's really no big deal, Oscar."

That, more than anything, was the final fucking straw. "Oh, well, thanks for telling me what I'm allowed to find a big deal, very helpful. It's not *just* kissing, it's not *just* beer, it's not *just* fucking if your grandma's going around telling people we're halfway married, and you can shove all of that up your ass, you prick."

I was shaking as I left the kitchen, and shaking harder by the time I got to my car. But I couldn't stay there, parked in front of the house, until I felt better. And I hadn't been carrying Xanax around lately, so even if I'd wanted to risk taking it before I started driving home, I didn't have it.

I started the car and drove slowly, gripping the wheel with trembling fingers, to the next block and around the corner. Then I rolled to a stop and just sat there, in the sun, in my hot car, and lost it. Fuck Jack, fuck his goddamn bullshit, fuck his house and his stuff and his job and he could go fuck himself if he thought I was going to be gaslighted by this goddamn "it's no big deal" thing, because it fucking *was* a big deal, it was a horrible deal, and he knew it, he had to know it, fuck, *fuck*, what if he didn't know it? What if it really hadn't meant anything to him? What if it was only me?

No, no, no, fuck this. Hands shaking, I turned the key enough to roll down the windows. Fuck this and fuck Jack. I would have my panic attack in my car, but I wasn't going to boil through it. And I wasn't going to give him the benefit of any fucking doubts.

He'd kissed *me*. On the *lips*. He couldn't act like it was a casual thing when in weeks of fucking it had never happened before. Screw that. Screw him. Screw relationships. Screw everything.

I slid my seat back and hunched over, trying to scrape together a small amount of privacy so I could cry and shake and gasp for breath in peace. My mind was a roughed-up and jagged landscape of words, not all of which made sense or fit together properly, and my body was in *I know we think this is a panic attack but we might actually be dying this time* mode.

This was just a moment, I told my lungs, and my heart, and my eyes, which were fucking crying from rage. A moment in my car. On a side street. And soon this moment, in my car, on a side street, would pass.

It will pass. It has always passed before.

Which didn't make it any better, but I kept telling myself that, and trying not to think about breathing, and eventually I was calmer, and I drove home.

Chapter Seventeen

I woke up Saturday morning with a pounding headache (apparently I'm so old I get hungover from having a fight with a guy I barely like) and an email informing me that Jack had sent me seven thousand dollars with a memo that read *For services rendered; job complete.*

The job…was not complete. There was the upstairs bedroom still to do. I hadn't seen everything it had to offer. It was still so full you couldn't open the door all the way. I'd wanted to know what Robin had started with, in the beginning of his hoarding. I'd wanted to see what was left of Jack's mom.

But *job complete* seemed pretty hard to misinterpret. I wasn't always great at understanding nuance, but there wasn't much nuance here to parse. It was the total amount he'd said he was going to pay me and now we were done, even though the work wasn't. Hell, he'd probably just hire the next guy he fucked to finish up.

I knew that wasn't fair, but I wasn't in a "fair" mood. I had cleaning and organizing blue balls. Which is a thing that probably only I have ever gotten, but I had it, and it was annoying.

Also, it occurred to me, my supply of strings-free sex had just poofed out of existence, which meant I'd have the other sort of blue balls soon. Yay me.

That was it, then. That was the whole thing over. I continued staring at the email, the cold, impersonal bank email, informing me that my services were no longer necessary because the incomplete job was complete.

Then I followed the link and accepted the money because I'm not a fucking fool. Seven grand was seven grand and I was officially unemployed. Again.

A twenty-five-foot-tall wave of anxiety threatened to crash down on my head, but I dodged, wove, and ended up with a controller in my hand and a *Call of Duty* game on my console. Sometimes you just want to fucking shoot some people. *Zen and the Art of Virtual Murder.* Would read.

Dammit. Jack was such an asshole. The memo line from his payment (in that impersonal bank email) felt like a censure. Like he thought *I* was the asshole. When I couldn't have been freaking clearer: no relationships, no strings. No beer after work. Except, okay, with the Motherfuckers, but that was different.

I could *feel* his judgment. The bastard. Judging me from the email his damn bank sent to inform me he'd paid me money. Serious dick move. Paying me. Before the job was done. Making me have organizational blue balls. Intentionally.

After getting killed multiple times for dumb reasons, I realized my mind was not focusing very well. It might have been the fight I was having with Jack in my head, in which I argued again that I'd been clear, and that all I'd wanted was sex, and that he was the one who'd fucked it all up by kissing me and then offering me beer. In my head it all sounded perfectly logical, logical enough that I was tempted to call him up so I could explain it all again for him, since he'd failed to be swayed by my perfect logic yesterday.

What the hell did paying me off even mean? He never wanted to see me again because I was annoyed when he crossed the lines both of us agreed to? I thought we'd been on the same damn page. No relationships! We'd agreed! Should I have not gone out to dinner with them? Except Evelyn was there, it's not like it was a date. Staying for dinner at the house with them wasn't a date either. Okay, the sushi thing had been a warning sign, in retrospect.

Also that night he came home in such a good mood and was all…all touchy and hot and sexy and—

Not. Helping.

Whatever, I didn't lead him on. If he failed to understand that I didn't want more than fucking, that was on him. Not me. And everyone knows sharing beers after work with your anonymous fuck buddy was the antithesis of the anonymous fuck buddy. That asshole. That fucker. That dick.

I fumed and shot more virtual people and got shot by

way more virtual people and then I got kicked by the jerks I was playing with (probably for being inept) and fired up *Red Dead Redemption 2* so I could side quest to my heart's content without anyone kicking me. Which lasted until Mason messaged to see if I wanted to play *7 Days to Die* with him, and since killing zombies sounded fun, I figured why not.

At least that was focusing. Mase did all the building and mining, I did all the traveling and looting. We were a good team. Mase was okay not being on voice chat, or if he was, not talking most of the time. We just went along doing our relative jobs, only speaking up to say things like "Can you scrap some cars? We need parts." or "Got a minibike schematic, you want it?"

I was slightly less ragey after a couple of hours and we'd made it through the first blood moon without getting killed, go, us. Then he had to go get ready for a date (Mason was *always* getting ready for a date) and I had to go feel sorry for myself.

I should have stayed in the game.

Insert additional disclaimers about fat guys and food issues. My old therapist told me that I didn't have an eating disorder, I had food-related self-destructive tendencies. Then she'd paused and said, "I'm talking diagnostically here. You don't *meet the criteria* for an eating disorder. But you might still benefit from some of the techniques." Sadly, she'd moved before we could really dive in on the techniques aside from the usual Cognitive Behavioral Therapy stuff.

Here I stand, having thoughts. *Jack is such a bastard and*

fucked everything up and now I'll never get laid again. Catastrophizing. Maybe also polarizing. I couldn't always remember the difference.

Here I stand, having feelings because of my thoughts. *I fucking hate Jack, I could kill him, I'm so angry I might explode.*

Here I stand, exhibiting behaviors because of my feelings. *I'm going to make a cake and eat the entire thing.*

So, I baked a cake. And made buttercream. And frosted the cake. And ate it. Not the entire thing. I made it through about three-quarters before I flopped back onto the couch and picked up my game controller again. Except since I couldn't think of anything to play, I hit YouTube and picked a let's play of other people playing shit. And sat there staring at it as three-quarters of a cake made its way through my system, resting my controller on my bloated belly, trying to forget the way Jack used to torture me by telling me how hot I was. What a fucking schmuck. Seriously. Goddammit.

Not so fucking hot now, am I? Full of cake and inevitably going to eat the rest. Fuck you, Jack. Take your bullshit and shove it down your fucking throat.

Annnd then I was fighting with him in my head again.

Sunday "dawned" around eleven after a restless night of tossing and turning, during the course of which I did, yes, get up and finish off the rest of the cake, which was crusty at the edges (from being left out), but way too soft in the buttercream (from being left out). By the time I dragged my ass out of bed and made coffee I was regretting the cake.

But not completely. It was never about the food. It was about this feeling, this endless, repeating feeling that I wasn't good enough to *not* be the guy who baked a whole cake and ate it. Eating a cake and aching physically from doing so was, y'know, better than feeling a lot of other shit, and arguably safer than feeling angry at Jack, since my brain could jump from "angry" to "suicidal" like I was some sort of depression savant.

Food was a familiar numbing technique. Still, I stuck with coffee and didn't hit the Chili Cheese Fritos until evening, when I was looting zombie corpses again so Mason could stockpile everything we'd ever need.

It was a nice video game version of events: taking what we needed, building what we needed, fortifying what we'd built to withstand attacks. Clicking a few things to kill, strip down, and cook meat. Soothing. I wished real life was a lot more like video games.

But it wasn't. I couldn't save and exit when I didn't want to play anymore. I couldn't pause time while I did something else for a while and came back. And I couldn't load from a previous save point in order to change my choices. Not that I wanted to do that. Well. Maybe I could not bake a cake? Except when that BAKE CAKE Y/N option came up, I'd probably hit Y.

I always do. Eventually.

TELL OFF JACK FOR OFFERING BEER Y/N

Fuck. I didn't even know what I'd choose on that one anymore.

And then, god help me, it was fucking Monday again. Last Monday I was on my way to Jack's house to work. And today? Today I was standing in front of my refrigerator looking for something to eat. Or make. Or do. Or be.

Nothing exactly presented itself.

★★★

I wasn't good without my routines. I knew this about myself. I'd never been good without my routines. Since I did know this, I tried to keep to my schedule. I dragged myself out of bed at the usual time on Monday morning. I made coffee. I put it in a regular mug instead of a travel mug.

Then I realized I was wide awake at six-thirty in the morning with…fucking nothing to do.

For a moment I was almost tempted to drive over to fucking Jack's fucking house like nothing had fucking happened. Because fuck that guy. Fuck him a lot.

I was not going to think about how much I missed fucking him. No. Bad road. Do not go down that road. Not going down the no-more-sex road. It had been nice, but it was over now. Consistently having good sex had been nice. I could admit that. I *was* admitting it. Right now. At six-thirty in the freaking morning. With coffee. And no job. And no income. And for sure no possibility of getting laid.

Fuck.

I took a pill and went back to bed.

The rest of the day was a hazy mess of sleep interrupted by food interrupted by checking my phone in case anything interesting was happening somewhere that wasn't my apartment. In one of those self-defeating psychological quirks of mental illness, I desperately wanted someone, anyone, to talk to me, but when Declan texted me a bunch of emojis just because he knew I hated them, I was unable to engage except by texting back a middle finger emoji, which was the standard response. He replied with a grinning face and the circuit was complete, leaving me alone again.

Later than that, when Mia sent a proposal for dinner, I lied and told her I was feeling sick because I didn't want to leave my couch, even though I also didn't want to be alone, except I had to be, except I hated it, except I didn't want anyone to see me like this, except I was starved for attention, except if they saw me they'd know something had happened and I didn't want to talk about it.

She told me to drink a lot of fluids and get a lot of sleep. I glared at what was left of the second pot of coffee and sent back a thumbs-up.

They're wearing me down. I used to be able to resist the emojis completely. "You can have my emojis when you pry them out of my cold, dead fingers," I'd said in college. But now, after years of the Motherfuckers battering against my anti-emoji fortifications, they're making inroads. A thumbs-up here, a middle finger there. I don't do the fucking faces, that's crossing a line, but the occasional thumbs-up expresses "yeah, okay, whatever" in a way that seems less dismissive than actually spelling it out.

And then I was alone again. Starving for attention, unable to cope with it when I received it, story of my life.

At least Mase was around later so we could play more *7 Days*. No chatting, no dinner invitations, no questions. Mase and I probably work best together while playing video games, to be honest. He believes in being a good person more than I do, which is one of those irreconcilable differences that generally break up a friendship. But by now we've known each other forever so we just keep going.

That and the Motherfuckers are a family. You don't get to have irreconcilable differences in your chosen family unless you want to be miserable, and Mason doesn't. But we're good at games because we can break up tasks between us and everything gets done. When Ronnie plays she likes to go scouting for new mines or cities, which is helpful, but she also likes chatting on the voice channel while we're all playing. She and Dec can yammer for hours.

Not that I don't like talking to my friends. Just that sometimes all you want to do is clear buildings, kill zombies, and loot shit.

Mase, of course, had to go to work in the morning, so eventually we stopped playing and I loaded a solo world, but I didn't like mining that much and I hadn't settled on a place to live. I had three different unfinished wood frame structures I wasn't attached to, none of which would hold up if attacked by a horde of undead.

Four hours later I had a well-fortified (if small) multilevel building with a roof from which I could kill, an extensive mine in the basement, and a dwindling supply of cooked food because I'd been mining and forgotten I had to eat and drink. Of course, the second I stepped away from my house I got mauled by a bear and bled out, so I figured it was time for bed.

Also it was almost five a.m. But what the hell, I was unemployed. Hashtag unemployed life. Or something.

Chapter Eighteen

My experiments in how to survive without a routine were not going well by the time drinks with the Motherfuckers rolled around. I'd slept the first half of Tuesday, stayed up again Wednesday but collapsed slightly earlier because I took a pill to keep from obsessively thinking about Jack and Evelyn, and what they were eating tonight, and if she'd noticed I tried to deodorize the armchair, and what he was telling her about my absence.

Did she hate me now? Did she think I was a terrible person? Did he tell her he'd screwed it all up? Probably not. Did he *know* he'd screwed it all up? He must. I'd explained it. In detail. The beer, the dinner, the kissing.

The kissing.

No. Don't think about that.

Except I kept thinking about it. Dinner. Evelyn's laughter, the way she teased him, the way he sometimes got huffy with her before a smile broke across his face, as if he was *trying* to be annoyed, but couldn't. The way he'd snapped at me about eating in the living room as if to do anything else was sheer lunacy. How uncomfortable he'd been at the idea of having sex there. Until we did. And it was amazing.

No. Scratch that. It was fine. Damn good after such a long dry spell, that was the thing. If I was getting laid on a regular basis, the sex I'd had with Jack would have been merely mediocre. Probably. Mediocre deep throating. Mediocre glitter in his eyes. Mediocre orgasms...

You can see why I took a pill. Again.

Thursday I ran out of snack foods. Which meant I had a terrible decision to make: face the store or face the pantry. A box of Kraft mac and cheese later I raided the last bastion of my usual hiding places and discovered, holy of holies, a half-pound bag of peanut M&M's.

I clubbed it over the head and dragged it back to my lair, aka the couch. Uh. Not to have sex with. To eat. Wow, that metaphor started out dark and then I brought in some kind of devouring thing that sort of implies cannibalism. Thank god I'm not a peanut M&M.

The isolation was beginning to get to me. Also the fucked-up sleeping and eating schedule. Probably also the *how many pots of coffee have I had again?* effect.

I tried to get out of drinks. I thought I had gotten out of drinks. I claimed to be sick again. Or still. And foolishly thought that would be good enough. Maybe I knew it wouldn't be and I was silently crying out for attention.

Hard to say. Whatever it was, I didn't do any laundry as a charm against them forcing me to come out (and they could assert a lot of pressure when they collectively put their minds to it, which they'd only do if they realized how close to being in crisis I was, and hopefully they did not realize that). If I had no clean clothes, my reasoning went, they couldn't convince me to leave the apartment.

Sometimes I think I'm clearly fucked in the head and no one notices. Other times I think I'm hiding my distress really well and then the old school lot of them—no Sidney, no Jack—show up on my proverbial doorstep with booze and fresh produce.

"Surprise!" Dec said, brandishing grapes. "Fruit salad time!"

"Um."

Mase gave me a once-over. "What *are* you wearing? And is that you I'm smelling or did you slaughter a wild animal and leave it out to rot?"

"I'm sure it's not that—" Mia's expression, which began with all the cheerful openness she was known for, contorted when she got in range. "Wow, that's pungent."

Ronnie didn't bother with commentary. She pushed past me and surveyed the scene of my wallowing. "Oh boy." She turned back and held out a hand to Dec. "Welcome to Oscar's Pit of Despair. May I take your bags?"

"Please do!" He handed off the groceries he was holding and turned to—*ugh*—hug me. "I knew something was wrong! Jack sent me this super condescending message about getting him off 'that fucking stupid message thread already' and since he hasn't gone full douche canoe at me in a while I knew something was up. What'd he do?"

The others invaded but Dec was still kind of holding my arms and looking at me, so I said, "He's a fucking prick, that's all. You shouldn't have expected anything else." *And neither should I.*

"Yeah, no, not buying it," Mase said, throwing himself on a pile of blankets that had slid from the couch to the floor. "What did *you* do? How'd you fuck up the thing with Jack?"

"Fuck you, I didn't."

He rolled his eyes.

"Okay, okay," Mia called. "I need someone on dishes. Dec, you're prepping—once I get some space cleared off for the cutting board—and Mase, since you're making yourself at home, maybe you can make room for everyone to sit." She clapped. Literally clapped. *Go, team.*

I escaped to the bathroom and stayed there until Ronnie pounded on the door and told me I had to come out.

She was standing in front of the doorway when I cracked it open. "We can leave if you want us to. Red or yellow?"

Normal people need safeword check-ins for kinky stuff. I need safeword check-ins for human interaction. I shook my head, indicating they might as well stay (or something), and pushed past her into my living room-slash-drinks with the Motherfuckers.

I wanted them to leave. I didn't want them to leave. I wanted to be alone. I was sick of being alone.

The subject of Jack had been dropped and we sat around eating fruit salad, which was just a fancy way of saying we all picked fruit out of a communal bowl while watching *America's Next Top Model*. And as much as I hated to admit it, hated to need it, their company was, if not welcome, at the very least tolerable.

At least it was until we'd watched two episodes, had a few drinks, and Mason turned to me during the ad break and said, "So what *really* happened with Jack?"

My back teeth clamped together but I managed to say, "He's an asshole. He was always an asshole."

"Yeah, kinda my point. Him being an asshole didn't seem to bother you before, so why'd it suddenly start now?"

"It didn't."

He blinked at me, too quickly, *pointedly*. "It 'didn't'? Then why does your apartment look like the first scene of a cop drama where they're investigating a home invasion and double murder right now?" He made a big show of looking around. "Not that we'd even notice if you had dead bodies lying around."

Mason watched way too much TV. Also he was a persistent jerk. When I didn't reply he said, "Yeah, sure, this is totally the behavior of a man for whom nothing has changed. Right, guys?"

Dec scooted closer to me. I scooted away. He reached out, his hand stopping short of what I assumed was going to be a reassuring pat on the arm or some shit. Maybe my deadly ice gaze forced it to freeze in midair.

Sadly, it did not freeze his mouth. "Aw. Is that what happened? He screwed up? I'm sorry I brought him around."

"*Is* that what happened?" Mia asked, and the undertone

of doubt in her voice affected me even more than the derision in Mase's.

"You think it's my fault?" I demanded.

"No! I didn't say that. I meant. You know. I'm wondering what happened. I thought you guys were…not you-guys-you-guys, obviously, just you two as people in each other's lives…um…were doing okay?"

I shot an unimpressed look at Ronnie, who shrugged. "You didn't actually tell me anything. It's possible I mentioned to Mia that your not-telling me anything might mean there was something to not-tell."

"And clearly there is," Mase added. "So tell. Spill the tea. What'd you do?"

"Look, *I* didn't do *anything*. I was very communicative about my needs and that bastard ignored them."

Dec leaned in. "Oh no, what happened? Are you okay?"

"What needs?" Ronnie asked.

"*My* needs. My need to not be in a stupid relationship. My need to not have strings attached. My need to not get emotions involved in something that was going fine. He's the one who fucked it all up."

"Huh." Now Dec looked confused. "*Jack* had feelings? Like, about you? I mean, not that you're not worthy of feelings, just that I'm not used to Jack having feelings. Or wanting relationships."

"He said he didn't!" I exploded, the words that had been swirling around in my head for days bursting out all at once. "I said I didn't do relationships, he said he wasn't offering a relationship, we had sex, multiple times, it was good, and everything was going really well until he fucked it all up! Suddenly it was dinner with Evelyn and the quilt and her stupid cross-stitch picture and—and he's such a fucking dick. We went to a nice restaurant, which I hate, but it was okay, and after that he fucking *kissed me*, which is not part of the deal, goddammit. Not the deal. So *he's* the one who fucked it up, not me. Which may be *rare*, but happens to be *true*."

I sat back and stared straight at the television screen and wished they'd go away.

"He…kissed you?" Dec's voice was light. "Um. That's what he did wrong?"

"After weeks of consistent sex?" Mia murmured. "Also um."

"Wellll…" Ronnie seemed to be trying to find a new take. "I can see how, knowing you, when you said 'no strings' you meant kissing. Even if Jack maybe didn't realize that's what you meant?"

"He did! We didn't kiss. There was *no kissing*. It was unnecessary. Antithetical even. No kissing. No fucking beers after work. No shooting the shit. We talked about the house, we hung out with Evelyn, we talked about the stuff in the house and what to do with it, but none of that invited fucking *kissing*." I clenched my jaw and sat there feeling nauseous.

It was true. Everything had been fine. Good, even. Before Jack screwed it all up.

"You know," Dec began, "I think maybe if you explained it to him—"

"*Fuck him*. I don't owe him shit. He can fuck off. I was

so clear and then he—" I waved my hand around. "I don't want to fucking talk about it."

"Of course you don't," Mase said. "Don't bother, Dec, it's a waste of breath. Oscar wants to be sad and fucked up and blame everyone else for it, so let him." He turned back to the TV and hit play on the video, effectively ending the conversation.

Which, you know what? I didn't need this crap. Not from Jack or from Mason or from anyone. "Just fucking leave me alone. Go home. I don't want company, you came here anyway, and now I want you all to leave."

"Sounds good to me, you miserable bastard." Mase tossed the remote on the coffee table and stood. When Dec opened his mouth to protest, Mase grabbed him and hauled him up too. "You heard the miserable bastard, let's go."

"But don't you think—"

"Nope."

Dec dodged away to kiss the top of my head before following Mason to the door. "Keep the fruit! It's good for you!"

I grumbled but was silently, secretly grateful. I could put off going to the store for another couple of days.

Mia and Ronnie gathered together everything they'd brought and said goodbye, Ronnie pausing long enough to say, "I'm sorry about Jack. It seemed like a good thing for you to have him, so I'm sorry you don't anymore."

"I hate him."

They exchanged one of *those* glances.

"Oh, shut up," I mumbled. "Plus, it's no fucking loss. I'm not sad he's gone. Fuck him."

"Yeah," Mia agreed gamely. "Fuck that guy."

Ronnie kissed my head where Declan had, not forcing me to look up or participate. "Love you, brother."

It hurt a little to hear her say it. Not like I was…feeling totally unworthy of love or anything. Just sometimes it hurt. To be loved. By people. "You too."

They walked to the door, opened it, clicked the lock, closed it. I'd have to get the dead bolt later for safety. I made a mental note. Also I should put away the rest of the fruit since it was still too hot to leave stuff out. I made a mental note about that too. Also I should go into the shared world on *7 Days to Die* and destroy Mase's stupid house. Just to be mean.

I didn't make a note about that because I wasn't planning to actually do it, though I was tempted. How dare he say the shit he'd said? Who did he think he was? I wasn't *trying* to be miserable, goddammit. This wasn't my fault! Jack was the one who'd messed this up. I told them the whole story. If, after all that, Mason could still act like I was somehow to blame, he was a dick.

Though really it had been Dec who'd tried to tell me I should talk to Jack, that I should make it better. As if that was my job. As if he'd listen anyway. (He wouldn't.) As if any of it fucking mattered. (It didn't.)

I ate the rest of my emergency peanut M&M's and went to bed.

Chapter Nineteen

Time.

Passed.

Endlessly.

I needed a job. I made a rule. Another rule. None of my rules had stuck yet (wake up early, wake up not that early but still morning, just pick a fucking time and wake up at it consistently—all good ideas that didn't pan out). But this rule needed to because I needed a job.

So I made a rule that I wasn't allowed to have a cup of coffee until I applied for one job. It didn't have to be a good job. Or a job I wanted. Or even a job I'd take. Since my anxiety is all about the doing of the thing, I needed to work up to applying for something I actually wanted to do. You know, when I figured out what that might be.

Until then I needed to exposure therapy myself into applying for jobs, period. Or change my feelings and thoughts about it or alter my neural pathways or *whatever the hell.* I started small, by filling out applications for retail stores I could never work in, figuring that at some point I'd get to the actual job hunt part of job hunting.

Stupid job hunting.

But it worked. Not to get me a job. But to make me apply to them. I'd put the coffee on to brew (more often than not thinking about the old Mr. Coffee in Jack's kitchen, and the day I'd broken it, and how I'd had to order a new one, and how he'd pretended he didn't care but I thought he was mostly lying to himself because he did care, Evelyn was right, he cared about all of it)...dammit.

I'd put the coffee on to brew and then I'd open my computer right there at the counter (if you don't sit down it's like you're not committing to doing it so your brain doesn't have to freak out) and fill out an application for McDonald's. Or Office Depot. Or Best Buy. Chain retail stores I didn't want to work at, which would have no reason to hire me.

Just. Do. The. Thing. Oscar.

Only after that could I drink a cup of coffee. And in the first few days of my new rule, that's all I did. After that one job application I'd be done for the day and I'd sit there drinking coffee and eating whatever I could scrounge up (pasta for breakfast, black beans directly out of the can for dinner), halfway wishing I was the type of depressive who'd just stop eating and get super skinny.

That was my mindset: *If I have to be a fucking depressive, why can't I be one of the skinny ones, waaaaaah.*

But I wasn't. And the longer I drank coffee, neglected drinking water, and failed at nutrition, the worse I felt, until my body was impossible to inhabit. Sometimes it felt like my skin was tight with dehydration, sometimes my stomach was bloated from processed foods and sodium, sometimes blinking hurt and my skin tingled and my face and chest and upper back all broke out in acne like I was fifteen again.

McDonald's didn't call back. Not that I wanted to work there. But you assume you'll have at least the satisfaction of rejecting *McDonald's*. But no. Neither did Starbucks. I wasn't even good enough to flip burgers or steam milk. Welcome to Oscar's Bell Jar.

I felt blah and bloated and boring (oh my), so I don't know why Grindr seemed like the thing to do. Sometimes when I'm feeling most *ugh* about my body/life, I go to Grindr to unfavorably compare myself to other people. Because that's super healthy. In this case I found a couple of guys with similar interests (fucking without caring) and hooked up with one of them.

This, *this* was what I needed. Not getting all up inside someone's life. But anonymously meeting up with him, fucking him, and leaving. There. Done. Orgasms were had by all. Good times.

Sort of. He wasn't exactly attentive. And I'd apparently grown so used to Jack's unfairly excellent blow jobs that going back to a Grindr hookup blow job felt subpar. Maybe it was this particular guy. But as they say, any orgasm was better than no orgasm. Probably. Though I felt a little tainted when I got home. Not in a *sex is dirty* way. In a…it was hard to pin down. I took a shower, covered myself in red plaid pajamas, and thought about my parents.

Okay, that sounded weird.

Just, my father had always worn this pair of slippers, brown, with fuzzy shit on the inside, and when they wore out he got new ones, same style. He preferred brown but one year for Christmas my mom had gotten him dark blue instead, I could still picture them sitting in the corner of his closet, never worn. Never gotten rid of either, as if he kept them as some sort of point, as a constant reminder of her failure.

I wasn't even sure why I was thinking about it, but the next time I looked at my phone I took Grindr off the home page. Whatever. No point in looking at it all the time, and it was still on the phone. I could always go back to it if I wanted to.

That night I dreamed of Jack. Which was irritating. And not even of Jack sucking my cock like it was his favorite thing to do, but of that moment up against my car when he kissed me. Which was worse than irritating. I wish my subconscious would wake the fuck up, so to speak, and at least send me dreams of the good stuff.

Not that being kissed by Jack had been *bad*. Not exactly. If I was into being kissed by hot men who liked my body and got off on blowing me it probably would have been nice. It's just not my thing. Kissing. The car up against my back. His hands resting on my shoulders. His fingers coming up to brush against my jaw…

It was a stupid, awful dream. A nightmare. What's worse is that my brain and my body weren't in line, so it also made me want to fuck Jack again, like a goddamn asshole. As if kissing was something I wanted and associated with sex, which it very well wasn't.

It was hard to get back to sleep after that, which meant I slept in late the next morning. By the time I got up I didn't give a fuck about applying to jobs and sucked down the first cup of coffee in a sort of dazed state of caffeine headache. And fired up Grindr again because fuck you, subconscious. I don't want fucking kissing, I want fucking *fucking*, there's a difference.

A week and three hookups later I dreamed of Jack again. This time we were grocery shopping. What the actual fuck.

I'd received two emails back on my Jobs I Don't Actually Want But Applied For Anyway list: one for a local fast food chain that always smelled like grease and onions (I sent back a polite *Thanks but I've already found a position* lie, mostly because lying about having a job was a very temporary boost in mood), and the other for an office supply store.

I'd copied and pasted my polite *fuck off* into an email before I sat back to think about it. And eat some wasabi-flavored dried soybeans. While thinking about it.

The next step to getting a job was interviewing for jobs. It was the part I hated most. Aside from starting a job, which was worse, but at least you got paid for it. My experiences in job interviews include a lot of freaking out in my car beforehand and self-soothing with ice cream after.

The question was: could I apply the same principle to

interviews that I'd applied to applications? If I went to a bunch of interviews for jobs I didn't want, could I at some point reach a less panicky state about jobs I did want?

Stupid idea? Genius idea?

I closed the office supply store email and set my computer aside to contemplate it. When contemplation didn't make things any clearer I sent a message to Ronnie outlining the plan and ending with *Am I making any sense?*

She replied that I was making sense and she'd come by after work to "hash it out."

I hadn't cleaned since…the last time I'd cleaned. Depression makes me a slob. Drinks had been at the Hole, our favorite bar, and I'd mostly gone just to show that I wasn't at all embarrassed about how I'd basically had a temper tantrum and thrown them all out of my apartment like a jerk.

Okay, maybe I was slightly embarrassed.

But I made myself go to drinks and act normal—normal for me, anyway, so barely making eye contact, handing over money for my round instead of going up and buying it, and generally not talking that much—and I did feel better afterwards. Or if not better, at least I felt like less of a prick to my closest friends, my legitimate family.

With Ronnie incoming, I did the usual haphazard straightening job and collected enough dirty laundry to wash, which I bagged and set next to the door. I'd barely generated any laundry in my days of unemployment, between lying around in boxers and a T-shirt most of the time and the weather being hot enough to not really need anything else, but my re-emergence into Grindrfucks had forced me to actually *get dressed.*

At the last second, I threw in two decent interview shirts that didn't make me look like a sausage (tight at the neck, tucked at the waist, ballooned out in between). They weren't dirty, but it had been a while since I'd worn them, and ironing seemed to go better when things were freshly washed. I didn't know if that was a real thing or an illusion, but whatever; if I was going to get the iron out, I might as well trick my brain into thinking it'd go well.

I did not have the energy to haul my laundry to the actual laundromat. Maybe tomorrow.

I washed depression dishes (plates that had held various forms of frozen food, many mugs of coffee, a handful of bowls with spoons dried to the last of the ice cream in the bottom) and overall felt a lot more human after spotty cleaning than I had before.

I took advantage of the moment and spontaneously sent back an email to the office supply place to say I was interested in the job. I could always lie if they got back to me and I didn't want to go to the interview. Springing the whole thing on my brain made it easier to do it and stop thinking about it.

When Ronnie arrived, I'd showered and put on actual clothes. Close to actual clothes: old, soft jeans I refused to wear outside my apartment and another T-shirt. Self-soothing clothes, but not flat-out depression clothes.

A nuance she noticed immediately. "Hey, you have on pants!"

I submitted to a kiss on the cheek. "Shut up. I wore pants last time."

"Only after Mase teased you for your Minecraft boxers."

"He's an ass. Those boxers are great."

She didn't exactly tour my apartment to make sure I wasn't burrowing into the corners and hiding food under the floorboards, but she wasn't subtle about her visual survey of the surroundings.

"I'm fine," I muttered after a long moment of Ronnie just standing there looking around.

"Yeah. Seems like." She sounded…surprised.

"I even agreed to a job interview today, so there."

Her eyebrows shot up. "No shit. Where?"

"I don't *want* the job. Remember? I'm practicing."

"Right, yeah, but *where* are you practicing?"

I told her, and she sat down, and I offered her the La Croix that gathers dust in the bottom of one of my cupboards because, contrary to literally everyone I know, I think the stuff is vile as fuck. Then I also had to offer her ice because apparently warm La Croix is "disgusting."

"All La Croix is disgusting," I pointed out, in a tone of pure fact. Still, I got her ice. And a glass. For her disgusting drink.

"I think your theory has some merit and is worth testing. The one about going to low-pressure interviews as a way to inure your brain to the anxiety-heightening effects of interviews in general."

I blinked. "Uh yeah. Is that what my theory was? Because that sounds better than *Maybe if I force myself to do a thing I hate that makes me want to die over and over again it'll eventually make me want to die slightly less.*"

"That's what I just said."

"Right. Sure. Glad we have that out of the way."

"So when's the interview?"

"Uh." I tapped my fingers idly on the kitchen counter. "I didn't actually schedule it yet. I mean. I sent back an email saying I was interested."

"They didn't email after that?"

"I guess I haven't checked?"

She waved a hand. "Well? Check now. Let's get you a throwaway interview."

I didn't want to look. It'd be too real. Saying *Sure thing, set me up a meeting* felt very different than saying *Sure thing, I'll be there.* But Ronnie was looking at me expectantly and also a little too knowingly, like she had some idea how close I was to scrapping the whole thing. So I did it. I pulled out my phone and loaded my email and wished on my unlucky stars that maybe they hadn't emailed back.

And…they had. In contrast to every experience I've ever had with jobs I actually wanted, this retail store assistant manager with a position I could probably not even actually *do* was all over me.

And, to be honest, she was funny. I assumed it was a she. Amanda-at-retail-office-supply-store-store-number-blah-dot-com. Huh. I kind of…didn't hate her. I handed my phone to Ronnie so she could read it too:

Great to hear from you! And thanks for using capital letters and punctuation, I seriously appreciate it! I'm eager to talk to you more. Can you interview Monday at ten? I'm "penciling" you in—let me know if I should commit and switch over to ink! Best regards, Amanda.

"I like this one! Too bad about not wanting the job, she

sounds cool. And no emojis, so you might get along with her."

I returned my phone to my pocket and considered things. "It's not that I don't *want* the job. I have to get a job and I can't be that picky since I pretty much hate everything. I just don't think I could really work in retail."

"Your last job was in retail."

"Yeah, but through the phone. This would be in an actual store. Like. With people in it. People who could talk to me. Shudder."

She smiled. "Shudder, nice. You should go to the interview. Maybe it'd be worse than the phones, but you used to have ringing-phone nightmares from the last one, so maybe it wouldn't be worse than that, you know? You can always decline the job if she offers it to you."

"Yeah. I guess. Isn't it a waste of time if I'm not going to take it?"

"The whole point was—" hand wave "—programming your brain until you could interview with places you did want to work without panicking, so no. It's exactly what you said you wanted."

"Right. Yeah. True." I didn't pull my phone back out.

"Right, yeah, true, and? Tell her you'll be there."

"I mean. This is going too fast."

Expressive look.

"What? It is! I mean. I just. I didn't think she'd want to interview me. *McDonald's* didn't want to interview me."

"Well, she does, so tell her you'll be there."

"Are you peer-pressuring me right now?"

"That's such a good idea!" Then *she* pulled *her* phone

out and I knew she was texting the Motherfuckers thread. "Oscar…got…job…interview…for… Monday…yay and send."

"You're such a bitch sometimes."

That got me a full-on grin. Because using "female-coded" insults always delighted Ronnie like so, so much. "I *am*! I am a bitch! I'm so good at it!" She brushed her nails off on her shirt and said, "Anyway, now you have to go to the interview, I told everyone."

"Fuck you, no, I don't." But I knew they'd be all gross and happy for me, and I'd end up feeling obligated to go. By the time I was waking up my screen again, Dec and Mia had already chimed in with happy faces and Mase had sent a gif of fireworks. *Not that big a deal, don't even want the stupid job*, I typed and ignored the rest of their responses while I, uh, went to email and sent a reply to Amanda agreeing to the interview at ten on Monday and thanking her for the opportunity.

I sent it before I could think too hard. "I can't believe you made me do that."

"I only made you do something you know you wanted to do in the first place."

"I don't know that!"

"Oscar, I came over here because you had this plan about job interviews for jobs you didn't want. And then I watched history happen right in front of my eyes as you took a job interview for a job you didn't want. I think I might be magical, not gonna lie."

"My fat ass you're magical."

"Super magical. Give me another problem I can fix."

"I don't have any problems that need fixing."

She raised one sculpted eyebrow. "No? But I could be your fairy godmother! I could conjure you a carriage and a prince!"

"Ew. No princes. Plus, I have Grindr, I don't need a fairy godmother."

"Grindr must have improved a lot recently, I don't remember you being super impressed by it before." She grabbed the last of the dried wasabi soybeans. "So? How's *that* going?"

"Shitty. I mean fine. Or no, mostly shitty. The usual mix of boring and eye-rolling and obnoxious." I shrugged. "I'd say it's better than nothing, but it's only slightly better than nothing."

"Yeah. I'm super glad Mia puts up with me. I would *hate* app dating."

"You're a lot easier to put up with than I am," I pointed out. "And I think I'm getting old. I used to be like, hey, a blow job is a blow job. And now my mind wanders sometimes, like I have better things to do than have some dude sucking my dick."

"Huh. Did that happen with Jack?"

I frowned. Aggressively. "What the fuck does Jack have to do with it?"

"I'm questioning whether this is a you getting old thing or a Grindr guys getting old thing." She did an impatient *This is so obvious I can't believe I have to explain it* hand gesture. "If it's you, then it must have also happened with Jack. If it didn't, then it's probably not you so much as the context."

Which I supposed made sense. "I don't know. No. I guess my mind didn't wander with Jack. But to be clear, Jack's cock sucking skills are basically unparalleled, so I might still be getting old."

Fuck, they really were unparalleled. At least in my experience. What if no one ever blew me as well as Jack had? That…ugh. That was depressing.

"It must be a bummer to not have him around anymore. For sex." She was watching me way too avidly.

"Why are you looking at me like that?"

"Because I think you're in complete denial."

"About Jack's sexual skills?"

"About how much you enjoyed them, maybe. About how easily you threw them away. Or threw *him* away." She crossed her arms. "Which you totally did, so don't bother trying to convince me you didn't."

"Um, excuse me? It wasn't like that at all. He's the one who threw me away."

"By kissing you." Flat, unimpressed tone.

"By fucking up our arrangement."

She sighed. "Oscar, honest to god, you're the most stubborn person I know. Do you or do you not miss fucking Jack?"

"I don't miss *Jack*." Oh fuck, that was a lie. I could feel it as I spoke, this bitter aftertaste, like the words didn't taste right. I swallowed. "Maybe I miss the sex, but only because when I thought it wasn't about feelings, I really enjoyed it."

"You seemed to enjoy it. You seemed to enjoy the whole thing. I think it made you happy, you know. At least that's how it looked from the outside."

I couldn't take looking at Ronnie, leaning back against the counter, arms crossed, staring me down across my kitchen like she had some kind of wisdom to dispense. I looked away. "I liked the house project. And Evelyn. And learning shit about their family. And yeah, fucking Jack, also good. Like, the...expectation of it. Not having to flirt or seduce or do any of that shit I'm terrible at, but knowing we'd have sex. That was nice. But it's over now."

"Right."

"It *is*."

She held up her hands. "Okay."

"What now? If you have something to say, just fucking say it." The thing Mase had told Dec the other night, about how I didn't want to change, I wanted to be sad and miserable, still echoed in my head. I really didn't want to be miserable. I took a deep breath and tried to make my tone less defensive. "What, Ronnie?"

"Look, I've known you a long time. And you *liked* Jack. I'm not saying you were head over heels in love with him. But you don't usually sit with people at Motherfuckers gatherings, and you did with him."

"We never stopped fighting."

"You seemed to have fun fighting. And you laughed with him too, you know. Fighting and laughing isn't a bad combination."

"No, but—you don't get it. I'm not saying any of that's wrong. I'm saying he took it to a place I didn't want it to go, so I left."

She nodded. "Okay. If that's how it felt, that's how it felt. I just wonder if some part of you *did* want to go there, and that's why you flipped out." A long pause in which she pondered something and I…

She didn't have a point. I was sure of it. She didn't get it, that was all. If I—if *any part of me*—had wanted to kiss Jack, I'd have known about it. Except my stupid subconscious, but that didn't count. Probably.

Ronnie cleared her throat. "Maybe I'm projecting. I know what it's like to be terrified of something that feels real and if that was true for you, I'd understand. Anyway, I'm glad you have a job interview. And don't forget you promised you'd come shopping with me next week. Maybe we can pick up some work clothes if things go well."

I made a face.

"Sorry, I mean, if things go badly and you're offered a job you don't want but feel obligated to take. You might need some clothes." She glanced at her watch. "I have to go grab dinner for my lady. Unless you want to come over?" She said it hopefully, like she genuinely wanted me to come over for dinner. I could do my laundry. Hang out. Watch the two of them stare googly eyes at each other even though they'd been married for months and together for years.

Yeah, no. "No thanks. But thanks for, y'know, inviting me."

"You're always invited." She pushed up from the counter and kissed my cheek, as she always did, as she'd been doing since sometime in college when she'd decided that kissing cheeks was something she wanted to make her thing.

No one had ever kissed me in greeting or to say goodbye before Ronnie. Even now it still kind of moved me. Made me appreciate her friendship more sharply.

I walked her out and went to sit in my much cleaner apartment. After a few minutes of thought I messaged Mase to see if he wanted to play 7 *Days to Die* with me. He did.

Chapter Twenty

The first problem was that I'd started to like Assistant Manager Amanda. Which made the looming job interview feel more high stakes than it should have, given I didn't want the job.

Or did I?

The second problem was I'd started to wonder if I could do it. Ronnie was right: I'd already been doing customer service. And I knew that the stuff people were willing to say over the phone was sometimes worse than the stuff they were willing to say in person, so there was at least a chance that a face-to-face customer service job wouldn't be that much worse. Maybe.

And it might mean I could have my phone ringer on again. I'd had it on vibrate since I started the last job because I got super twitchy every time any phone rang in my hearing. Even in grocery stores, if a phone rings somewhere I jump and feel a heavy ball of dread in my guts, as if I'm the one responsible for answering it.

Not that there wouldn't be any phones, but it'd be different. Not my whole job in the same way.

But I'd probably hate it. It didn't matter how I did at the interview. Or how much I liked Assistant Manager Amanda. I'd probably hate the job and fantasize about crashing my car on the way to work every day. The interview was irrelevant.

Then again, if they offered me the position, could I really say no? When I had no other prospects? I was tying myself in knots. The "take all the interviews in order to practice" experiment was only executable if I was offered more than one interview. If I wasn't and I blew this one, or said no to it, I'd be fucked. Completely.

I blamed Jack. Though not really. Because if he hadn't paid me off before I was done with the house, I still would have been done by now. It'd be the same damn thing: me drinking coffee and applying for shit jobs I'd hate and agonizing over job interviews. Welcome to Oscar's job hunt, any year since I was sixteen and got my first job at a burger place.

I'd left that job off my application to McDonald's. Self-sabotage or just getting out ahead of a job I already knew I'd hate? You be the judge.

Sunday was a day I'd earmarked to hate life and wallow in my unfulfilled self-destructive tendencies, but Ronnie invited me over for dinner again and I said yes this time.

Partly because I recognized it was healthier than sitting in my apartment freaking out…but also partly because now my laundry was really piled up and I had exactly one ratty pair of underwear left.

You should never go to a job interview in terrible underwear. Even if you actively don't want the job. It's just bad form.

Dinner, laundry, they made me laugh a few times, I went home.

And tossed and turned all night because knowing you have a job interview in the morning is the perfect recipe for not sleeping basically at all, and I didn't. I dragged myself out of bed at six thinking at least I'd be wide the fuck awake by ten, but then I fell asleep on the couch with my coffee literally in my lap (or, okay, between my legs, where I'd put it because reaching out for the coffee table was too much to ask in my state).

I jolted awake a little after nine and almost figured fuck it, why bother going if I was going to be frazzled and/or late, but I tried to *reframe* it like a good shrink would tell me to do, and told myself that instead of seeing this as a bad sign I should act like all the pressure was now off and I wasn't likely to get the job anyway so I was free to completely bomb the interview, no problem.

I didn't. Bomb the interview. I didn't stun Assistant Manager Amanda with my brilliance and charm or anything. But I did manage to answer the usual questions in a way that didn't make me sound like too big a dumbass. And she was cool in person. When I left I almost wished

I'd gotten sleep and ironed my shirt for longer than five minutes so I'd have a shot at getting the job.

Which I did. Not. Want. Dammit.

My phone vibrated as I was just pulling up to a Starbucks drive-through in celebration of having survived a job interview—and it had worked, my plan to not care and thus not panic; I'd been nervous-sweating and my hands had been shaky, but I didn't have a panic attack either before or after. Go, me. Not that having a panic attack would have been some kind of personal defeat, I'm not new. Just that on balance it's nicer to get through your day without one.

Since I didn't recognize the phone number I let it go through to voicemail, expecting it to be spam or something like that.

It wasn't.

"Hello, this is Analise Broderick from The Meadows. I'm trying to reach Oscar Nelson. Please give me a call back as soon as possible." She left her number, repeated her name, then repeated her number again.

The Meadows was Evelyn's apartment building-slash-senior community. What the hell?

I hate phones I hate phones I hate phones I hate phones. I really fucking hated phones. Making calls. Answering calls. Returning calls. But I couldn't think of any reason someone would be calling me about Evelyn and…it was Evelyn. Did she need something? Whatever it was, I couldn't let her down. I didn't *want* to let her down. Even more than I didn't want to make a phone call.

Fuck, I hated phone calls though.

Palms sweating, I carefully dialed the number she'd left, which was of course not the number she'd called from. When she answered, I realized I hadn't rehearsed what I was going to say. Rookie mistake. "Um, I, you, um..." I gulped. "Someone left me a message? About Evelyn... Phillips? Um. This is—my name is Oscar. Nelson. Oscar Nelson."

"Oh yes, I'm glad you called me back. I'm trying to get in touch with Jack Phillips and Evelyn has you listed as the only other contact."

"Wait, she what? Why? Why would she do that?"

"It's common to list the partners of the next of kin."

"She what—no—I'm not—"

"I've been trying to reach her grandson and he's not picking up his phone. Is there any other way to get in touch with him? He hasn't updated his work phone number and I really need to speak with him."

Shit, Evelyn. "Is she okay? Is everything all right? Why isn't Evelyn calling Jack?"

"I'm sorry, you're on her contact list but I still can't share information about her health with you."

"Her *health*? Oh my god, what happened? Is she okay? Please tell me she's okay."

"It's not an emergency, but I do need to speak with her grandson. Unless—are there are other relatives you know of?"

"No. Um. Not that I know of. It's just the two of them." *And also she has a daughter somewhere in Florida who totally abandoned them, whose name I don't know so it's not like I could call her even if I wanted to and I don't.*

She sighed. "I'll keep trying his phone, but if there's any way you can contact him and tell him to get in touch with me at this number, I would appreciate it."

"Sure, yes, of course. I'll—I'll do whatever I can." I swallowed hard, thinking of facing Evelyn down over her chessboard. "She's all right, though?"

"I really need to speak to Mr. Phillips."

"Okay. I will find him."

"Thank you. I'll keep trying from my end as well."

We hung up.

Shit shit shit shit shit oh god oh fuck shit shit shit. Also I was awkwardly pulled off to the side of the drive-through lane and needed to move my car before caffeine-starved drivers flipped the fuck out at me for inconveniencing them on the way to their fix.

Parking space. Breathe. Roll windows down. Breathe again. This was serious and I had to make sure I had a plan. I called Jack but it went straight to voicemail. Midmorning on a Monday. He'd be at work. Did I know where he worked? How would I know where he worked?

Except I did. I'd seen pay stubs in the kitchen, in the neat little pile of paperwork he kept there, a stark contrast to the rest of the house. I closed my eyes and pictured the yellow walls, the Mr. Coffee, the chipped sink. Yes, I had it: Baker and Associates.

I looked them up and Google mapped the address. If he wasn't there—if he was at the gym, or on a break, or having an early lunch—I was fucked. I had no clue what he did during the day besides work. But this was at least a start.

Everything was terrible. Parking was the worst. I ended

up in a lot I had to pay for six blocks away. I was sweating and disheveled by the time I got to the cool, modern office building where Baker and Associates were located. Then, because there were two floors of Baker and Associates, I then had to navigate a calling system in the lobby to reach an admin person who was at first reluctant to tell me where Jack was ("If you don't have a meeting scheduled…") until I mentioned it was with regards to his grandmother.

Then it was elevators and hallways and signs and office suites and finally after all that I still had to ask someone else where Jack would be.

And then there he was. In a dark gray suit. With a silver tie. Hair neatly in place, back straight, shoulders tense as usual. For a moment I couldn't walk toward him, couldn't speak, as if time paused so I could take him in.

I'd fucking *missed* him. The bastard. I hated that I'd missed him.

He nodded at something the woman in front of him was saying. He started to move. He glanced away from her, raising a hand and saying something else, his body already angling in a walking-away direction. Which is when he saw me.

His eyes went wide with surprise but in that first moment I thought he was—pleased. To see me. Maybe as pleased as I was to see him. Except then the expression was wiped off his face and he made an aggressive beeline for me.

"What are you doing here?" he demanded, low-voiced, grabbing my arm and frog-marching me to the outer corridor.

"Evelyn." I was breathless with anxiety and uncertainty

and Jack's proximity. "They called me. Her place. Where she lives. The Meadows. She needs you. Or they need to talk to you, but it's not an emergency situation. That's all they'd tell me."

"You? Why did they—" He patted down his pockets. "Fuck, I plugged my phone in and got called to a meeting. I used to be so good at keeping it on me all the time but after Grandfather— And she never calls me during the day, and—" He broke off, starting to walk.

Since I didn't know what else to do and didn't want to be abandoned in a hallway with tasteful architectural prints in frames, I followed.

"But why did they call you?" he asked over his shoulder.

If I'd been secretly hoping to be hailed as a knight in sweaty job interview clothes, I'd have been disappointed. "She must have put me down as a contact or something. I don't know."

We'd gotten to a cubicle. "That's exactly the sort of thing she'd do. She's so stubborn." He grabbed his phone and cursed again, waking up the screen and holding it to his ear.

So this was where he spent his entire days? I'd assumed he at least had an office, but he was in a cubicle like everyone else. It was a *nice* cubicle, not as small as some, with decent furniture and a nice chair. No personal touches of any kind. Small container of lotion, dry hand formula. Box of tissues. Pens in a holder, both blue and black, as well as mechanical pencils, but the cheap plastic kind.

He exhaled and lowered the phone. "She fell down. They think she may have broken her wrist, but she's mostly okay, just shaken up and in pain."

"But she couldn't call you herself?"

A troubled expression crossed his face. "She was apparently disoriented. She couldn't find her phone and when they tried to get her to call on a landline, she insisted that she could only call me from her cell. I don't know."

That didn't sound great. "But she's okay? I mean. Now. She's all right?"

"She's probably got a broken wrist, they don't think she's broken her hip, but she's taken a serious fall and they're still 'assessing her injuries.' She's in a lot of pain, and she couldn't figure out how to call me, but other than that, she's fine." He focused on me again. "You can go now. Thanks for coming and finding me."

"Well—but—" I wasn't ready to go. "Do you need a ride?"

"Why would I need a ride? I have a car."

"Yeah, but..." I shifted from one foot to the other. "I mean. Should I come with you?"

"Absolutely not. Why would you come with me? You don't want anything to do with me. Or Grandmother."

"That's not true. I love Evelyn. She's great." Wait, was that what I meant to say? "It's not like I—I didn't mean I didn't want anything to do with you. I just. It got. I wasn't. I didn't know—"

"Oscar, I have to go. I need to talk to my boss and then get to Grandmother. I don't have time for this. You did what needed to be done, I'm grateful, now you can leave."

"But I didn't mean everything I said. And it was good. What we were doing. I mean." I lowered my voice. "You know? After work, not having to do the apps, I'm sure that was good for you too—"

"Are you seriously talking to me about sex right now? While my grandmother is lying in a hospital bed?"

Oh fuck. Was that what I was doing? "I'm sorry, I didn't mean—"

"I have to go, Oscar. I need to talk to the doctors and whoever else. I need to—" He cleared his throat. "I need to see her. I need to know she's okay."

"I know, I'm sorry, I—"

"I don't care."

He turned, grabbed his briefcase, and started walking down the hall back toward the elevators.

His jacket was still hanging over the back of the chair. I grabbed it and dashed—okay, awkwardly quick-walked—after him. "Jack, you—"

"I *said*, go away."

I tumbled into the elevator after him, ignoring the glower, and handed over his jacket. "Forgot your jacket."

He took it and jabbed two buttons: lobby and garage.

There had to be something I could say, some brilliant apology, some…some something, but nothing occurred to me and the elevator was fast. Within seconds we were at the lobby and he was holding the doors open. "This is you."

"Right. Okay." I stepped out. "Will you at least let me know how she is?"

He stood there, face blank, for a long moment, still holding open the doors. Then he stepped back. "Yeah."

The doors slid shut. I stared at the seam of the outer door, wishing…wishing I hadn't lost my shit about the kissing.

Wishing I wasn't dumb enough to miss the sex. Wishing I hadn't had a whole fantasy in my head that I'd save the day and he'd be grateful. Because it was gross, and also because I hated myself for wanting him to smile at me.

Since I had nothing left to do I trudged back to my car and got in.

Relationships were not for me. I'd always known that, but I guess… I guess sometimes you just needed a reminder. About how you didn't deserve nice things. Like relationships. Not that relationships were nice. Obviously relationships were horrible. Which was why I wasn't interested in them. At all.

None of which explained why I felt so hollow driving away from Jack's office building. As if I was leaving him behind. Him, and Evelyn, and the house, and the sex, and the laughter, and the bickering…

Best not to think about it. I drove home and engaged bell jar mode. Fuck it.

Chapter Twenty-One

I'd gone numb. I didn't care. About anything. Time passed. Or maybe stood still. Didn't know, didn't care. Assistant Manager Amanda called. I ignored her message. Ronnie called. Ignored her too. The only time I perked up was when Jack's name flashed on my screen.

Grandmother will be fine. Thank you for coming to get me.

And that was it. It was better than *Fuck off and die*. I was surprised at how relieved I was to hear Evelyn was all right. I mean, I may or may not have googled "old people broken bones" and gotten a little freaked out. But that was in the past. The distant past. However many hours ago it was.

Too long. Not long enough. What did it matter? I had my couch nest. I stood in my kitchen for an embarrassing amount of time confused about what I should make to eat.

Or not confused. Ambivalent. I had another cup of coffee standing there. Lukewarm, no milk because I couldn't be bothered to open the fridge. Didn't microwave it because I couldn't be bothered to cross the (very small) room. Didn't put ice in it because getting ice out of trays was too much work. In the mug I'd used earlier because what the hell, it was a mug, it was in my hand, it was clean enough.

What was I saying?

Evelyn was okay. Jack…might still hate me, but he'd gone back to hiding it. Actually, maybe *Fuck off and die* would have been better, since at least that would have meant he felt something. A bland *thank you* by contrast meant…nothing. At all.

I checked my phone again, hoping that somehow my desire for Jack's emotions would magically make them happen. But randomly texting *I despise you and everything you stand for because that is how strongly I feel about you* was not exactly Jack's way.

And wanting someone to feel strongly about me was the polar opposite of *my* way. That alone was awful enough to drag me back to reality: the kitchen. The physical need for food. The emotional need for comfort. This time it wasn't a cake, it was a huge tray of nachos. Not because I'm Mexican. My mom has never made fucking *nachos*. But because it was delicious and you didn't need a bunch of specialized ingredients on hand.

Baking sheet, foil, tortilla chips, refried beans (out of a can), diced green peppers (out of a can), cheese (pre-grated in a bag), topped with salsa (from a jar) and avocado, which I cut all by myself. It'd be better if I had (and was willing to dice) fresh tomatoes, but I neither had nor was willing to dice tomatoes, so salsa it was.

Then I laid out a towel, took the whole thing to the couch, and settled down to eat…dinner? Midnight meal? Whatever the hell it was, after this fucked-up day I was going to eat a whole sheet of nachos in front of *Bojack Horseman* and I was going to enjoy myself.

Or stew in my feelings of ugliness, whichever. One of those things came more naturally to me than the other, no points for guessing which.

I crashed at some point. When I woke up again the baking sheet was on the floor beside the couch, I'd drooled down the side of my face, and my head was pounding. So. Here we fucking were. Portrait of the man who tried to apologize to a guy he didn't even care about that much but liked fucking, and whose apology was rejected.

Except that wasn't quite it and I was having trouble pretending it was. Seeing Jack again, especially that flash when he saw me and nearly smiled, had fucked me up. More than I was usually fucked up. It had *seriously* fucked me up.

How dare he…how dare he…fucking exist. In this timeline. Where I also existed. And how dare he not accept my apology. Did he realize how fucking rare it was for me to apologize? It was *rare*, goddammit.

No. Not going there. Not thinking about it. Going to bed was a much better plan. I tugged my clothes off and fell into bed—my actual bed, not my couch nest—where I stayed. For a long time. And missed, like, eighty-seven messages from everyone on earth. Or at least Ronnie, Mia, Declan, and Assistant Manager Amanda.

I didn't listen to any of them. I didn't delete any of them. I ate two bowls of Lucky Charms and sat down in my nest again for another grueling Netflix marathon.

Which is where I still was when there was pounding on my door. My apartment door. The door that led to the hall that led to the stairs that led to the locked downstairs door. What the hell, man. Can't a guy feel sorry for himself in peace anymore?

Short answer: no. A guy cannot. Especially when it's *The Love Study* night and Declan is on and ohhhhh goddammit the Motherfuckers always watched Sidney's show together when Declan was on.

"Who the hell let you assholes in?" is how I greeted my nearest and dearest.

"Not you," Mason said, pushing a pizza box into my arms. "And we brought dinner."

"I already had dinner." If you counted two bowls of Lucky Charms.

He narrowed his eyes. "You don't want to eat pizza, fine, don't. I don't give a fuck." Still, he didn't take back the box and did push past me to get to— "Oh Jesus, are you fucking stewing over Jack still?"

"Oh, honey," Ronnie said, kissing my cheek. "Are you? Why didn't you call?"

"We would have come over," Mia added, also kissing my cheek.

"I didn't need to call, I don't need anyone to come over, and it's not *still*, it's *again*, to be clear." I shut the door and fought a very real urge to hide in my bedroom until they left.

"Again?" Ronnie called over her shoulder as she began dismantling my nest.

Sometimes I worried that my friends' role in my life was to right things I'd wronged or fix things I'd fucked up, even when that thing was me. Like Ronnie telling me to go get my meds changed. Or the many times she's listened to me bitch about things and told me they were going to be okay. Or Declan making me food and/or inviting me over for food, sometimes both at once, inviting me over for food and then giving me leftovers. Or Mia always ready to come to me if I needed anything, even way back when we were in the dorms and it was a walk across the entire campus.

Even Mason playing *7 Days* with me was support of a sort. Not that he wouldn't otherwise, but I knew he played even when he was annoyed just because it was how we related. And I wasn't sure I'd ever done the same for him.

"What happened?" he asked as I slouched into a corner of my very small, very crowded couch.

"Job interview. Call from the place Jack's grandmother lives. Went to find him. Found him. Apologized. He told me to fuck off. Came home." There. Succinct. Concise. Other words for *succinct* and *concise*.

"Did you get the job?" he asked after a moment full of unasked questions.

"Dunno. Haven't listened to my messages."

He rolled his eyes.

Ronnie held out her hand. "Gimme."

"I do not want to listen to—"

"We know," Mia said, patting my arm gently. "But we really do, so can it."

"*TLS* in thirteen minutes, so have your crisis fast. I am not missing the new season kickoff, especially because Mara is great and totally deserves a *Love Study* of her own." Mase navigated to YouTube on my TV and searched for Sidney's feed. "You know what you and Jack are? *The Hate Study*. You two have been pretending to hate each other ever since you met, it was never true, and if you fuck this thing up because you're both 'commitment-phobic'—" intense air quotes "—then you both deserve to be alone."

I opened my mouth to retort something terribly clever but was interrupted by Ronnie and Mia shrieking.

"Call her back! Call her back right now!" Ronnie thrust the phone at me. "You got the job, call her back."

"She couldn't technically offer it to your voicemail, but you totally got it," Mia agreed, waving her arm around in what I assumed was a *call her back* hand gesture. "I have *left* that message, call her back right now."

I did not take my phone. It looked like a foreign object up to some devilry, held out in Ronnie's hand with the intention of being used.

"I will *dial for you*," she said, pulling up the call app. "Mia?"

Mia rattled off the phone number (she had a freaky short-term recall for stuff like phone numbers and license plates, but give her twenty minutes and she'd have a total blank where that had been). Ronnie dialed it. I glared at her but she just shoved the phone into my hand.

I didn't even get up from the couch corner. I grudgingly, even angrily, put the phone to my ear and waited through the ringing, my heart rate climbing. Didn't have time to rehearse, didn't know who would answer, didn't know what they'd say—

An anonymous voice answered with, what else, the name of the store, and asked if they could help me.

My brain was blank. Entirely blank.

"Amanda," Ronnie whispered.

Right. I knew that. "May I please speak to Amanda? I'm returning her phone call."

"I think she might have left, but let me check real quick. Is it okay if I put you on hold?"

"Sure."

Click.

I avoided looking at any of my friends. "I'm on hold." Did I want her to be there? Did I want her to be gone so I wouldn't have to talk to anyone? If she was gone did that mean they'd given the job to someone else? Wait, I didn't even want this job! "Ronnie! I don't think I can work there," I said in a furious whisper.

"Then you'll find something else, but you don't turn down a fucking job offer, Oscar!"

I curled more tightly into my corner. *Please don't be there, I need to think about this, I can't do this right now—*

"Hello, this is Amanda."

Oh fuck. I swallowed, nearly injuring myself somehow, then managed to say, "Hi." What, what, this was why I needed to plan these things. "This is Oscar." That was it. My name. So she'd know who the hell I was. "Sorry, Oscar Nelson." Because maybe she'd interviewed a dozen Oscars.

"Oscar, I'm so glad you called back! And I was just going off-shift too."

I picked at the couch. "Um, sorry, I had a family emergency." Which was true. Even if it wasn't *my* family.

"Oh no, I hope everything's all right!" She sounded nice. But I knew, from the interview, that she also had a dark sense of humor. It's why I'd liked her.

"Everything has been resolved, yeah. Yes. Thank you." *Say as few words as possible and get off the call.*

"Of course. Should I get down to business?"

"Please." I grimaced in anticipation of...whatever she was about to say.

"I enjoyed our interview and I think you'd be a good fit for the position we have open in the copy center. Technically you interviewed for a cashier role, but I discussed it with the manager and I'd like to offer you the copy center position instead. You indicated you'd like to start immediately, I know, but that position actually won't open up until two weeks from today." She paused.

My brain, processing rapidly, was unable to make enough sense of what she'd said to respond.

"So is that at all a possibility for you? I know it's incredibly inconvenient given how long ago you were laid off, and I have an alternate plan to get you in sooner if you need to, but it would involve training you on one thing and then pulling you out of that right around the second you finally got comfortable doing it."

"Um." I swallowed, mouth dry, my world narrowed to a thread on the couch and Assistant Manager Amanda's voice in my ear.

"Is there any way you can hold off another two weeks before you start working? I will understand, completely, if you can't."

Seven. Thousand. Dollars. "I can." I swallowed again. "That would be fine."

"Wonderful! That's great. Hours would be the same, so a mix of early and late shifts, nothing before seven or past ten. We'd start you on Monday, in two weeks, at twenty hours per week."

"It's part-time?"

"That's what we're hiring at the moment. Almost everyone here started at part-time and worked their way up to full-time."

Translation: *we try not to pay anyone benefits unless we absolutely have to.* Did I care? At part-time at least Obamacare would kick in. "That's fine for the moment."

"Fantastic. And of course there are often shifts available during the week for people to pick up if they want to, and inventory a few times a year, and other opportunities. Twenty hours will be the base."

"Good. Thank you." I had to get off the phone. My heart rate was climbing again. A new job. Clothes? Food? Where was the store? I'd have to figure out how to get there, and how long it would take at peak traffic times, and retail schedules were hell on my routine, and—

Thump. The TV remote landed in my lap after hitting me on the chest. Mase stuck his tongue out at me. Ronnie giggled. Mia shot him a severe look.

Fuck it. I tuned back in.

"—welcome you to the team and I look forward to seeing you in two Mondays at nine."

Obviously now I had to say something. "Um, I look forward to seeing you too. Thanks. Thank you. For the job."

She laughed. "Thank you for taking it and saving me another round of interviews! Have a good night, Oscar."

"You too."

Then. It. Was. Over.

I sort of melted back into my couch. "Fuck. I'm dead now."

"You're *employed* now, son. Hit the volume up, would you? We're missing the show."

In another universe Dec and Sidney were streaming on YouTube right now with a friend of theirs who was the new subject for Sidney's *Love Study* show. My brain was buzzing, but I managed to turn up the volume, setting the remote down immediately after because I didn't want to be responsible for it.

Ronnie and Mia both congratulated me in low voices, Ronnie reaching over to squeeze my hand for a minute.

I had a job. A job I didn't really want or think I could even do. But it was *a job.*

And I didn't start for two weeks. Maybe it would feel more real by then.

The day had been endless. And a roller coaster. That was probably why I was so raw listening to Dec and Sidney answer relationship questions on YouTube. I didn't mind watching them most of the time—and unlike Mase and Ronnie, I didn't watch Sidney's show unless Declan was on it—but after a day that started with a job interview, progressed to a health emergency, skipped to a rejection, and ended with me getting an actual job, I was unprepared for all the feelings.

With Dec, you always got feelings. It was one of the reasons we thought he was a popular guest on the show—Sidney was a lot more battened-down, so they made a good contrast. And when Dec went *feelings*, sometimes Sidney followed, which always threw their commenters into a tizzy.

On the other hand, sometimes they went the other way, which always threw Mason into a tizzy. He leaned toward the screen. "Hell yes, I love it when they do this."

The question had been about how to know if you're "on the same page" with your partner. I was barely listening, my mind flying in different directions (was I happy I had a job? was I terrified of having a job? was I sad that Jack had rejected me? was I pissed at Jack for rejecting me?), but then Sidney started talking about the most valuable relationship skill in any relationship.

"What's that?" Dec asked, both because he was the perfect sidekick and because he adored them and always wanted to know what they were thinking.

"Learning how to fight effectively."

Mase hooted his enjoyment. Ronnie and Mia laughed. Dec looked flabbergasted. "Wait, you think the most valuable thing in our relationship is knowing how to *fight*? I hate fighting with you! We never fight!"

"If we never fight, how do you know you hate fighting with me?" Sidney's *I'm being super logical right now* tone was so deadpan I couldn't always tell when they were intentionally trolling someone with logic versus when they were genuinely just making a statement.

If I ever found a shirt that said, *Trolling you with logic*, I was buying it for Sidney.

Dec sputtered, but they put him out of his misery with a smile. (They *had* been trolling that time.) "Would you feel better if I said 'communicate intensely' instead of 'fight'?"

"Yes! That's different!" He turned to the camera. "That's different, right? You guys know that's different. Anyone? I'm gonna put up a poll or whatever." He turned back to Sidney. "Wait, can I put up a poll?"

"Not unless you plan on editing this later and adding one."

He made an exaggerated sad face.

They smiled again. "Okay, I'll put up a poll. Anyway, back to the point: you can't have a successful relationship with anyone—and this is any kind of serious relationship, not just romantic or sexual—if you don't know how to communicate with them."

"Intensely!"

"Yes, intense communication is really important when you care about someone. The more you care about the person, the more you'll care about what they think and how they feel. If two people feel that way about each other, or three, or more than that, you have a setup for intense communication that might end in damage if you haven't put in the time and effort to learn how to fight effectively."

"It's not—"

"Sometimes it *is*," they countered. "Sometimes people fight. Even people in love with each other fight. That's a feature, not a bug. That's the way you learn how to talk to each other. Sometimes it's the way you learn how much you care about each other."

"Uh, yeah—" Dec eyed the camera again "—just in case you're both super commitment-phobic, not that *we* know anyone like that, no way, no how..."

"We're speaking from observational experience," Sidney agreed solemnly. "In no way have *we* ever had a fight that resulted in both of us realizing how much our relationship meant to us."

"Right. That would never happen to us." Dec lowered his voice. "Spoiler alert: it totally did, it fucking sucked, and we're so much better off now, seriously, Sidney's right, it's a necessary evil."

"It's not an evil at all! That's literally the opposite of my point."

"Really?" He tilted his head to the side. "Tell me the point again? Maybe I missed it..."

My friends laughed at Sidney's *If we weren't livestreaming I'd hit you in the arm right now* expression, but I sort of drifted away.

Fighting was the end of things. My parents never fought. They handled all disagreements by swallowing their rage (Mom) or going out to the garage for four hours to hammer things (Dad). Ronnie said she thought I was always confrontational because I'd decided as a kid that it was the best way to keep people away from me, and keeping people away from me felt safest.

I fought with the Motherfuckers pretty much constantly and they hadn't run away yet. Or maybe they were just the only ones not put off by me being…the way I am. At least with Jack I hadn't worried about hurting him or offending him, because he was as confrontational as I was.

Unless… I'd managed to fuck it up by hurting him anyway.

We ate pizza and they left soon after the show was over, which was a relief. Though even once I fell into bed I couldn't sleep.

Intense communication. Jack and I had communicated intensely. With our barbs, our bodies, and sometimes in other ways that I hadn't thought of as communication at the time. His teasing. My more-than-absolutely-necessary organization of his family papers. Invitations to dinner with Evelyn, which communicated…what? On his end that he felt we were friends close enough to share a meal with his grandmother. On my end…that maybe I felt the same way.

Could I have felt the same way without actually knowing it? And if I did, what the hell did it matter now?

Chapter Twenty-Two

I'd promised Ronnie I'd go shopping with her back in better days, the days of semi-consistent sex and having a purpose in life. And by "purpose in life" I mean that I was cleaning out someone else's house and inadvertently becoming the family historian, like some kind of weirdo.

Fuck, I missed having a purpose.

Ronnie picked me up one day the following week and forced me into a department store. We did her thing first—she needed a dress for…something. Some work thing of Mia's. She'd told me about it but I, selfishly absorbed in my own crap, hadn't paid close attention.

The thing about shopping with Ronnie was, no matter how much I bitched, I also…just, it meant something. That we could now walk into the women's section without feeling like we were going to be arrested. Without her panic-clutching my hand and whispering, "I can do this, I can do this, I can do this" over and over again. The first time we'd ever done that (in a Walmart, not a department store; we wouldn't have dreamed of going to a mall), I thought she might faint from the general fear. She wasn't passing, she hadn't started hormones, she was just this eighteen-year-old girl who desperately needed some damn clothes.

And now? She kept holding things up to her and asking me what I thought even though she knew I didn't have any thoughts about dresses.

"Oh, what about this one?" She turned to me, and the fabric got a little flowy. "I love it."

"It's, uh, flowy? I guess?"

She turned back to the mirror, totally unperturbed by my lack of investment. "Right? Totally not right for this event, but I might get it anyway. I should try it on though." She made a face at my reflection. "Needs must. Let me grab a couple of other things first so I only have to do it once."

I waited outside the dressing rooms (we wouldn't have dared do that back in the day either), not taking her up on the option of doing my own shopping while she was evaluating her choices. She emerged triumphant and smiled widely at the gargoyle standing outside. "Two out of four aren't bad, are they?"

"Not at all, dear," the lady replied.

I have seriously no idea how people just talk. To other humans. Without planning first.

"Your turn, bestie!" She looped her arm through mine.

"Oh, gross." Still, she dragged/led me to the men's section, where I proceeded to whine and fume about pretty much everything we saw.

"I'd look like a bloated corpse in that color," I muttered when she held up a beige shirt.

She plastered her hand over her mouth. "Oh my god, Oscar."

"What? I would. Like I'd maybe been knocked out and tossed in a river and my body had been floating around in the reeds for a few weeks before some school kids found me while they were looking for treasures."

"Sorry, let me just clarify—in this scenario you lived someplace where *schoolchildren* wandered around in *reeds* looking for *treasure*?"

"And found my dead body, yes."

A woman passing us holding a little kid's hand looked back in curiosity. "We're plotting a novel," Ronnie explained, waving.

"Fun!" the lady said, waving back.

"How do you *do* that?" I asked.

"Do what?"

"Randomly talk to people. Strangers."

She shrugged. "I don't know. It was kind of a funny moment. I didn't, like, think about it." She nudged me, still holding the corpse shirt. "What's up with you? You got a job, I thought you'd be, I don't know, at least a little bit reassured that you're going to have an income again soon."

I forced the hanger for the corpse shirt back onto the rack and moved to the next one. "Nothing is up with me."

"Liar."

"I have a job. Things should be fucking great, right?"

"I don't know about 'fucking great,' but..." She surveyed the rack—polo shirts—and pushed me toward the next one.

"This one?" I asked, poking a blue button-down.

"You have to ask yourself: are you a man who wears a short-sleeved button-down shirt or aren't you?"

"I...have no idea?"

She studied me for a long moment. "Maybe you will be at the new job. And it's on sale, so."

I grabbed it. "How many more am I supposed to buy?"

"Two more. Oh, what about this one?"

"It's fucking canary yellow."

She tried to hold it up to me but I ducked away, so she just held it up in general, as if she was trying to see it in different lights. "It'd look good on you. A little cheery, though. Might give people the wrong impression."

"That I'm cheery?"

She grinned. "We wouldn't want anyone thinking that."

I picked up a black long-sleeve. "I'll get three of these and then no one can get the wrong impression."

"Black's not as unapproachable as it used to be."

"What's unapproachable now?"

"Cargo pants? I don't know. Hipsters? Here, what about this one?"

Dark red with subtle darker stripes in it. "Oh. It's not terrible."

"Yes, thank you, Oscar, it's not *terrible*." She put that one over my arm as well. "Is it about Jack? Your mood, I mean. Not the shirt."

"I haven't accepted the premise that I have a mood."

"Uh-huh."

We browsed to the next section, which was maybe too business-y, though one of the shirts was soft and felt nice.

"That's a good one. Long sleeves means you're prepared for weather, not super formal, not super casual, and the color is good on you."

"It's black."

"It's dark gray and has depth."

I rolled my eyes but picked the shirt out anyway, checking I had the closest-to-correct size on all three. "Can we leave now?"

"Do you have pants for work?"

I analyzed my current mental state. "I have enough pants to get through the first week. I want to get out of here now, though."

"Got it." She linked her arm in mine again. "It's about Jack. You miss him?"

It was such a stupid question. No. And yes. And the sex. Also his laughter. And his blow jobs. And I hated him. And I…

"It's not like I want to get married or something," I said.

"I know."

"And I wasn't looking for a soul mate or some stupid shit."

"I didn't say you were."

"I wanted to get laid. No strings."

"At first anyway."

I shook my head. "I don't think I stopped wanting that?" I could hear the doubt in my own voice. "I don't want to stop wanting that. I want to go back to wanting that.

Where do I get a ticket that will take me back to just wanting to fuck random people and never get to know them?"

Our conversation, such as it was, was interrupted by encountering a salesperson with a cash register. Ronnie got her stuff and I paid for mine, grateful the cashier didn't want to make customer service small talk, and we emerged into the open air after what felt like three hours (but had only been about forty minutes).

I assumed the previous topic was dropped since we'd changed settings and moods and whatever else.

"I don't know that you can go back," Ronnie said.

"Go back to what?"

"To wanting anonymous fucks after having something you liked more than that."

"I did not! I don't *like* Jack. I just…the sex was good."

"Uh-huh."

"Don't 'uh-huh' me in that tone of voice, Veronica!"

She unlocked the car and we got in. Maybe *now* the topic would be over. "So you had good sex with a guy you disliked for a consistent period of time and now you miss it. The sex. Not the guy."

"Right."

"Okay."

I tilted my head back and closed my eyes. "What *okay*?"

"What what okay?"

There was no point in glaring at her so I kept my eyes closed. "What's your fucking point?"

"I don't know. You went over to the house every day for weeks. You sorted through his private papers, and his grandparents' private papers. You made decisions about what to keep and what to donate. All of that is kind of intimate, you know?"

I said nothing.

"You met his grandmother and had dinner with her and when Jack needed someone to hang out with her you volunteered."

"No, that was Evelyn. Jack had nothing to do with that."

"Right. Yeah. I mean. Maybe you and Evelyn are like Harold and Maude over here—"

Okay, that wasn't fair. I punched her in the arm. Without opening my eyes. Because I was talented. And because my brain had punching-Ronnie-in-her-car muscle memory.

"I'm just saying, you hung out with Jack's *grandma*. You don't hang out with your own grandma."

"My grandma isn't as cool as Evelyn is."

"Oscar, come on. You were happier. When you were fucking Jack."

"Sex is good for endorphins," I muttered. "Endorphins are mood-boosting. And I got on new meds. It probably had nothing to do with Jack."

"Right. Except. You miss him a little."

I finally opened my eyes. "I fucking don't! I don't miss Jack! Fuck Jack!"

"You're saying that you would have cared that much about any random guy's, like, many boxes of decades-old credit card statements and pay stubs?"

"I was doing a job."

She sighed. "I think the only way you spent that much time and energy on the job is because you cared a little bit about Jack. Which also, incidentally, explains why you were massively hurt when he—"

"I was not hurt!" I cringed, realizing the sheer volume of my protest probably undermined my point. "I mean. He was busy."

"What did you actually say, though? I hope it was something along the lines of 'Sorry I cheapened the developing intimacy between us by pretending all I wanted was a quickie after work.'"

"Okay, no, that would be *dumb*."

"And yet accurate."

"I didn't cheapen—I mean—there's nothing wrong with only wanting sex from someone!"

She pulled into the Starbucks drive-through, which was my usual reward for going clothes shopping. "I didn't say there was."

"Which means it's not *cheapening*."

"Unless it's the way you pretend you aren't into someone when you actually are." She turned away, saved by the voice of the barista through the ordering speaker.

I stewed while Ronnie ordered our usual drinks and an iced tea for Mia, who'd opted out of shopping in order to plant vegetables. Or harvest them. Or prune shit. Or... something-gardening. When we pulled away from the speaker I was ready with my defense. "I like Jack fine. I liked the sex more than fine. I don't think you add those two things up and get a recipe for soul mates."

"I also didn't say *that*. But you wouldn't have been this bummed if you didn't care at all, ergo you must care at least a little. Right?"

"I cared about the sex."

"Oh my fucking god, Oscar."

I stared sullenly out the window. "I didn't ask him to kiss me."

"You didn't stop him from kissing you either. Did you want him to?"

"Kiss me? No."

"Did you want him to *stop* kissing you?"

"I…" The streetlight. The car at my back. His lips. His fingers at my jaw, more gentle than I'd felt them before. "No," I muttered weakly. "No. I didn't want him to stop kissing me."

She didn't say anything. We got to the window. Ronnie paid. I took Mia's drink, then mine. Ronnie set hers in a cup holder and drove away.

"I hate this." I didn't know what else to say. "This is why I didn't want to give a fuck. Because the second you give a fuck someone can hurt you and disappear from your life never to be seen again leaving you with nothing but fucking question marks."

"Orrrrrr you could do something super complex with a lot of moving parts like saying, 'What I want has changed and I didn't realize it until now, do you want to try again?'"

"Oh my god, no. Never. Not gonna happen." The thought of it, of groveling to fucking *Jack* of all people, was appalling. "I'm not begging Jack for a second chance, that's absurd."

"More absurd than giving up good sex because you guys had like one spat? Okay, then. Priorities understood. You're not thinking with your dick, you're thinking with your fragile male ego, well done."

"Um, fuck you?"

"Sorry, did you imagine you were taking some sort of moral stand against Jack kissing you? Or what, you were drawing a dark, moody guy line in the sand so you'd never be hurt again? Good plan, you can be the star of your own early-two-thousands MTV show."

I hit her again. "Shut up."

"I speak the truth."

"You speak bullshit."

"What'd you really say to Jack the other day?"

I slouched down in my seat. "I don't remember." I tried to remember. "I think whatever it was he was like, 'I don't have time to talk about sex right now.' Which indicates it was maybe not a super sincere apology."

"Ya think?"

"Ugh. What are you saying? I should, like, call him? Text him?"

She shrugged. Suddenly now she had no bright ideas? "Even if you don't ever speak to Jack again, I think it's worth you reassessing how it made you feel to enjoy someone's company."

"We literally only bickered and fucked."

"And ate dinner with his grandma and talked about what he should do with his house and had sushi that one time."

And laughed. Dammit. "Fine. I'll think about it. But fuck that guy, it's over."

"Okay, fine. It's over. I won't bring it up again." She glanced aside at me. "But if you want to talk about it—"

"*No.*"

"Kay."

And that was it. The last time I'd ever have to talk about that bastard. And how good the sex was. And how I'd maybe accidentally liked the man, not just his body, his mouth, and his dick. Never have to think about any of that again.

Chapter Twenty-Three

I couldn't stop thinking about it. Him. It. Jack. The sex. The dinners. The anticipation of him coming home. His stupid fucking laughter. The way his voice rose when he was mocking me and how unfair it was that thinking about him mocking me still made me want to fuck him.

This was Ronnie's fault.

I lay in bed at five a.m. on my last Wednesday of unemployment and wondered if he was up yet. Since we'd never spent the night together, I didn't know when he got up in the morning. I bet it was early. I bet he drank a whole pot of coffee before work and, like, read the news or something. He probably caught up on the latest headlines around the world so he'd be well informed. Did he walk around in bare feet? I couldn't remember ever seeing his bare feet.

Or thinking about his feet except for that one time he offensively left his socks on during sex just to prove he could.

Maybe he had slippers. He seemed like a slippers type of guy.

Padding in slippers to the kitchen, pouring out his first Mr. Coffee of the day. With fancy almond milk. Did he drink it in bed? At the kitchen table? On the couch? Maybe he read a book. Something nonfiction and deep, with a lot of philosophy to it. Or maybe science.

There was something disturbingly compelling about my mental picture of Jack in slippers and a bathrobe drinking coffee at his childhood kitchen table while reading a book about, I don't know, botanical classification systems or the greater colonial implications of the spice trade. I had no way of knowing how accurate it was, but it made me want to fuck with him. To settle on the other side of the table and eat a crunchy bowl of cereal. Or put on a podcast with a lot of swearing.

Or come up behind him and grab his cock. He'd be horrified. *No sex in the living room!* It was unsettling to realize that I wanted to horrify Jack. That I still wanted to put him off his game. My brain had put that desire on hold but not abandoned it as if nothing had happened between us.

No. *No*, goddammit. I wasn't going to let Ronnie get all up inside my head like that.

But it was hard to pretend I wasn't thinking about alternative timelines where I'd never gone off on him about the kissing. What if? What if I hadn't done that? What if I'd kissed him back? What if I'd grabbed his coat and pressed *him* up against the car instead?

What if when he came home the next day I'd greeted him like that? Right up against the wall, before he even put his briefcase down?

The idea of exposing myself like that—of opening myself up to him saying "No" or "Jesus, Oscar" or, god forbid, laughing—made me shudder and tug the blankets more tightly around my shoulders. How fucking horrible would it be to kiss someone and have them reject you? Way worse than being rejected for an admittedly somewhat half-assed apology.

And yet…wasn't that exactly what I'd done? He'd kissed me in this moment. This moment after having dinner in a nice restaurant with Evelyn, and everyone treating us like we were a couple all night, and even worse, not hating that everyone was treating us like we were a couple. And then not hating the kissing either. Or the way he was taller than me, the way he'd pinned me gently to the car. The way his body had framed in mine, his fingers had held my jaw steady, his lips…

I pulled a pillow over my head and tried not to think about it.

Except.

If what he'd done was risk something to kiss me and what I'd done was basically throw that back in his face… I felt uncomfortably shitty about that. At the time I'd kind of short-circuited because I didn't want to admit I'd liked it. Or whatever. But I hadn't really considered that maybe it had been legit crushing to be Jack in that situation.

It's not like he'd been trying to trick me into anything. I'd gone along with the kissing. I'd *responded* to the kissing.

Ahem. And then I'd flipped out a little when I thought he might do it again.

I pulled the covers over the pillow over my head.

I might be the asshole. Make a note.

Not that realizing it did anything but make me feel worse than I had before. It wasn't like I could text him *Hey, by the way, the kissing thing was actually good, I just flipped out because commitment issues, no biggie.* And he'd made it pretty damn clear he wasn't interested in talking to me again. So that was that.

I didn't want that to be that. I wanted…fuck. I didn't know what I wanted. To go back to having sex with him. To make him laugh. To turn him on in places he didn't think he should be turned on. Like the kitchen. To go out to dinner with him and Evelyn again. Or maybe even just with him and me.

This was the literal worst. And it was obviously still Ronnie's fault for making me feel things. Or Jack's fault for existing. Or my fault for not realizing how much I'd liked him until I'd already fucked everything up.

Go team.

I'd scoped out the drive to the new job a couple of times. For the purpose of rehearsing my route at different times of day. And alleviating my anxiety about doing new things. The fact that it also, with a very small detour, took me past Jack's house was a secondary advantage. Or point of interest. Or…something.

Since most of my excursions had been in the middle of the day on weekdays, there hadn't been much activity. Any activity. No For Sale sign. No cars out front. The house looked slightly less haunted in daylight, but it still hadn't been painted, and still looked like it had seen much better days. The yard where we'd made our initial piles was still dirt and weeds. The big garbage bin was gone now, so someone must have cleared out the upstairs bedroom. Otherwise, it looked the same as it had before.

Not much of a surprise. Given houses aren't sentient beings, they mostly don't change that much.

I'm not sure what I expected. I knew there were other things Jack wanted to do before selling it, like increase curb appeal or whatever, so I guess I figured at some point I'd drive past and it would look different. Better. Cleaner. More curb-appealing. There'd be a For Sale sign. I'd accept that it was over and move on. You know. The usual stuff that happens when you feel a compulsion to drive by your not-ex's house. Which is a normal, non-stalkery thing to do.

I figured I'd try a commute time, uh, commute, and drove all the way to the office supply store, adding about seven minutes onto my non-commute time average for the drive. Which, given it was a twenty-five-minute drive otherwise, made me glad I'd tested it. I almost didn't drive by Jack's again, but, well, it was Wednesday after all. Maybe… maybe…

A huge moving truck was outside. I could see it from down the block. Fuck. Had I somehow missed the whole sale of the house? No. It had only been a few weeks! Right? Houses didn't sell that fast. And it still didn't have curb appeal.

My heart was beating faster than it should have been as

I drove slowly past, and then—the garage door was open, Jack's car inside.

I impulsively pulled over and just idled there, foot on the brake, car still in gear, heart pounding. Jack's car was there. A big truck outside. As I sat there, two people came out with a bed frame held between them and loaded it into the truck.

Sure. Movers for the stuff still left. Okay. That made sense. The house wasn't sold—yet. Not that it should matter. If I wanted to talk to Jack, I had his phone number.

But I'd never use it.

And sitting here outside the house made him feel…closer. Than he did as a name on my phone screen.

"Do not do this," I said aloud.

I put my car in park.

"Seriously, this is really stupid."

I pulled the emergency brake.

"This is so fucking dumb that literally no one has ever called Sidney for advice on whether or not they should barge into a guy's house uninvited to apologize to him. Even *YouTube* is not this dumb."

I opened the door and sat there for a long moment, the heat of the day rolling over me.

I got out of the car.

No. Don't. Do not.

I closed the door. And locked the car.

What the fuck are you doing right now?

Sweating everywhere, from the weather, the lack of breeze, the epic fucking foolishness of what I was doing.

At this rate by the time I reached the door I'd look like I'd walked through a car wash.

And yet my legs kept moving.

Voices rose. Not from the house, from the garage. "I'm telling you it should be lime tart."

"I'm not painting the house green, Grandmother."

"You're thinking kerry green, but I'm saying a happier green."

"There are no green houses on the street."

"All the more reason for us to paint the house green!"

"I spoke to the Realtor—"

"Oh, what do they know?"

"I think this falls squarely in the realm of what they—"

I'd turned away from the front door toward the garage right as Jack and Evelyn rounded the corner of the garage toward the front yard.

Jack's face froze in a mask of displeasure.

Evelyn clapped her hands gently, one of her wrists splinted. "Oscar, you're here! Wonderful! Please inform my grandson that the color I've picked out is perfectly appropriate and will make the house stand out so that people remember it."

"That's literally what I'm afraid of," he retorted. Then, to me: "What are *you* doing here?"

"He's saving the day." Evelyn took my arm. "Let me show you the paint chips. Now, Jack wants to paint the house a boring shade of blue."

"It's gray-blue."

"It's boring."

"Whereas you want to paint the house bright green, which we're absolutely not doing."

"Stop being so dramatic."

"Oh, *I'm* the one being—"

Her voice rose over his. "Don't listen to him, Oscar. I know you'll see things my way."

"Oscar doesn't get a vote," Jack said flatly.

"Nonsense. I value Oscar's opinion." She led me back into the garage, where at least a dozen paint chips were laid out in various shades of blue and gray and green. "Now this is the obvious choice, it's not that bright at all, it's *refreshing*."

The one she'd pointed to was refreshing, I guess, in a sort of *if mint julep were a color* sense.

"It's nice..." I said.

"He hates it," Jack said.

"I don't hate it. I do think that it might...look better on a paint chip than it would on a house?"

"Well, that's a failure of imagination, but in any case, you're entitled to your opinion. You have to admit, though, that Jack's is utterly lacking in character." She pointed out a, yes, muted gray-blue color.

I dared to glance out at the street, but Evelyn *tsk*ed and, like a trained dog, I came to heel and looked at the paint chip again. "I guess this is probably what comes to mind if I'm thinking about the most neutral paint color to paint your house if you're selling it..."

"Oh, Oscar. Honestly. You boys disappoint me. I can't believe both of you are so intent on such a dull color." She shook her head. "It makes me sad. I'm taking this outside. I'm sure if you see it in the light you'll agree with me."

She waved the splinted arm. "You two gather up the others, would you?"

I stared at her back. Beside me Jack said, "Count on Grandmother for subtlety. Why are you really here? Assuming she didn't call you and tell you to drop by for a paint consult."

"Oh. Um. No. I…" *was creepily driving past your house and saw your car and thought I'd stop by.* "Um. I'm not sure. I guess I wanted to…"

I didn't rehearse this. I had no idea what I wanted to say to him. Or how I wanted to say it.

"I think I might have…"

The way he was just looking at me, eyes clear, face still as a lake on a cloudless day, like he felt nothing.

Still not better than anger.

"Dammit, why are you looking at me like that?" I snapped.

He blinked. "Like what?"

"Like *that*, like nothing, like we barely know each other!"

"I was under the impression you felt we barely knew each other."

"Your grandmother wants me to help pick the paint color for the house, I think we've met."

He shrugged, but it looked a bit forced, like his shoulders were too stiff for it to be a real shrug. "I don't want to make you uncomfortable by acting too familiar."

And ouch. That was a barb. A barb I might deserve. I should accept it with grace. "Oh, fuck off, Jack. That isn't what happened and you know it."

"Do I? Because for me what happened was I kissed you,

you kissed me back, and the next day you flipped the fuck out and stormed out of here like I'd hit you in the face."

My fists were balled up, clenching and unclenching, and I realized I'd leaned forward, almost as if *I* might hit *him* in the face. "You kissed me! Why did you do that? We had a perfectly fine thing going on without kissing."

"Okay, one, the kissing was good, so fuck you. Two, you must have thought so too since you totally kissed me back. And three, if you didn't want us to kiss you could have just said, 'No kissing, even though it was good, and I liked it, I don't want to kiss anymore.' Like a fucking adult."

"Right, sure, yeah, good call." Shit, I didn't have a counterargument. "If I'd said that you would have what? Said it was fine?"

He frowned. "Yeah, obviously. What's the alternative? I wouldn't have thrown away amazing daily sex because of a temper tantrum."

"Fuck you! And it was good, but I'm not sure I'd say it was *amazing*."

He came in close, lips brushing my ear. "Me deep throating you wasn't amazing? Because I'm pretty sure you literally called it that on more than one occasion, Oscar."

The bastard. Practically whispering *deep throating* in my ear. I flushed and skittered away toward his car. "Whatever. I don't—I didn't—"

He followed me but didn't touch. "You seem confused. You don't what? You didn't what? You didn't want me to kiss you? You don't want me to blow you? What are you trying to say?"

"I—We—Evelyn's right outside!"

"Oh, for fuck's sake, you asshole, I'm not offering!" He shook his head, looking more exasperated than angry. "What the hell do you want from me? Why did you come here? Why are you even in this part of town?"

"I, uh, got a job. This is my new commute or whatever."

His eyes widened. "Congratulations. Do you like it?"

"Haven't started yet. Rehearsing the drive. You know, it sort of makes me feel better when I've done it a few times first."

"Right, yeah. That makes sense."

Now, suddenly, we were just…talking. "Uh, you're clearing out the last of the upstairs stuff?"

"Yes. I hired people to do it. Again." He half chuckled. Air-chuckled. "They're almost finished. Then it'll be a matter of painting the interior and exterior. And Grandmother thinks we'll do better if we get the floors done in one of those high traffic laminates, but I'm going to ask the real estate agent if the cost of doing that will bring the value up enough to bother." He glanced out at the rest of the houses on the block. "It might. This won't be a fixer-upper, so people will probably expect flooring that's been replaced in the last three decades."

"I heard that, young man!" Evelyn called.

"Good!" he called back. He added, to me, "We've had seven disagreements today alone over what to prioritize, it's exhausting."

She came back around the corner, towing a young guy in a backwards baseball cap along with her. "I asked Mario if his crew could do the backyard since they're here and he said no problem."

“Did you tell Mario what was in the backyard?” Jack asked wearily.

Mario glanced in between them. “More furniture?” His voice was lightly accented, though I couldn’t tell from where.

“See? It *is* more furniture!” Evelyn said triumphantly.

Jack addressed poor stuck-in-the-middle-of-feuding-relatives Mario. “You should see it before you commit. And don’t let my grandmother force you into anything. That stuff has been out there for decades, it’s not resellable.”

“You don’t know that!” Evelyn took Mario’s arm. “Come, dear, I’ll show you.”

He looked back over his shoulder at us as she led him into the house.

“I don’t know what kind of crew I need for the backyard, but it’s not these guys. Anyway.” Jack turned to me. “Congratulations on the job. I’m still not sure why you’re here except you missed fighting with me.”

“I didn’t miss you.” Except…fuck. Why had I even bothered to pull over if I was going to keep lying to myself? “Maybe I missed you. Okay. I missed the sex. Maybe the fighting too.” Fuck, fuck, fuck. “And yes, the kissing was good. Fine. I just…wasn’t ready for it. And then I didn’t know how to deal when you…wanted to do it again.”

“You realize there’s actually no difference between ‘the kissing was good, let’s do it again’ and ‘the sex was good, let’s do it again,’ right?”

Maybe he had a point.

I considered it.

He did not have a point.

"You know that's not true, don't be a dick about it. You can have good sex with anyone, but good kissing is different. It's—it's more—intense or something. More fucking *intimate*." Something passed over his face, I wasn't sure what, but I thought it might be recognition so I pressed forward my point. "I didn't know you were going to kiss me and it was good, fine, yes, but then it seemed like it *meant* something, and I didn't know what, and I handled it badly, I'm sorry about that, but don't act like it was the same as a blow job when you fucking know it wasn't."

His jaw went tight and I thought he was going to fight with me. Instead what came out was "Okay. I grant that. It wasn't the same. For me it was...better." A wry smile directed more at the wall than at me. "I assumed, and here I was misguided, that it was also better for you. If it wasn't, I apologize."

But that...didn't quite feel right either. Even though I'd ranted and raved about how much he'd fucked up and how everything was his fault. "Don't...fucking be sorry you kissed me."

"You've left me with very few choices. Kissing you was wrong but I shouldn't be sorry about it. Kissing was good but you never want to do it again—"

"Technically I didn't say that."

"Um, yes, well, when a man flies out of my house and stops speaking to me I don't feel like I need that sort of thing spelled out."

I wished I had—anger or passion or something behind me right now instead of all this awkward lack of rehearsal and not-knowing what to say. Or do. "I…" I swallowed. "If I had any courage at all I'd kiss you right now. But I don't. So I guess we'll just stand here."

His jaw relaxed. The muscles around his eyes softened in the split second I saw them before I had to look away because I couldn't stand the fact that he was looking at me. "Oscar…"

"Don't fucking feel sorry for me."

"I don't. You're a damn fool, and you're for sure the reason I haven't had sex in weeks, but I don't feel sorry for you."

"Well *you're* the reason I haven't had decent sex in weeks, so—so fucking fuck off."

I was no longer looking at him but I could feel him roll his eyes. "Excellent stance, well spoken."

"Thanks," I replied sarcastically.

"Boys! Boys, I need your help back here!"

If she'd been listening again (and I wouldn't put it past her), Evelyn's timing couldn't have been worse. Or maybe better. Depending on your tolerance for awkward silences in which you wish you could take back the super childish thing you just said.

My tolerance was high for that sort of thing, but Jack was probably relieved we had an excuse to leave the garage.

"I was just telling young Mario—" at some length, judging by his glazed expression "—that most of what's under here is almost certainly still salvageable."

"Oh for fuck's—" Jack shook his head at Mario. "I'm so sorry. Please finish the job I actually hired you to do and don't worry about any of this. I can almost guarantee *nothing* in this pile is salvageable."

Mario nodded and smiled and slipped past me, looking ten pounds lighter as he retreated to the back hallway.

"Grandmother, stop it. I'll get someone to take care of this."

"You've been saying that for months and it hasn't happened yet, so I was attempting to *help*." She frowned at him. "Sometimes I think this is your way of holding onto the house, Jack. It won't do for you to keep hanging onto the past like this, it's time to move on."

He sighed. "I'm not afraid to move on. Just because I love this house for both emotional and practical reasons doesn't mean I need therapy."

I wanted to edge away back down in Mario's tracks, but I also… I don't know. I felt bad for both of them. In different ways each of them was trying to do what was right, and from an outside perspective it seemed like they kept missing each other.

"Oh, pah, what practical reasons? You could make good money off a nice house in the Bay Area, Jack!"

"It's your house and we will sell it if that's what you want." He sounded weirdly resigned.

Fuck, what was I in the middle of?

She threw her hands up, but a lot more dramatically than he had. "I'm going to go check on the upstairs. I'd appreciate it if you came up with a plan for this so that I can finally make a date to put the house on the market."

"Yes, Grandmother."

She walked off, not looking at me as she passed.

I thought I should say something. You know. Because that was awful. And both seemed hurt by it. I gestured to the pile of partially grassed-over junk taking up much of the yard. "We could probably get the Motherfuckers over here again. And another dumpster. Might take a couple of days, but we could get it done."

He ran a hand through his hair. "I accept your olive branch of offering the manual labor of other people."

"I wasn't. I just meant—" I broke off. "You okay?" That seemed like an appropriate thing to say. I was pretty sure.

"No. Yes. I'm fine." He shook his head. "You don't have to ask me how I am. I'll be fine. I'll figure this out."

I took in the sagging fence, the larger pile of junk next to the house, the smaller lumps around the back of the yard that indicated other dumping places. "Did you play out here as a kid?"

"No. It was dangerous. Probably more dangerous than it is now that it's been reclaimed a little by the weeds." He toed a clod of dirt and roots, which crumbled under the pressure of his shoe. "About the other stuff. I accept your apology."

I stared at him, momentarily unable to speak. "I…you… I…"

The bastard had the indecency to smirk. "I'm glad you dropped by to apologize for your seriously messed-up behavior—"

"Okay, you can go—"

"—and I think we should talk about it, but I can't right this second. Between the house and Grandmother and work I need some time to think. About a lot of things."

"I wasn't apologizing for my *behavior*, I was—"

He stepped forward and rested his hand at my jaw, effectively shutting me up. I thought, I was certain, he was going to kiss me again. All signs pointed to kissing.

Instead, he just looked at me. "You should have the courage of your convictions, Oscar. Kissing me was the move back in the garage." He ran his thumb over my lips. "I'm sincerely happy you stopped by even though this house is not actually on the way to your new job. I'll talk to you soon. But right now I need to corral Grandmother before she starts dismantling anything else."

The brush of his thumb was tantalizingly close to a kiss. But not quite. I had no clue what to say and hardly any breath with which to say it.

"Come on. I'll walk you to your car."

And he…did. Walk me to my car. He even tried to open the door for me, though obviously it was locked, so he looked like an ass.

I elbowed him out of the way and unlocked the door and opened it myself and then… I drove away. Away from Jack and the house and Evelyn and everything that had to do with them. That was it. It was over.

Chapter Twenty-Four

I started work on Monday morning and it wasn't as bad as I'd expected it to be. For one, Assistant Manager Amanda had taken on my training herself and she was dark-funny to me, but light-funny to most of the rest of the employees, and even though I knew that sort of thing—being singled out like you're special for inside jokes—was kind of BS, it also totally worked, making me feel like I had a place there even though it was only my first day.

She wasn't intentionally manipulating me, I didn't think. But she definitely seemed to like having a partner in gallows humor. (You wouldn't think you could have that in a basic retail environment, but customers are the same everywhere, and you totally could.)

By the end of the shift I'd only had three seriously close

calls to a panic attack, mostly because I was in training and thus couldn't hide in the bathroom to calm myself down very easily.

"Only three near-panic attacks!" Ronnie cried when I called her from my car. "Oh my god, Oscar, that's fantastic!" Her voice lowered while she relayed information to Mia. "He only got close *three times*! No, never even had a full panic attack! I know!"

Real friends are the ones who rejoice for your victories. All of your victories. Even the ones that to a non-panicky individual might sound less like victories and more like psychiatric emergencies.

"You should come over! We're making this salad with soybeans and garlic and—"

"I want to *celebrate*, not eat freaking soybeans."

"You're missing out, they're delicious. And the rice! Yum. Anyway, we love you, I'm super happy today went well."

"I didn't say it had gone *well*—"

"Are you still employed?"

"Yeah."

"So there it is. Yay!"

Her enthusiasm was so complete and sincere that I couldn't help smiling. "Thanks, Ronnie."

"Anytime, sweetheart. I'm so happy for you."

"I'm..." What was I? "I'm not excited to go back tomorrow, but I'm not completely sick to my stomach about it. That seems okay?"

"It's more than okay! You sure you don't want soybeans over fried rice?"

"Repeat the thing you just said over to yourself and ask if I would want it in a *million* years."

She laughed. "Okay, fine, your loss. Call tomorrow!"

"Yeah, yeah, whatever you say, Mom."

We hung up.

Declan, far more clued into my culinary needs, was sitting outside my building with a tray of cupcakes. "I gotta run to Sidney's! Ronnie said you had a good first day?"

Because naturally the first thing she did was message the Motherfuckers thread. "I didn't say *good*—"

He grinned and hugged me, forcing the tray into my hands. "I'm super happy for you. Love you! Enjoy the cupcakes!"

I virtuously ate a banana before diving into cupcakes. Mase messaged me two hours later to ask if I wanted to play *7 Days to Die* so I pulled up the game and got to exploring, looting, and scrapping stuff. At least I had a mini bike now.

Sometime into playing he texted, *Work okay then?*

Yeah. Didn't die. Didn't faint. Didn't hyperventilate.

Sweet deal. See if you can find truck schematics?

Okay.

End of feelings with Mason. Except. As the last remaining single in our friend group…

I apologized to Jack. More. Better this time.

?? What'd he say?

Uh. He has a lot to think about? He was a dick about it too, but also almost kissed me. So.

That seems…something.

Yeah.

Pause for a long time. Like. I'd found a factory and was

most of the way through clearing it before his next message came through.

I like him. Jack. He fits in in a weird way.

My fingers tapped the keys for a really long second before I typed back, *Me too. He fits me in a weird way. It's kind of obnoxious.*

Lucky asshole.

Sorrynotsorry.

He sent back a tongue-out emoji, I sent back a middle finger emoji.

We went back to playing.

I got a phone call Thursday night. Evelyn. I didn't answer it. Stared at the phone like it might bite me and sent it straight to voicemail, like a normal, phone-avoidant person. If she was calling me this time she couldn't have broken anything, right? And after four days of new jobness I was exhausted and looking forward to the weekend, which was my actual weekend this week, though my schedule for next week had me off Wednesday and Friday.

Fuck. Retail. Now I remembered why I didn't even want this job.

But it was fine. I was doing it. Whatever.

Anyway, Evelyn called and I ducked out of answering, but curiosity got the better of me and I almost immediately listened to the message.

"Hello, dear, this is Evelyn. I'd like you to come to the house for lunch with us Saturday, if you're free. We're having the godforsaken Realtor over and for my troubles I've insisted Jack order us lunch. You have no idea how *te-*

dious trying to sell a house is. These people want you to pour your entire savings into the thing that you no longer wish to own!" She huffed in my ear on the recording and I smiled, thinking about her impatience. "In any case, I know you boys have had your challenges, but no one has put more effort into readying the house to sell than you have, and I would like you to be there. Of course you can text me if you don't want to call, and don't worry about Jack. He's always happy to see you even if he expresses it badly. Hope to see you Saturday, dear."

Click.

I sat there with my phone in my hand, trying to figure out how I…felt? Was I feeling things? Maybe I was thinking things? I wasn't sure.

Evelyn had called me. Left me a message. Invited me to lunch on Saturday. On one hand, it felt somehow less formal than eating dinner with the two of them on those Wednesday evenings—had it only been two or three times?—when I stayed after working. On another hand, it felt more…intentional. I'd never gone out of my way to eat dinner with Jack and Evelyn. I'd been working at the house. Or I'd gone over to The Meadows to hang out with Evelyn. And they'd just sort of scooped me up in their wake.

This, though, would be going out of my way. On a Saturday. My first day off since I started working. Which I'd planned to spend on the couch in a nest playing video games and watching YouTube videos to self-soothe from a week of being around people, which had seriously depleted my ability to like…cope. With other people. Or even myself.

So why wasn't I texting back *Sorry, can't, busy* right now?

I listened to the message again, trying to make sure I wasn't missing anything. But it seemed…very Evelyn. *I know you boys have your challenges.* That was putting it mildly. *Don't worry about Jack. He's always happy to see you.* That couldn't possibly be true. And anyway, she couldn't say *always* since she hadn't seen him see me every time he did. See me. Or whatever.

It was hard to deny that I *kind of* wanted it to be true. That Jack was happy to see me. He'd told me himself that he was happy I'd stopped by. But he'd been joking or maybe sarcastic or at least trolling me when he'd said it.

I put my phone down carefully, as if at any moment it would spring to life and Evelyn's voice would come out of it, like a passive-aggressive howler out of *Harry Potter*, telling me I must come to lunch, please, and don't worry about Jack.

The bitch of it was I could picture the whole thing. I could see myself parking where I'd parked all the time when I was working at the house. Approaching the garage, which Jack used to open for me because apparently they never used the front door and he thought it was weird to let people in that way. Going in through the back hallway, now cleared except for Evelyn's *Remember the secret* sampler on the wall. Listening to them argue with each other, regardless of the company. Helping get plates down for food, then helping to put them in the sink afterwards.

It was all so freaking *crystal clear* to me. I could almost feel the slightly cool air in the back hallway, that moment of thinking, *Maybe it* is *a haunted house* before the life of the living room and kitchen took over things.

And Jack's bedroom door, his childhood sign, which, despite all of his protests against sentimentality, he'd never taken down.

I would probably regret it. Come Saturday morning, going to lunch at the house while they talked about how they were going to sell it off to the highest bidder would probably sound like the worst idea on earth.

I texted Evelyn back: *Let me know what time and I'll see you there.*

Then I turned the phone on silent, put it facedown on the coffee table, and covered it with a pile of junk mail just to be safe. You know. So it couldn't influence me into any additional social excursions.

Chapter Twenty-Five

Saturday.

Eleven-fifty-three a.m. Aka "around noon."

Me. In my car. Two blocks from Jack's house. Having second thoughts. Or, more aptly, twentieth thoughts.

This was a dumb idea. He didn't want to see me. I… couldn't deny that I did want to see him, but I knew it was a bad call. Whatever our conversation had been the other day—last week—years ago—whenever that had been, now the whole thing was a no-go. I'd drive home. Where I was safe. My own apartment. My nest on the couch.

I didn't *need* to do this.

I didn't *want* to—

I did, though. I wanted two things. And I didn't know how to deal with wanting them.

I wanted to be a person who could go to lunch at the house, with Jack, with his grandmother, with some Realtor I'd never met, and be okay with that. That was the first thing. I just wanted to be able to do it.

And the second?

Slow inhale. Slow exhale.

I wanted Jack. I wanted to be the guy Jack wanted. I was full of so much want it was almost drowning me. If I went to lunch and he acted like we barely knew each other…

It would be way worse than not seeing him at all. I couldn't face that. I'd have to hide for a week. I'd hate myself.

Or, okay, I'd probably just have a lousy night, eat a cake or something tomorrow, and then, y'know, go to work on Monday. Like a grown man. Who'd been dumped.

Not that he'd dumped me. Then again, not that he *hadn't.*

Time ticked down. What to do. Two blocks. Around the corner. I had to. Needed to. Wanted to. Something.

I closed my eyes and put my key in the ignition by touch. Turned it. Settled my hand on the gear shift. Put it into drive by touch.

Right. Drive. Two blocks. Turn. Pull over. Park. Get out. Walk to the house. Garage door if it was open, front door if it wasn't.

I could do this. Wanted to do this. Wanted to see them.

So I did it. Drove. Two blocks. Turned. Pulled over. Parked. Got out. Walked to the house. Garage door was open. Walked through the garage. Knocked on the back door.

Which opened almost immediately to a youngish Asian

woman who had a sort of hunted look about her. "Sorry," we simultaneously apologized.

"I was just leaving," she said, and slipped past me. I thought she was muttering something about "indecisive old ladies" but it's not like we were about to become besties.

I had not planned for the event of me standing in the doorway, knob in hand, door open, without having been invited inside. Um. What was I supposed to do now?

"Hello?"

No answer.

Right, well, if no one was there to hear me call out, obviously no one was going to hear me knock again, so no point in doing that. I stepped inside and pulled the door shut behind me.

Yep. Here I was. Back hallway, where I'd spent hours going through papers and hauling out boxes and making new piles out of old ones. Sampler on the wall. I'd have to ask Evelyn about it. Jack's door halfway down. Backyard door at the far end.

I called out again, still no answer. Right, so, this was me, walking into the house unannounced, no big deal, could happen to anyone.

They were not downstairs. But when I paused in the living room I could hear their voices, which I followed to… Jack's mom's room. I was braced for argument and contention, but what I eventually made out as I climbed the stairs was…laughter.

"But they're terrifying wooden horses that escaped from a carousel. Did she have nightmares?"

"Oh, you be quiet, it's very cute. She liked it just fine."

"It's a nightmare in wallpaper form."

"*You* are spoiled for choices, Jack. You don't know what it was like when there were only a few varieties of each thing from which to choose."

I grinned at their bickering and waited until a pause to call again, "Um. Hello?"

"Oscar's here!" Footsteps, and then Evelyn stuck her head into the hallway. "Come defend my honor, Oscar. Jack is telling me that I put nightmares on his mother's walls. Nightmares!"

I dutifully followed her into the little bedroom, now utterly empty and aired-out. It was a compact square, with a tiny-looking closet stuck like an afterthought in one corner, and a small window, still cracked open.

Jack gestured at the walls. "Oscar's going to side with me, Grandmother."

"He will not." She narrowed her eyes in my direction.

The wallpaper was peach, with a print on it of merry-go-round horses who seemed to be going off on a merry-go-round-less lark of their own.

"It's terrifying, isn't it?" Jack prodded.

Evelyn, on the other side, said, "Don't lead the witness!"

"I don't think I'd find it terrifying if I was a little kid who'd always had it on my walls," I said slowly. "I think it does have a sense of…um…playfulness to it."

"Ha," Evelyn said triumphantly. "Oscar likes it!"

"He didn't say that." Jack grabbed my shoulders and pushed me to face the wall. "Seriously, look at that. The horses look rabid. And they have *poles* impaling them. You really think that's not terrifying for a kid? I hated those horses when I was little." He shuddered.

I patted his hands. "I'll protect you from the rabid horses, Jack." Then I realized what I'd said and wished I could take it back.

He didn't speak for a second before replying, "No way, these bastard horses are being torn down as soon as I can get someone in here to do it. Anyway, should we get lunch?"

He pulled away his hands and I missed them immediately. "That sounds good. Also did you two scare the Realtor away? Or was she, um, running from the wallpaper?"

"She has problems with change." Evelyn, assuming the air of someone who has better things to do than contemplate wall decor, swept back out of the room and down the stairs. Her wrist was no longer splinted, but it still had some sort of brace wrapped around it.

"Grandmother isn't willing to set a date to put the house on the market," Jack explained. "Which Linh was understandably a bit annoyed by, considering she's been working on this listing for months and stands to make no money on it unless Grandmother commits."

I kept my voice low. "I thought *you* were the one having trouble letting go?"

"Sometimes I think Grandmother only accuses people of things she's actually doing herself, but don't tell her I said that."

"Don't tell me what?"

He held up a hand as we walked downstairs. "You can't invite Oscar over for lunch with every intention of us getting back together and then object when we have a private conversation, old woman."

"Oh, well, in *that* case." She checked her watch. "Shouldn't that delivery thing be here soon?"

"It's DoorDash, and it will be here any minute." He added, to me, "I ordered sandwiches, a few different kinds. I know Declan's held a sandwich buffet before, so I figured you'd be okay with that."

"Sounds good."

Evelyn, mischief permeating her tone, said, "I wanted Mexican food, but Jack told me that would be insensitive."

I rolled my eyes. "I know you're trying to do some sort of trendy white lady accidental racism thing, Evelyn, but it's not going to work. I already know you're doing it on purpose to cause drama."

"Who, me?" She took my arm. "Come sit with me and tell me everything that's happened since you and my Jack had your silly fight."

I glanced at him, but he shook his head, presumably indicating that she knew nothing about our "silly" fight. "Um. I got a job?"

My own grandparents were a lot closer to what I thought of as grandparenty. Talking to Evelyn felt more like getting into a conversation with the eccentric but cool senior next to you in line getting coffee and realizing halfway through that you weren't even pretending to enjoy talking to her, you actually did.

I did, anyway.

I filled her in while Jack coordinated dishes and, eventually, DoorDash. She filled me in on everything that had happened at The Meadows, completely skating over the whole broken wrist thing, and only deigning to say it had "pinched a little" at first, but now she was perfectly fine and she only wore the brace so she wouldn't be badgered by people, cue: significant look at Jack.

"It was only *sprained*, for goodness' sake." This time I glanced at Jack, which didn't escape her. "Do you doubt I know my own body, mister?"

"No, no. Um. I just thought Jack said it had been broken."

"They *thought* it was broken, but it was only strained. A few days of rest, that's all."

"Which you didn't take. And then you're supposed to be doing hot and cold compresses and stretches, none of which you're doing. And the splint you're supposed to be wearing is on your kitchen table, replaced with that cloth thing you got from Amazon." He set the food down. "But it's your wrist, Grandmother, as you keep telling me."

"Well, I wasn't going to sit around not picking anything up or opening anything for weeks just hoping to feel better! Studies show that people who exercise live longer. Or something." She took a plate and began unwrapping a sandwich. "Who wants turkey?"

We parceled out the food and ate, conversation returning to lighter topics. While Jack was probably right about her lack of following doctor's orders, she didn't seem to be having any trouble holding onto her sandwich. Which was reassuring. Though she was drinking water with the wrong hand, leading some credence to his scolding.

I still wasn't sure why she'd invited me, aside from making more comments to the effect that Jack was happier when I was around, which I assumed was meant to make me propose marriage or something. Both of us pretended we didn't get the subtext.

Evelyn sat back after slowly eating half of her sandwich and surveyed us in a frankly alarming manner. "Well, boys, I think it's time I tell you my plans."

I looked at Jack, who was frowning at her. "What do you mean? What plans?"

She seemed to be coming to a decision, right then and there, as we watched. A long moment. A long look. A deep breath. "I'm giving you the house, Jack."

"*What*?" he all but exploded, as if she'd told him she was planning to join the circus. "You can't give me the house! It's not a puppy!"

"I would *never* give you a puppy. As you well know." She turned to me. "He always wanted one, argued that he'd be completely responsible, he'd take care of it and feed it and walk it and everything, but we weren't worried about that, it was more—"

"*Grandmother.*"

She shot him an exasperated look. "I'm telling Oscar about how you never got over not having a dog as a child."

"Yes, I realize, but could we curtail story time for a brief moment so you can tell me what *the fuck* you're talking about?"

"I couldn't have possibly been clearer. I'm giving you the house. I still think you should sell it—in fact, I'll think less of you if you don't—but I was planning to sell it and give you the money and at this rate it appears you'll just turn back around and buy it again." She shrugged. "I will arrange for whatever makes sense to legally put the house in your name. I do feel bad for that poor young woman, though. Imagine having to work with me for *months* and still not make any money. We should do something nice for her. Do you think she likes flowers?"

Jack began to rub his temples with what couldn't have been a helpful amount of pressure, judging by how white the skin was around his fingertips. "No, I don't think she likes flowers, I think she likes money, which she'll get when she sells the house, because you really can't *give me* a house. That's not a thing."

"Oh, pah, of course it's a thing. Rich people do it all the time, why can't we?"

"Yes. But. You." Rubbing, rubbing, rubbing. "You can't possibly..."

"Why on earth not? Who else should have it but you, dear? I honestly don't understand what the big deal is."

"The big deal is you're *giving me a house*!"

She waved a hand. "I've hardly given you anything your whole life, Jack. You insisted on getting a job and buying your own car—do you remember? You didn't want to be a burden. We could only afford to give you a little bit of money for college, so you did the rest yourself. Even when you were a child you didn't want to ask for too much." To me she said, "Other kids ask for bicycles and robots for Christmas. Our Jack asked for a book, maybe a game he could play on his mother's old Nintendo."

"Nintendo 64," he corrected. "And you guys already

did so much for me. I didn't need a robot. And I always had bicycles."

"That your grandfather picked up at garage sales." She shook her head. "This is the same thing. It isn't as if I'm giving you a *new* house, silly boy. I'm just passing down the old beast we've been holding together with duct tape and bubble gum for years."

"Yes, but you can't *give me* the house."

Evelyn pursed her lips in a stubborn expression that looked an awful lot like Jack's. "Too bad, Sonny Jim, I'm doing it. Now it'll be your problem. Sell it, or don't sell it, but at least I won't have to think about the old thing anymore."

Jack looked…stunned. Still. Continually. Moved by something—mercy, or discomfort, or awkwardness—I said, "Evelyn, can I ask you something? I never figured out what the sampler in the hall meant. The one that says *Remember the secret*? Maybe this would be a good time to, y'know, tell us what that means."

She smiled, her face relaxing in a way that made me feel I'd done my part. "Oh, that. Hmm, I suppose you might be ready to hear it. I made that for Robin when we were just married. It was something of a joke between us, that we knew the secret to a happy marriage. Of course the sampler was a joke—he knew how much I detested and was terrible at needlepoint. But then he framed it and put it in the hallway, that cheeky man."

I shook my head. "But what *is* the secret? Not that, um, I'm getting married or anything. But I'm curious."

"Ah, that's easy. It's obvious if you think about it." She

paused dramatically and I began to regret my instinct to interfere in their argument. Evelyn's dramatic pauses were often followed by something slightly horrifying. With a flourish she said, "Exceptional lovemaking. People will tell you it's communication or commitment or any number of other things, but none of that much matters if the lovemaking isn't there." She eyed us, and I didn't know about Jack, but I looked away fast. I wouldn't put specific questions past her, and while I liked Evelyn a lot, I really didn't want to discuss my sex life with her.

"I'm sure plenty of relationships have good sex and shitty everything else," Jack said.

"I didn't say *sex*, boy, I said *lovemaking*. And if you don't know the difference by now, well, I'm not sure there's anything else to say." She was still eyeing us. Beadily. I could tell. "You can have *sex* with anyone. But lovemaking—that's a skill you learn with a specific person, and while you can make love with different people it will never be *the same*. It's a thing you build. At least that's what Robin and I told each other early on in our marriage when our entire lives were before us. And I will say I've never seen anything to steer me differently."

"I miss Grandfather. Um." Jack's forehead creased in consternation. "Not, uh, that's not related to the lovemaking thing. Now this seems weird. Just he could be kind—more kind than me. And I miss that."

"I miss him too." Evelyn patted my arm. "He would have liked you and you would have been dreadfully uncomfortable around him, thinking a man that quiet was judging you. But he wouldn't have been."

It was an unsettling and somewhat uncanny read. I felt a bit naked at her words, aware now that Jack was looking at me, and I needed to say something. "I'm sorry I didn't get a chance to meet him." To my surprise, it was true.

"Well, you did, in a sense." She waved around. "This was his creation, you know. Not only the unfortunate parts, but all of it. Over the years we lived here he must have replaced, repaired, or repainted practically everything in this house at least once. You know him as well now as anyone who didn't meet him in life ever will."

It seemed like the thought should be vaguely creepy, but instead I found it almost comforting. And, on the heels of her announcement that she was giving Jack the house, even a little hopeful. I nudged his plate with my fork, which was about as close to an actual nudge as I could get. "So? Are you going to keep it?"

He groaned.

Chapter Twenty-Six

I'd vaguely hoped Jack might…say something at lunch. About me. Him. Our exchanged apologies. Ever having sex again. Anything at all. He'd left it at *I'm overwhelmed, I need to think about this* and it's not like he'd properly ghosted me since his grandma had invited me over to lunch. He acted like he was fine with my existence. So…what did it mean?

I hated uncertainty. Hated it. It spread through me with the destructive power of a vat of acid and ate away at me, undermining even things that seemed obvious. He wouldn't have let Evelyn invite me to lunch if he hated me…right? He'd laughed with me, hadn't he? And the lovemaking thing—he'd been uncomfortable in the way I had been, because maybe some lines weren't totally obvious to us even if they were to Evelyn. Unless Jack had been uncomfortable because he realized I'd managed to want him *more* somehow in the time we'd been apart and now he had to deal with this awkward reality in which he was completely disgusted by me and I was…not at all disgusted by him.

But I didn't hear from him for the next day…two days…three days. I didn't text him either, which both Ronnie and Declan told me to do, the latter attempting to enlist Sidney in his efforts, but they only shrugged and offered the opinion that while it wouldn't be inappropriate to check in, it also made sense to give someone who asked for time, y'know, some time.

So yeah, that's what I was doing: giving Jack time. And totally not going bugfuck while waiting to see if he'd ever speak to me again. Picture of patience, that's me.

Wednesday rolled around. Were they eating at the house again? Nothing had really changed, but Evelyn announcing her intention to give it to him might have…shifted something? Probably not. Or maybe they were going out to dinner to celebrate transferring ownership. I had no idea how long that thing took.

Stop thinking about Jack, raged part of my brain. *But I wonder what he's doing right now*, responded another.

Work was a good distraction. Mase had built us a fortress in 7 *Days to Die*, so we had to turn off our various sorta-cheats in order to let the zombies have a fair crack at killing us. Time moved steadily forward.

Until Friday at about five-thirty, when I was about to leave the store at the end of my shift.

A text.

From Jack.

You have to see what she's done. A picture would not do it justice. I will send one if you can't stop by but you should really see it in person. No emojis so I wasn't sure what to make of the message. Apparently the Motherfuckers had worn me down over the years and now my brain required emoji clues in order to figure out what tone was being conveyed via text. Was this a toothy eek-face? A laughing-so-hard-I-cried face? An upside-down smiling face?

Leaving work, be there in a few. What the hell. I almost asked if he wanted me to pick up food, but one, that would be a whole other social interaction that I didn't feel prepared for, and two, it also felt like I'd be presuming a whole lot. "Stop by" wasn't the same as "come over for dinner." Ditto "I'm just stopping by" wasn't the same as "I'm just stopping by...and I brought dinner."

I was just stopping by. No expectations. To see what Evelyn had done, since she was the only *she* who would be understood as the subject of a text like that. To see what was so wild a picture couldn't do it justice. I definitely wasn't on any level wondering if this was an excuse to get me to the house. That would be perilously close to *hoping* this was an excuse to get me to the house, and I was not, certainly *not*, going to hope for anything.

With my brain—and, okay, probably "heart" as well, or whatever—barred from experiencing any intrusive projections about what might happen, I drove to the house. Well. To the street. I turned the corner and my car slowed to a stop right there in my lane, though thankfully no one was behind me. I managed to pull to the side, but by then I was laughing pretty hard and my parking job was off.

She'd done it. Mint julep green. Brightest house on the block, practically highlighter-colored if your highlighter was lime without being neon. I was wheezing with laughter by the time I realized Jack was standing outside my door glowering down at me. He opened it, probably in the spirit of glowering more intensely.

"She—oh my god—that's—amazing—" Breathing, breathing was good. "Oh fuck, Jack. It's glowing. The house is *glowing*." I couldn't talk again I was laughing so hard.

"I know it. Dammit." He looked up at the incredible shining beacon that was his house. "I can't tell if this is her way of forcing me to sell it because it's so awful, or if she actually believes it somehow increases curb appeal."

"It's fantastic." I wiped at my eyes. "Oh fuck. It's. I can't. Wow. Um, was it supposed to be a surprise?"

"It's a surprise all right," he muttered grimly. He pushed the door open further. "You should see it up close. It's worse than the paint chip."

I bit down hard on my tongue. "It's…a statement."

"Just the statement I always wanted my home to make."

"I don't think you have to worry about ships crashing into it at night, anyway. I bet it's highly reflective."

He growled, a low rumble of non-words that I knew was meant to be forbidding.

I elbowed him. "Hey, it doesn't look haunted anymore, though. They did a really, uh, thorough job. Turning the house into a glow stick."

"I thought you might be a little bit sympathetic."

I laughed again. "You did not. You just wanted someone to make you laugh before you have to talk to Evelyn about what she's done. You know she'll act like she did you a huge favor."

"She will. And nothing I can say will in any way prove to her that it now looks *worse* than it did before."

"It does not." Though up close it did sort of give you a headache if you looked at it too long. "Look, they did a bunch of prep work. If you want it to be a different color, just hire people to repaint it. Easy."

"Do you know how much that would cost?"

"No, but I know you make enough to pay for it."

He exhaled an irritated breath as we entered (through the garage, of course). "Yes. But I shouldn't have to. If she'd only *listened* to me."

"Sorry, is this the part where I express sympathy about your grandma straight up giving you a house but then paying to have it painted the wrong color? Because I'm new to feeling sympathy for people who are just *given* a house, so it's going to take me a minute to plan out how I'm gonna feel sorry for you." I pretended to think really hard.

"Oh, shut up. You know that I—that I—you know I..." He huffed into the kitchen. "Just shut up."

"Yeah, I do know that you, that you, that you, dot dot dot," I agreed, nodding. "I know all about it."

"Seriously, Oscar, shut up." He opened the refrigerator and leaned in, calling from behind the door like he wasn't sure he wanted to look at me as he said it, "If I offer you a beer are you going to leave?"

"Do you want me to?"

"No."

"Then I'll take a beer." *Also maybe a pill to keep my heart from pounding. In case it starts. Which it might. Maybe.* Was it already pounding? Shit. I did not have a pill. I took the beer he offered but didn't open it.

"Oscar?"

"Just a little anxiety." Breathe. Air.

He sat down beside me at the table. "Why? Is that an unhelpful question? I guess it doesn't matter why. Unless maybe it does? I have literally no idea. Sorry. Tell me how I can be helpful and I'll do that instead."

"Nothing. I mean. Hang on." I gripped the cold bottle in both of my hands and focused on the sensation of it: cold, glass, hard, wet. If I gripped tighter my fingers went white. The glass was unyielding. That felt good. It would not let me down. I could be that. I could be strong and firm and not fall apart right now.

At least not too much. Goals: *if you're going to fall apart, don't fall apart too much*. Right. "Sorry. I think I'm worried you'll kiss me again. And also worried you'll never want to kiss me again. Basically, I'm fucked up."

Jack clinked his beer against mine. "Cheers to that. I take it that's a 'there's nothing I can do to be helpful,' then?"

"Um." There wasn't. Well. "Ronnie and I have a code. Like a safeword, but for anxiety. We use stoplights."

"Like red, yellow, green?"

It sounded stupid just...spoken like that. "Yeah. I wish I hadn't mentioned it. Jesus, I'm a fucking wreck."

"It sounds like you're actually managing, which is the opposite of being a wreck."

I choked on a laugh. "How do you figure? Isn't the opposite of being a wreck, like, being well-adjusted or something?"

He gestured around with his beer. "Do you see anyone well-adjusted in this room, Oscar?"

Which: point. "Fair enough. I just feel like I'm a lot more of a mess than most people. I have anxiety safewords so I can let my friends know when I don't want to talk about something."

That seemed to perk him up. "Okay. Like if you say green that means you're willing to have a discussion and red means you aren't?"

"I…guess." I might not have fully thought through telling Jack about my anxiety safewords. "Yellow is most common. Which mostly means 'I should probably talk about this at some point but maybe not now.'"

He nodded. "That's helpful. So kissing—is that red, yellow, or green?"

"Kissing itself or talking about kissing?"

"Either. Both."

"Um." Shit, shit, shit. "Kissing is… I want to kiss you again. Yes. But talking about it is yellow. I don't really know how to talk about it. I don't know how to talk about most of this shit."

He eyed me for a long moment. "Will you try? I think I at least have to know more about what happened before we kiss again. If we kiss again, though for the record, I am also green when it comes to kissing." His brow furrowed kind of…fuck. Adorably? Was that a thing? No, right? Shit, that was not my thought. Maybe Declan would think something like that but not me. Plus, Jack was not adorable. In any way. Like, at all.

Sometimes when he was smug with his mouth on my cock he was…appealing. Appealingly smug. But that wasn't the same.

"That sounds weird," he said, in no way adorably. "'I'm green when it comes to kissing.' Like I'm a frog or something."

"Oh for fuck's sake," I muttered.

"Sorry, I didn't mean to make light of your anxiety. At all. I'm just trying to understand better what happened and how we can…"

Uncomfortable pause while both of us pondered that "we."

"…avoid it. In the interests of continued sex." Jack sighed. "And kissing. And spending time together, which you know, I actually enjoy, and I'm just going to say it."

I couldn't let that pass. "You think I wouldn't say it? Screw you, I enjoyed spending time together too, but then you basically told me to go away, so I did."

"*After* you lost your shit because I offered you a beer."

"That wasn't what it was, damn you! It was a beer and kissing and *more* than just sex, and you fucking knew it. You acted like it was nothing to you and I thought… I thought…" Anger deserted me. The bastard emotion. Never around when I needed it. "I thought maybe I'd made it up. That you hadn't felt what I felt. So I got scared and I left. That's what we do in my family when we feel things: run away until we can pretend we didn't feel anything. Except then you paid me and said the job was done when it *wasn't*, and it was like you were never going to talk to me again. And that was shitty, Jack. Seriously shitty."

"We fight. In my family. If one of us is pissed we stand our ground and fight until we've said everything we need to say."

"I am totally not surprised," I said after a second. "I can't really see Evelyn going for a drive when she's upset."

"Ha. No. She gets sarcastic. That's how I always knew when I'd pushed her too far." He hesitated. "I'm sorry. I guess my coping strategy and your coping strategy had a head-on collision."

"Fuck. Yeah. Apt. Anyway, I flipped out a little bit and blamed you—like a lot—and then I finally saw you and I tried to apologize but it went to hell and I decided we were just never going to see each other again. And that I'd never know what Evelyn's secret was."

He raised his eyebrows. "Which would be tragic."

He was joking, but I shook my head. "Ronnie said I was happy. When we were—you know. Doing whatever we were doing. She said maybe I got scared because I liked where it was going and I'm not used to liking that. Kissing. Laughing. Whatever."

"That would make sense. I mean, I got scared and pretended it didn't mean anything." He shifted a little in his chair. "I want to kiss you again but I'm worried you'll hate me if you let me. Also I wish I'd at least tried to talk to you instead of just going for it."

"You were probably right that kissing after weeks of having sex made sense."

"You were clear that it wasn't your thing."

"Stalemate," I said.

He smiled crookedly. "I think that means we're both wrong, doesn't it?"

"Knowing us? Yeah."

"Okay. So, starting from the premise that we're both wrong, does that mean we should kiss? Or that we shouldn't?"

"Do they cancel each other out?" I asked. "If it's true that we should kiss and it's true that we shouldn't kiss does that mean that us kissing will cause an avalanche somewhere?"

"Schrödinger's Chaos Theory? I don't think that's how it works." He put down his beer.

After a slight hesitation in which I felt my heart double up for a few beats I put down mine. And cleared my throat. "Um. Green. Like. For the record."

"Good to know. The thing is—" his eyes seemed to be on my lips "—now it's too deliberate and it might not work."

Since he wasn't meeting my gaze I looked my fill. He had thinner eyebrows than I would have thought if I'd been trying to draw his face from memory. But longer lashes. The concentration line in his forehead was familiar to me, though. The wave in his hair. The way his lips parted, almost like an invitation.

Apparently I was also looking at his lips. "I guess if it doesn't work we'll just have to go back to sex without kissing."

"You bring up an interesting point."

"That we should have sex?"

"That we should figure out the secret." Now his eyes

rose, catching mine. "It may not be the same as my grandparents' secret, but we ought to give it a shot, don't you think?"

"Jack…are you proposing we *make love*?"

His cheeks went slightly pink but he held my gaze. "I mean, not if you're too scared."

"Um, fuck you."

"Not yet." He leaned in and this time, okay, fine, this time I kissed him back. This time I felt the kiss tingling along my lips, lighting up something in my brain that made me feel brighter than the house. "Okay," he said, pulling back after a second. "Now."

"Now?" I murmured. Kissing. Maybe kissing *was* good.

"Yeah. Now. You know. What you said."

"What I said?" Had I said something? What happened to the kissing?

That line in his forehead disappeared as he leaned in to kiss me. Then he pulled my head closer to speak directly into my ear. "You said, and I quote, 'Fuck you.' And I'm consenting. So do it."

"What? Here in the kitchen? Jack, in this house, as I understand it, sex is only permitted in the bedroom." Humor, ridiculousness, such good ways to hide my heart pounding.

"I'm turning over a new leaf now that the house is nominally mine."

"And lime tart. It's yours and lime tart, don't forget that."

A side of his mouth quirked up. "Are you *afraid* of fucking me, Oscar? Because I did invite you and you seem to be stalling."

"I'm not fucking *stalling*. You brought up making love,

so apparently that's a thing now, and I'm just—I'm just processing."

"Oh. Wait. You." His hand curled along the back of my neck, but only lightly, so it felt good, not like it was a trap. "Is this your first time?" He kissed me, far too gently.

I mauled him, an aggressive battering of teeth and tongue, to show my displeasure. But he only accepted it, his fingers sliding through my hair, his other hand landing on my side. I tried to squirm away but he kissed me again and I…got distracted.

"I want more than no-strings fucking," the bastard whispered in his I'm-about-to-blow-you voice. "I want sarcastic text messages and suggestive looks across the room and your cock in my throat as often as possible. I want to take you apart until you admit that's what you want too." He went back to kissing, his hand moving to the fly of my work pants. "You think you can handle all that, Oscar?"

"I think you can go fuck yourself," I said, but weakly, my own voice sounding like sex and need.

"I could do that." He leaned back a little and stopped touching me, his hand now shifting to…to himself, pressing over the front of his much nicer work pants, where he was hard.

Fuck. Jack. Hard. Fingers moving over his cock.

"Goddammit." I batted his hand away and opened his fly, reaching inside with my own damn hand, since he obviously wasn't going to do it right. "You're such an asshole."

"I'm pretty sure you calling me names when you're—ahh—stroking my dick makes them endearments."

I ramped up my efforts, and he ramped up his, until kissing and touching and intensity and arousal all got wrapped up together, snowballing, the moment turning into something different. Not, for fuck's sake, making *love*, but… suddenly my hand was on the back of his neck, gripping him as I kissed him, or he kissed me, and his hand was in my hair, and our other hands were…other places, and…

I broke away by mere centimeters. Just enough to say, "You're such a jerk."

"Admit you want me."

"Shut up."

His hand—when did he start playing with my balls through my pants *oh fuck*—moved abruptly away. "Admit you want me, Oscar. Tell me you want me to fuck you. No. Tell me you want me to kiss you."

I growled and went in for a kiss myself, but he shifted his face so my lips only grazed his ear. "You are such a prick."

He laughed. "I know. It's what you like about me. If you tell me you want to kiss me I'll do whatever you want."

"Does that include shutting the fuck up?"

"No. Shutting the fuck up is a hard limit. I'll do anything you want that isn't a hard limit."

I slumped. Okay. I slumped against him. Even though he was an asshole. "Kissing you isn't the worst thing I've ever done."

"Try again."

"Kissing you…" I wracked my brain for something not-too-revealing to say. "Kissing you is okay. For kissing."

"Fail. Try again."

"I…you…asshole…"

He kissed the side of my face. "I like-like you too, Oscar."

"You're insufferable."

Fuck, fuck, he was nuzzling my ear. "Tell me to kiss you."

"Goddammit, you weren't like this before! I didn't—I don't—" Except I did. "Fuck you, you bastard, fucking kiss me already."

And he did, his need equal to mine. I tried to make a joke of it, in my head—*two grown men making out in the kitchen over here*—but somehow it had no sting to it, no edge. We were two grown men making out in the kitchen, yes, and it felt...fuck, it felt wonderful.

"Why are you making me like this?" I whispered when we broke apart to breathe.

"Because it's fun. I don't know. Because..." He shook his head slightly. "I got used to it. Teasing you. Being with you. And when you left I didn't laugh as much. I'm making up for lost time."

"By making me beg you to kiss me?"

"Oh, that wasn't *begging*. Don't tempt me to make you beg, because you'll hate it."

And I knew exactly what I was doing when I dug my nails into the back of his neck and said, "I'd like to see you try."

So he did. And, before long, I begged. But by then it didn't feel like he won and I lost anymore. It felt like, y'know, both of us won or whatever.

Fuck. That was what "lovemaking" was, wasn't it? Super annoying. I'd think about just how annoyed I was later. Because I was busy lying in bed with Jack after the first time we'd had sex in weeks and had…other things on my mind.

Like kissing him more.

He was turning me into a monster. And I was kind of… all for it.

Chapter Twenty-Seven

The house color delighted the Motherfuckers.

"It's *amazing*!" Dec called loudly.

I did a *lower your voice* arm movement, which was a thing. "I'm sure the rest of the neighborhood is equally invested in your opinion, but maybe keep it down."

"I don't hate it," Sidney added. They raised their eyebrows at me. "Do you hate it?"

"I can't hate it because Jack hates it, so I get to enjoy how much he hates it while secretly liking it. At least, it's growing on me."

"I heard that!"

"No one's talking to you!"

Dec covered his mouth. "Ohmaghhh."

I glared at him. "What?"

"You guys are *adorable*." He dodged my too-slow punch and went into the house.

"You guys aren't really *The Hate Study*," Sidney said. "I know that's what Mason thinks, but he's wrong."

"Um." I waited for them to bust out with some deeply insightful crap about how we'd never really hated each other blah blah always were secretly in love *cough* BS.

"It wasn't a *study* so much as it was a *project*." They smiled. "Yeah. That's much more accurate."

Oh my fucking god. "You know you're becoming one of the Motherfuckers when you start randomly trolling me about my relationship."

They shrugged, but there was a quality of smirkiness in their face. "Thank you. I like becoming one of the Motherfuckers." Somewhere upstairs Dec laughed and Sidney, as if through some instinctive response, smiled.

I looked away, because it seemed almost private, but just as privately I listened for Jack's voice in a lower register, not laughing at all, and smiled myself.

Ronnie and Mia arrived next, bringing an enormous bowl of fruit salad, which they deposited in the fridge, and a bottle of champagne.

"Jack told us we couldn't get him a housewarming gift for a house he already lived in, but we thought this was a good compromise," Mia said as she handed it to me. "Also oh my god, I love the new color! I'm a little surprised, but I love it!"

I told them the story of Evelyn having the house painted while he was at work and both of them enjoyed it.

"Yeah, but when do *we* get to meet Evelyn?" Ronnie asked.

"Um. Why. Uh." It was a nutty idea. Wasn't it? But Evelyn would love the Motherfuckers. And it went without saying they would adore her. "I don't know yet."

She kissed my cheek. "I'm so happy for you, baby. This feels like a really good thing."

I pushed her away. "Shut up, nothing's happening, go away."

In the two weeks since Evelyn had gotten the house painted—and Jack had used that as an excuse to invite me over because he missed me—a lot had happened. While, simultaneously, nothing had changed. We were having sex, so that was back to our type of normal. At least, when I was off work at a decent hour I stopped by, and sometimes spent the night (which was logical, considering the house was a lot closer to work than my apartment). If he'd picked up food on his way home I might come over to share it…even if sometimes I was off much later and he'd already eaten.

I went to the house a lot, fine, but it's not like I was moving in. That would be foolish. He thought so too. Except shortly after we mutually agreed that me moving in was a terrible idea, he'd bought the desk I'd liked at Ikea when we had gone for home office supplies (he was moving into the master bedroom and turning his old room into his office), and installed it in the spare bedroom upstairs.

When I demanded to know what the hell he was pulling, he said he just figured this way we could spend time in adjacent space for sex reasons, but we'd be at opposite ends of the house and wouldn't get sick of each other. And he said it in such a rational sounding way that it took me hours to realize that no one in the history of ever had set up a home office for their non-cohabitating boyfriend.

Jack was a tricky bastard. I'd always said that.

And then, in a rare trip to my place, he'd discovered Evelyn's old quilt. Uh. On my bed. Where I'd put it. Because that's…where quilts go. And he'd looked at me with this, like…sweet, touched, just slightly vulnerable thing in his face, and it had been way too intense so obviously I'd blown him to make him stop looking at me like that. But those weird sex/lovemaking wires were all tangled up and I wasn't sure if my plan had worked.

The housewarming party was my way of getting back at him for making me feel things. He'd complained that Declan had added him back to the Motherfuckers list without consent and I'd taken the opportunity to remind Dec that Jack was officially coming into ownership of a house and didn't that call for a celebration?

The string of angry emojis Jack had sent me made listening to the details of party planning worth it. Mostly.

The others had gone out back by the time Mase arrived. "Sorry I'm late. Your house looks like a peppermint popsicle or something."

"I don't think that's a thing."

"You know what I mean." He smirked. "Also please note you didn't even argue when I called it your house."

"I live *at my apartment*."

"Sure, sure." He went out to say hi to everyone and I went upstairs to, well, hide.

I loved them more than anything, they were my family,

and oh my god I needed like five minutes of quiet. Except both "my office" and the bathroom had windows to the backyard, and wow, did my friends' voices carry. I slipped into the bedroom instead and sat down on Jack's bed. I could still hear everyone, but they sounded farther away and much less vivid.

Sometime later the door opened and Jack came in, closing it behind him. "Hiding?"

"No. Yes." I pondered lying and figured there was no point. "A little, yeah. You?"

"Completely. I like all of them, but together they're *a lot*." He sat beside me. "You spending the night?"

"Are you asking because you need help kicking them out later and you're afraid I'm going to run away?"

In the past he might have snarked back at me but he'd discovered a new way to be irritating, so instead he said, "I'm asking because I want to *make love* to you later. With my mouth. And lips. And tongue. And throat."

I swatted at him. "Oh my god, shut up, everyone's here."

"It turns you on when we *make love*, doesn't it?"

There's a whole level of hell reserved for people who make me blush. "Fuck off, asshole."

"What? I'm asking innocent questions." He waggled his eyebrows in no way innocently. "I like turning you on, Oscar. I also like making love to you. With you. At you. Around you. Inside you." He reached out and it was a sign of how much he'd conditioned me with sexual pleasure (and, like, companionship or something) that I didn't flinch away from the kiss. Or the way his thumb caressed my lower lip. "You can run away if you want. There's always phone sex."

"Oh. My. Fucking." But I didn't finish because kissing him seemed like a better idea than inserting dramatic pauses between words. "You're a jerk."

"I'm amazing. You said so yourself."

"Did not."

"I'm pretty sure you did."

"Never."

We kissed again. For a while. The kind of continuous kissing that, when you don't have a house full of people (or, okay, a backyard full of people) becomes something else.

But we did have that. Jack had that. Not me. I didn't live there. Obviously.

"We should probably go outside," I mumbled against his lips, loosening my grip on his shoulder. I'd developed a… thing for Jack's shoulders. His broad-shouldered handsomeness used to bother me, but apparently having sex with a broad-shouldered handsome guy inclined me toward being less judgey of his broad-shouldered handsomeness.

Especially when at every opportunity he slid his hand under my shirt in a way I was beginning to get used to (that conditioning again), which usually led to sex.

"Stop teasing me," I mumbled. More. More mumbling. Mid-kiss mumbling.

"Hmm?" His eyes were clear of the usual pointed eye-commentary.

"We should go outside. Guests. Stuff."

"You're probably right." He kissed me again. "Spend the night. Please? No strings."

"You mean we can just fuck instead of making love?"

"We can watch YouTube and fall asleep on the couch if we want. I don't care."

I swallowed. Jokes were the way I usually got through moments like this. But right now? "Yeah. Sounds good. YouTube, fucking, kissing, whatever." I kissed him to seal the deal. "But right now we should—"

"Entertain our guests, I know. Ugh. Guests. Let's never host another gathering, okay?"

"Thank god. I was worried you'd own the house and suddenly want to invite people over all the time."

He laughed. "Who are you talking about? Have we met? Come on."

So we went downstairs, in the house that was more his than mine, but not *totally* his, to guests who were more mine than his, but not *totally* mine. And later, much later, we lay still and sleepy beneath Evelyn's quilt, our arms resting against each other, breaths slowing, the night settling in around us. I'd never wanted this with anyone, not until Jack. And now? I never wanted to be without it.

★★★★★

Reviews are an invaluable tool for spreading the word about great reads. Please consider leaving an honest review on your favorite retailer or review site.

To discover more books by Kris Ripper, please check out zir website at krisripper.com! You can also find more Ripper books at the usual places where ebooks are sold.

Acknowledgments

I have no idea where this book came from. Oscar's voice was so clear, his dynamic with Jack so immediate, that I was consequently convinced the book must be terrible. Two early readers—General Wendy and Alexis Hall—assured me that it was not, in fact, terrible. Actually they seemed to think it was quite ~~okayish~~ good. My thanks to both of them, as always. Being a writer of long-form stories is an odd sort of occupation and it's entirely possible to get lost in one's own fears and insecurities. When this happens it's incredibly helpful to have honest friends around to either confirm you fucked up—or, in this case, to counter all those insecurities by pointing out, you know, that you should get out of your own damn way.

In less feelingsy notes, because Oscar would *hate* ending

the book with feelings, Jack's shower curtain totally exists, hit me up on Twitter and I'll send you the link. It's all over tentacles and thus delightful.

Also available from Kris Ripper
Gun for Hire

Being an assassin is all well and good…until you're hired to kill the only man you ever loved.

In the not-too-distant future, governments all over the world break down, leaving society uprooted, the prey of war lords, gangsters, bullies, and bosses.

But Chester Horowitz—Witz to his friends—doesn't care about all that. He got an early start at eliminating people and he's supposed to be one of the best, but he's getting tired of looking over his shoulder. There's a real nice beach down south and one of these days he'll score big enough to go there. For good.

When the shit hits the fan he takes a job out of pure desperation. His sister's in a coma (beaten up by a couple of goons trying to get at him), he owes serious money to one ruthless boss, and he's dodging another one. This job would fix everything for him and his family—everything that matters.

Until Witz sees who the target is. They used to say you never forget your first love. Well, if your first love is the heir of the biggest gang in the darkcity, that goes double. If your first love also happens to be the guy your sadistic prick of a father just manipulated you into agreeing to kill, it's *triple*.

Why the hell couldn't this one job have been simple?

To check out this and other books by Kris Ripper, please visit Ripper's website at http://krisripper.com/reading-order-book-list/.

Some people can't wait to have babies. They're ready for it—
with their perfect lives and their pregnancy glow...
Poppy Adams doesn't have a perfect life, and she wasn't
ready for the positive test. An unexpected baby—
Poppy's unexpected baby—won't exactly have her family
doing cartwheels. But she's making the right choice.

Right?

Keep reading for an excerpt from
Knit, Purl, a Baby and a Girl *by Hettie Bell*

Chapter One

If this were one of those mid-00s R-rated bro comedies, my story would begin two months ago, the night I got sloppy drunk and succumbed to a 2 am text from my ex. Our sex would be comical, full of the usual "realistic" comedy-sex pratfalls: bumping heads, limb-entangling clothes, and downright terrible dirty talk, but never crossing the realistic and/or comical line where I as the female party stop looking sexually appealing for even a second of screen time.

I'd also inexplicably have sex with my bra still on, and as soon as my schlubby not-nearly-hot-enough-for-me ex rolled off to instant sleep, I'd have my genitals—but never my shiny, shaved legs—covered by his artfully tousled sheet.

Like he'd ever have a flat sheet on his bed, but I digress.

Luckily for all of us but especially me, this isn't a mid-00s

R-rated bro comedy. It isn't the story of a lovable loser man-child who, in spite of how bitchy and irrational his harpy nag of an ex is about everything, still manages to barely grow up and come into himself, just in time for said harpy to renounce her nagging ways and meekly accept all his faults, negating any need on his part for personal growth. It isn't the story of a guy who not only gets the girl, but gets to keep his video game and pot habit, too. It isn't the story of a *guy* at all.

It's mine.

About—among other things—knitting, having sex without a bra on, and not only *not* having permanently shaved legs, but going several months without even *touching* a razor.

And it starts at a Planned Parenthood.

"You don't have to talk to them," the woman in the neon pink vest tells me and flashes an edgy smile. "You don't have to listen to them. You don't even have to look at them."

"Okay." I nod, already shell-shocked. We're standing sheltered by the door of my cab, but it might as well be tissue paper for all it protects me from the sounds of shouting and singing. There's one particularly throaty woman who keeps reciting a version of Hail Mary that would be more at home in a horror flick than a church.

"I'm Rhiannon. I'm gonna be with you every step. If you want me to hold your hand, I can. If you want me to make small talk, I can. If you want me to recite *Monty Python and the Holy Grail* including the moose jokes from the opening credits, I can. I also have a very large umbrella."

She gestures to the four-foot-long neon pink *staff* she's leaning on. "Sadly I'm not allowed to use it as a weapon." This time her smile seems ever so slightly more natural, and I find myself smiling back.

"Okay," I say again, a little more confidently.

"You ready?"

The question isn't funny, not in the phrasing or the delivery, but it still makes me laugh. I am the absolute opposite of ready. Not ready to face the fire and brimstone waiting for me on the sidewalk (which I assume is what Rhiannon is asking about), not ready to commit to the irreversible decision I'm somehow supposed to make today, and sure as hell not ready to be a mother. I don't even consider myself ready to be an *adult*, and yet here I am, twenty-two and on my own regardless.

Rhiannon opens her very large umbrella.

She may not be allowed to use it as a weapon, but she's still damn good with it regardless. One minute she's twisting it to hide my face from some asshole recording me with a handheld video camera. The next, she's using the pink fabric of it to block my view of a particularly gory five-foot poster before my brain can register the image. She doesn't recite Monty Python to me, but she does talk my ear off with her excitement for tea latte season.

"Tea latte season?" I ask. "You sure you don't mean that lesser-known season… What do they call it? Oh yeah, 'Fall'?"

"Nope. Tea latte season," she repeats without hesitation.

"Not *pumpkin spice* season?" I continue, hoping that even though Rhiannon and I are strangers to one another, the in-joke will be one we can still share. Surrounded by hate and harassment on all sides, I'm desperate for kinder human connection, even if it means bonding with a clinic escort over stale memes.

"Oh God no. Not that I have anything against Basic girls—some of my best friends wear Uggs!—but little known fact, pumpkin spice syrup? Not the best choice for the lactose intolerant among us."

It may be impossible for either of us to be loud enough to drown out the noise, but the light talk is still a welcome distraction.

Rhiannon even manages to get me to laugh—right as some geriatric asshole is calling me a whore, no less—by regaling me with the story of the day said lactose intolerance met a disbelieving barista and a latte that *definitely* wasn't soy.

I'm so damn glad she's here. I can't imagine running this gauntlet with Jake, assuming he didn't smoke up and flake like that time we were supposed to go to my grammie's funeral. I certainly can't imagine being here with my mother or sister, because that would mean admitting to either of them why I need to be here in the first place.

Yeah, no thanks.

Not that anyone in my family spends their weekends wailing and handing out pamphlets like this Costco-sized pack of nutbars, and I know if I called my mom she'd be here in a flash, even pay for the procedure if I needed her to, but none of that means she'd be over the moon happy that her college-dropout youngest daughter got herself knocked up by her loser ex-boyfriend. And the thought of admitting my shame to my big sister, the 4.0 student and lawyer, isn't much better.

The last thing I need in my life is to disappoint my family even more than I already have.

But unlike when I'd very conspicuously needed my mom to come and help pack up my dorm room two months before the end of semester, she doesn't ever need to know about this. As long as I do what I'm *supposed* to do and get this abortion, she'll never have to know. None of them will ever have to know.

"Remember," Rhiannon says in parting as she drops me off safely at the door of the clinic, "Whatever choice you make, it's always the right one."

It's a nice sentiment, but is it still true when your choice isn't a choice at all?

When is a choice not a choice?

I think it over as I fill out my medical history form, drumming out a tattoo on the clipboard with the end of my pen. It's an old habit from my days of high pressure tests, even though the hardest question on this sheet is *Starting Date of Last Period*.

Six weeks, four days ago, for the record. I'd figured *that* one out the day I finally gave in and forced myself to buy a two-pack of digital tests. Because, you know, there was totally a chance of the results being inconclusive, right?

I hand my form in with the guilty smile and head-duck of someone who's just finished answering every multiple choice question with *C*.

This isn't a multiple choice test. The "choice", for me at

least, is an illusion. I should be sure about this. It's simple and straightforward. I know what I'm here for, what I'm supposed to do. So why do I feel like I've taken a wild stab in the dark and flunked?

I'm still mulling it all over when the receptionist calls out, "Poppy?" In fact, I'm *so* caught up that it takes her two tries to get my attention.

"Th-that's me!" I blurt out, raising my hand like I'm still in grade school. Every other person in the quiet waiting room turns to look at me, and even though their expressions are either smiling or neutral, I want to crawl under the carpet. Instead, I laugh nervously, put my hand back in my lap. Fix my skirt. Wish Rhiannon were still here, telling me more about her dietary restrictions. Anything to release this pressure building up inside me, this horrible impending sense of doom that comes from knowing that in the next hour I'm going to have to commit to this—*my*, dammit—choice.

My choice that nonetheless feels like it's already been made. The last time I was put in this position was when I chose my college path...or rather, agreed to the path my mother set out for me. And we all know how *that* turned out.

My mother isn't here to voice her opinion on this particular choice, but I can still hear her voice loud and clear in the back of my mind:

"Just because college didn't work out doesn't mean you don't still have your whole life ahead of you!"

"I know things aren't going according to plan for you, but that doesn't mean you have to give up!*"*

"Sweetheart, do you really think you're ready for a baby? I know they say nobody's ready for a baby, but that doesn't mean there isn't such a thing as being not *ready!"*

Thanks, Mom.

And yep, I am the definition of not ready: single, living in a studio apartment, working a cushy receptionist job I only landed because of my mother's meddling—which has health insurance at least, but isn't exactly where I pictured myself being when I was sixteen and not yet a failure.

What could I possibly have to offer a baby? By the time she planned to have me, my mom was the head of her department at the hospital where she worked, was married, owned a home and two cars, and already had a contingency fund set aside to pay for the various unexpected costs of having a baby.

What would I do, bring my baby home from the hospital on the bus?

PS, note to self: stop calling this thing "baby".

The receptionist, who introduces herself as Tammy, buzzes me through a heavy steel door to the left of the glass-fronted reception desk and leads me to a small bathroom, where she points to a specimen cup on the counter. "Go ahead and get this half full, screw the lid on, and leave it on the counter for me. Then you can head over to patient counselling room 3, where someone will be in shortly to discuss the results with you."

I already know what those results will be, but I suppose they have to do their due diligence. Although why anyone would put themselves through this unless they were *absolutely certain…*

I slip into the bathroom and close the door behind me. Squat awkwardly over the toilet with my tights around my ankles and my peecup in hand. On the wall next to the toilet is a notice that reads:

Are you being abused? Coerced? Is your partner/family controlling your reproduction? Take a sticker and attach it to your sample for confidential counselling.

I stare at the little sheet of red dot stickers while I wait to pee and think about Jake, who's probably still asleep or, at the very most, on a wake and bake right now. Not abusive, not coercive, not controlling. Just…not relevant at all.

If I have this baby, I probably won't even put his name on the birth certificate.

Except I'm not having this baby.

Except it's not a baby! Fuck!

My pee makes its debut all over my hand, barely splashing the insides of the stupid cup. So much for half full. I'll be lucky to get my cup even a quarter full. I hope they don't have to test my blood instead.

At least my fear of needles gives me something new to agonize over when I head to the patient counselling room.

It's small and beige, with three chairs set around a desk, a bowl of hard candy, and various medical posters papering the walls comparing birth control methods or advertising the importance of breast exams. Unlike my regular family doctor's, there's no saccharine Anne Geddes print to face down. Thank God. Er, or maybe not God, considering the hymn-singing creeps outside.

I unwrap and eat three candies in the time it takes a nurse to arrive. She has my chart tucked under one arm and gives me a handshake with the other, then seats herself across the desk from me.

"All right. Poppy. Hi. I'm Janine, I'm an RN here. So I see you took a pregnancy test at home before you came in?"

My palms are suddenly sweaty. "Y-yes. That's correct. Two of them, actually. If that matters. Although I guess it probably doesn't since the result was the same both times."

Why am I acting like she's interrogating me?

"And that result…was positive?"

"Yes."

She opens my chart but doesn't really look at it. "The test we just did here today came up the same." She pauses, looks me directly in the eye. "Poppy, you're pregnant. And you've come to the right place."

I wish I could wrap myself up in her validation like a blanket, let it give me the sense of relief she obviously intends to impart.

But I don't.

I can't.

So I put my face in my hands and cry.

Chapter Two

I can't remember the last time someone told me I'd done something right.

Well, Rhiannon, of course, who'd said that thing about any choice I made being the right choice.

But before that?

My mom, back when I'd accepted the admissions offer from her and my sister's alma mater. Back before I'd flunked out.

So how come instead of validation or relief at Nurse Janine's praise, I'm sitting here hyperventilating and bawling my eyes out?

Because I don't know. I'm not sure. This decision is supposed to be obvious, but it's *not*.

I don't know if I'm in the right place.

I don't know.

Nurse Janine hands me a tissue. Lays a hand on my shoulder.

"Tell me why you're crying," she prompts, gently. "Let's talk it out."

I sniff and dab my eyes, manage to blubber, "I don't know!"

"That's okay," Nurse Janine consoles me. "That's perfectly okay. Emotions can be unpredictable."

"No." I wipe my runny nose. "I mean, I know why I'm crying. I'm crying because *I don't know.*"

"What don't you know?"

"I don't know if I'm in the right place. I feel like I should know, I feel like the answer should be obvious. I feel like, I know what I'm *supposed* to do, but I… I…"

Back to wailing again. Nurse Janine takes the seat beside me. Sits silently while I cry, her hand still on my shoulder.

When the crying turns to gasping, and the gasping to sharp but controlled breaths, Nurse Janine finally speaks. "Poppy, can I give you some advice? You're not *supposed* to do anything. 'Supposed to do' implies there's an expectation that someone else has set for you, something that's required of you by outside parties, and you don't have to bring that crap into this room. In this room, it's just you. What you want, what you need, what you think is best. Not what you're *supposed* to want, need, or think is best."

I heave a shuddering sigh.

"So you don't know. That's okay. This is your body. This is your life. For some people it's simple, but for others it's a big decision. It's okay not to know."

"But what do I *do*?" I ask. My voice is high, needy. I feel like a little girl.

"Whatever you feel is best, Poppy."

"That's kind of a bullshit copout answer, Janine." My body tries to laugh and sob at the same time, and it comes out as a hiccup.

Nurse Janine laughs with me. "Sorry. It's kind of my job to stay neutral in these kinds of questions."

"And here I was thinking I'd come in here and you'd have a banner and balloons that say 'abortion is the best, you'll love it'."

"Ummm, no. The best I can do is, 'For *some* people, abortion is the best *option*.' Which isn't what you're looking for me to say to you right now, is it?"

"And you can't pick a side, you know, just between you and me?" The tears have stopped for now, replaced by a wobbly smile. I hope she realizes I'm joking.

Trying to joke.

While also trying to decide if I want an abortion.

I am a mess.

"I *have* picked a side," Nurse Janine says. "Yours. Whatever you decide to do, I'm in your corner. That's what I'm here for. But it has to be your decision, Poppy. Yours. Not mine, not your family's, not your church's, not society's, not your partner's or your sperm donor's. So here's what we're gonna do. I'm going to give you a couple of options on ways we can move forward, and you're going to put aside the *supposed to*s, and tell me what you, Poppy, want for yourself. Is that enough direction for you?"

"I'm still holding out hope you'll just grab me by the

shoulders, give me a hard shake, and yell 'Get the abortion already' into my face like a drill sergeant, but… I guess this is okay, too."

"Okay." She smiles. "Here's the deal, then. According to the dates you've written down here, you're just about six and a half weeks along into this pregnancy. At this moment in time your options are wide open. You can carry the pregnancy to term, you can have a medical abortion with pills, or you can have a surgical abortion. The longer you wait, the fewer options you have, but you still have time. If you're local, I can give you some literature, let you go home, sleep on it. If you're leaning toward the medical abortion over the surgical, though, then we should probably do an ultrasound today to be doubly sure of your dates, and that way you know for sure how much time you have to make up your mind. That's a requirement one way or another, for medical reasons, but it's strictly for the physician's and my use. You don't have to look at or hear anything if you don't want."

"And if I want to?"

God, why did I ask that?

"If you want to, then I can do that, too."

I shouldn't want that. I shouldn't want to see the baby—the fetus. Being forced to look at an ultrasound or hear a heartbeat, that's a cheap guilt-trip tactic out of the playbook of those assholes outside.

But it's not being forced on me. I *want* it, just like I *want* to call this thing inside me baby, not fetus or mistake or parasite or clump of cells—all equally valid alternatives, depending.

And thinking about what Nurse Janine said, thinking about leaving behind the *supposed to*s and the obligations and what-would-my-mother-say, I'm not left with any compelling reason for doing what I've come here to do. Sure, I'm single. Sure, I'm a college dropout. Sure, I'm working a boring nine-to-five job that doesn't leave much for savings after I pay my rent and bills. But if I told Nurse Janine I wanted to keep the baby, she'd say "Go for it." And if *I* were Nurse Janine and someone in my exact situation came to me saying "I want to keep the baby," I'd say "Go for it," too. Heck, I'd say "Go for it," to a woman in a substantially *worse* situation than my own, if that's what she wanted.

Rhiannon's words: *Whatever choice you make, it's the right one.*

Well, for now, I choose to see this stupid ultrasound.

"I'm going to turn the monitor around now," the ultrasound tech says. "Unless you tell me not to."

I clench my teeth. "Do it."

I have no idea how this is going to feel, if it's going to change anything, if I'm going to look at the screen and cry at the sublime beauty of the life inside me and hate myself for even considering extinguishing it, or if I'm going recoil like I've been infested by an alien chestburster, or if I'm going to feel nothing at all, as detached from the image on the screen as if I would be looking at an X-ray of my arm.

The tech turns the screen to face me.

I'm looking at… I don't know what I'm looking at, actually. A blob? It kind of looks like a baby hamster.

Whatever it is I'm looking at, I feel myself smiling. I

don't feel awed, or amazed, or disgusted, or transformed. It's not profound or life-changing. I can see how people can look at it and still be solidly sure that abortion is right for them. It certainly doesn't inspire me to splash the pictures of it all over Facebook for my relatives to coo over.

I don't feel love or hate.

Only one thought, one word, runs through my mind:

Hello!

A tentative, shy greeting to the little stranger inside me. That's all.

Just…hello.

I don't say anything aloud.

The tech fills the silence by explaining my dates were off by only one day.

Nurse Janine adds, "That means you have a solid two weeks until the cutoff for a medical abortion, which gives you time to think things over, if that's what you want. Either way, we'll have to see you sooner or later, whether it's for whatever procedure you choose or to get you set up with prenatal care."

In that moment, at least, I don't need the two weeks to make up my mind.

I don't tell Nurse Janine, not just yet, but this hamster thing of mine? This little stranger? I'm keeping it.

I'll figure out how to handle the *supposed to*s and my mother and Jake and my studio apartment…later.

I thank the ultrasound tech, then Nurse Janine, who hands me a paper envelope full of pamphlets. "Some reading," she explains, "Or there's a confidential number you can call, 24/7. Be careful googling."

Yeah, no, definitely not googling.

I smile at the people still in the waiting room as I'm escorted out. Teenage girls and middle-aged women, a couple of guys, one massively pregnant lady fanning her belly with a magazine.

Will that be me?

I wonder if she came here with a head full of *supposed tos* and a disapproving family. If she's single, too. Or if she has other reasons, explanations for why she shouldn't have a baby but she's doing it anyway.

Or maybe she didn't have any doubts at all.

Rhiannon comes to get me at the door. "Your cab's here," she says. "All set?"

I jiggle my paper envelope. "All set," I say.

The protesters are still here. A couple of them hiss and boo, a couple others "pray for my baby". I don't tell them I didn't get an abortion today, that I'm keeping my baby, even though it might take at least some of the heat off. I don't want them to use me to justify what they're doing. I don't want them to think they had any say in my decision. Sure, I'm starved for approval, but not at that cost.

Rhiannon's very large pink umbrella is angled just right for the light filtering through it to turn her pale skin the color of bubblegum.

She doesn't ask me about what choice I made. Doesn't ask about what happened inside at all, just smiles and resumes our conversation about tea lattes right from where we left off, like my life hadn't completely changed in the space between. She's probably used to that, meeting people before and after life-changing events and decisions, acting as the constant point between two worlds. Charon, safely bringing us from one world, one life, to the next.

Or maybe she just feels really strongly about people having the right to reproductive care without being harassed and intimidated for it.

I'm barely pregnant and I'm already over-sentimentalizing everything and everyone around me.

Hormones, that's why I suddenly want to take Rhiannon up on her earlier offer to hold my hand.

Closest I can get is a brief little squeeze to her palm after she tucks me safe and sound into the back seat of my cab. "Take good care of yourself," she says with an unexpected gentleness, that contrasts with but doesn't contradict her brash confidence from before.

"Thanks." I'm unable to manage anything remotely close to expressing how I'm feeling just now.

She shuts the door, drowning out the sidewalk noise in an instant. The protesters are gone, but so is she.

I'm alone.

Don't miss Knit, Purl, a Baby and a Girl *by Hettie Bell, available now wherever Carina Adores and Carina Press books are sold.*